I0556140

Raw
A novel

By Steven Revare

Published by
Inknbeans Press

Raw: a novel
©2011 Steven Revare, and Inknbeans Press
© 2017 Steven Revare and Inknbeans Press

ISBN 13: 978-1-946841-05-6
ISBN 10: 1-946841-05-6

Inknbeans Press
25060 Hancock Avenue
Bldg 103, Suite 458
Murrieta, Ca 92562

*For Polly and Virginia and Graham
And Frank and Henry and Russell*

Prologue
Shredding Party

Paper overflowed the offices and cubicles, spilling into the hallway. A check clung to an air intake grid on the wall: $85,000 from West Egg Holdings. Some had crosscut their files into confetti. Others sliced green ledger paper into long ticker-tape strips. As he passed one office, a woman spoke to her computer, "I'm well aware this operation can't be undone. Why the hell do you think I'm doing it?" She jabbed the mouse with her index finger.

Someone moaned in mock orgasm over the paging system. None of the firm's senior partners were around to be offended.

He found her in her office, facing the window, which after dark offered more reflection than external view of the Empire State Building. "Bland's not going to hire us," she said. "Acted like he'd never heard of us."

"I thought your 'special friend' had it all set up."

She turned around. "I'm out."

He looked behind him at the paper-strewn hallway. "At this point, there's not much here to stay in."

"I mean I'm out of our marriage."

Chapter 1
A Late Model Student in Bad Pants

Even before any other grad students walked into the reception, Carl Krauthammer worried he had chosen the wrong pants. A cross between business casual khakis and Saturday morning cargos, their freshly ironed pleats battled over formality with the whimsical thigh pockets. He did not want to attract Jules Frye's attention. His pants wouldn't help this cause.

To determine the makeup of his back-to-school wardrobe, Carl had created a spreadsheet of the largest apparel retailers serving the eighteen to twenty-four-year-old market, comparing data points on each company like stock price, market share, and EBITA (earnings before interest, tax, and amortization). The data showed two clear winners: American Eagle and Abercrombie & Fitch. His research had revealed *where* to buy new clothes, just not *what* to buy once he got there. He had received no guidance from the sales staff at Abercrombie, put off perhaps by his age. He was on his own to pick out something "young," or, dare he dream, "hip."

A dark-haired woman named Rosalie, who served the English department in some administrative role, showed up first to set out the food. He helped her load soft drinks into a tub of ice. As they worked, they made the connection that his new roommate was her boyfriend.

Students continued to file in, their ages falling between twenty-two and maybe thirty at the top, and he placed himself as the oldest by seven years. A ten-year difference would just seem like too much. As he watched them congregate around the platters of melon and grocery store sushi in room 012 of the English/Counseling Services Building in Manhattan, Kansas, Carl Krauthammer determined he should've worn flip-flops.

He got a Pibb Xtra from the tub and hovered near a conversation between Rosalie and a professor, hoping to think of something pithy to say. The professor's dirty-blond hair and round glasses made him look like John Denver before he died, which was, Carl imagined, a lot more pleasant than the way he looked *after* he died. At this thought, Carl snorted some Pibb, probably the Xtra part, up into his nose. He barked a cough, and his eyes watered at the searing in his nose.

They looked at him with expressions of mild concern.

Carl could think of nothing pithy to say. "I'm not dying," he finally croaked.

"Dr. Grey, our acting chair of the department," Rosalie said. "This is Carl. He's just starting the graduate program in Creative Writing. Be nice to him. He knows my boyfriend."

Grey shook Carl's hand. "Well, some of my best friends are friends of Rosalie's boyfriends."

"Carl used to be with Ogilvy & Standpipe."

"The accounting firm?" Grey asked. "And you're not in jail?"

Carl emitted a courtesy laugh but said nothing, being familiar with the pedestrian joke. He'd heard several variations of it since the investigations started.

Another student buttonholed Grey, and he turned away.

"I always try to picture someone from their application, but with your business background, I simply couldn't. So, I Googled you and found your picture and resume on the Ogilvy website." Her face pruned. "I take it that picture must've been old?"

Carl remembered the picture because he had intended to update it for four years. It was taken the year he had moved to New York. The photographer had slightly underexposed the shot, making his short dark hair a mass of solid black. It also accentuated his five o'clock shadow.

"In real life, you look less like Kevin Jonas," she said.

"I've been compared to C. Thomas Howell."

"I don't know who that is," she said, before excusing herself to refill a bowl of M&Ms.

2

As if by previous agreement, the students avoided the Lit'l Smokies en masse. Earlier when Rosalie had plugged in the slow cooker containing them, she had extracted a promise from Carl that he would try one. He liberated three sausages from their Crockpot cauldron of bubbling barbeque sauce. He put one inch-long link in his mouth. Once he pierced the skin with an incisor, he found it dry inside and a little chewy, though not exactly bad.

A woman's voice rang out from behind him. "I can't believe it. Someone other than Julian actually eats Little Smokies!" She drew out both syllables of the "Little."

At the mention of the name Julian (which certainly referred to Jules Frye), Carl stopped chewing the sausage and swallowed with some effort. He wiped his mouth on a paper napkin and turned to see a woman, approximately his own age, gathering her shoulder-length blond hair behind her head. Instead of looking directly at him, she set her blue eyed gaze vaguely up, her arms back over her shoulders wrangling a ponytail into an elastic band.

Carl stole a look down the neck of her shirt. A purple lace bra struggled to contain her breasts, which pushed toward him as a side effect of her hair-adjustment posture. He noted a defined tan line, milk-white as it plunged into her cleavage. He could see the top border of a greenish tattoo extending out from the material of the bra. He felt a pip of excitement, and just as quickly smothered it. He hadn't escaped his former life to have an affair. Not right away.

She caught him looking, but said nothing. Carl thought he saw her eyebrows rise.

"That was the first Lit'l Smokey I've ever had, believe it or not."

"They have them at every one of these receptions," she said. "In fact, I wonder if Rosalie just reheats the same batch every semester."

"You couldn't have made that observation *before* I ate one?" He put his plate on the table. "I'm Carl Krauthammer."

"You're a student." She hesitated, an uncertain pause, possibly even a slump of the shoulders. She appeared genu-

3

inely baffled by the situation, to the extent that she couldn't decide what to do with his extended hand. Once she finally committed to shaking, her hand felt warm and dry, her grip firm. "I'm Susan Hirschman."

"I'm in your Romantic Era class this semester."

"Just my luck," she said. "I was going to ask you out but the department tacitly discourages that sort of thing. Plus, I've sworn off men with Little Smokies breath. At any rate, it's nice to meet you."

"Likewise. And it's 'Lit'l.'"

"What is?"

"Smokies. It's 'Lit'l' not 'Little.' I must say they aren't bad. Let me get you a couple."

She shuddered. "No thanks, I don't eat beef."

"There are plenty of things from a cow in there, but I doubt anyone would call it beef."

"Thanks anyway," she said, laughing. She put her hand on his shoulder.

A man spoke from a few feet away near the Crock Pot, scooping sausages onto a paper plate. "How gratifying it is to see one's ex-girlfriend on the rebound so soon, talking up a late model student in bad pants."

Carl studied this new arrival. Frye always used his old high school portraits on his book jackets, so Carl was not sure how he would look now. The best one (on the first edition of *Again With the Voortmans*) had featured a skinny tie, hair that covered his ears, and the faint wisps of a teenage moustache. This guy looked to be the right age, fifty, but some-thing in his demeanor seemed too tentative. He wore black-rimmed glasses, perfectly round, a little large for his face. The lenses adjusted their own tint, the kind that looked neither fully dark in the sun nor fully clear inside. His graying hair swept back over his head and extended down almost to his shoulders. This physical appearance neither confirmed nor denied that he was Jules Frye, but the tweed blazer definitely did not fit the image Carl had in his mind.

He slid a link off a toothpick with his teeth. "Who do we have here?"

4

"Julian Frye, meet Carl Krautenheimer."

Carl no longer bothered correcting the pronunciation of his name.

Frye saluted with a toothpick to the temple and then used it to spear another link. His posture caused his blazer to open, revealing an Indiana Pacers jersey underneath. He asked Susan how she was holding up.

"Remarkably, Julian, I've had a great summer without you. Excuse me. There are some new students I haven't hit on yet." She smiled at Carl and walked toward the cheese table where most of the students stood. Frye placed his plate tottering on the edge of the table without looking, occupied with watching Dr. Hirschman walk across the room.

His expression of light amusement vanished when his eyes met Carl's. "Remind me about your writing sample."

Carl straightened his posture. He felt especially proud of the short story he had sent in. A friend in his writing group in New York had described it as "Frye-ish." He assumed it was what got him into the program. "Mine was the one with the cows stampeding through the office."

He nodded. "Yes, the one that should've ended after about four pages. Excuse me, I think I've had about enough of this event as I can take." After a short wave, he walked through the crowd and out of the room.

Carl had hoped their first meeting would have been more intimate, perhaps in Frye's office over coffee. He would've told his story, careful not to bombard with too much detail, but enough to provide a positive thumbnail impression of the Future Aspirations of Carl Krauthammer. He wanted it to feel more like a job interview than an informal chat next to a Crockpot. Still, Carl could tell the meeting had made an impact on Frye. He now knew whom Carl was, and that his ex-girlfriend found him interesting. And what about Dr. Hirschman? She clearly had the physical and intellectual appeal, but did she have the same allure as the famous women Frye had dated: Susan Sarandon, Natalie Maines, or any of the others? The fact that Frye considered her in his league made them both a little more interesting.

Frye's plate teetered off the edge of the table, splattering barbeque sauce on the floor. Carl got a paper towel and wiped it up.

Within half an hour Carl had left the reception with-out speaking to anyone else. He headed west through cam-pus toward the rental house he shared with Keith Lancaster, a friend from his undergrad years at Indiana. Keith and Carl had met in some English classes and shared an odd pairing of dual majors: Carl in Business and English, Keith in Biology and English. They'd kept in touch throughout the years, and Keith now taught in Biology at K-State. When he learned Carl was moving to Manhattan, Keith offered the second floor of his house for very little money. The price suited Carl. He would live there until his apartment in the West Village sold and freed up his capital.

Once he got to his new home Carl finished unpacking. He put his enormous five-by three-foot magnetic whiteboard up next to his desk and opened the box of assorted dry erase markers. He arranged them in order of the spectrum (ROYGBIV) along the bottom lip of the board. Looking at the shelves he had MacGyvered out of a few boards sup-ported by bricks, it didn't feel like he had been away from college for so long – he had used the same setup as an undergrad. Only instead of the Realistic brand cassette shelf stereo, he now had a boom box with an iPod dock and a 3-CD changer. He surveyed his space from the back corner of the room. He scowled. With nothing adorning the walls, it had the appeal of a minimum-security prison cell. Perhaps he'd take some black and white photos of the campus and have them blown up and framed. He scowled again, know-ing he would never actually do that. Elizabeth, his wife, had custody of the camera. Anyway, he didn't have anything budgeted for decorating.

"You'll miss the money," she had said the last time they talked.

He missed it all: the corner office, the apartment with a view of downtown New York, and the money. He had six months of cushion cash, of which his wife withdrew half from the ATM. Three months of cash in the Manhattan he'd just left would last six months in this Manhattan. He would make it work. Now things were about progression.

He'd read an article describing the place Frye did all his writing, a room painted entirely in beige - the walls, the floor, the ceiling, the desk, and the computer. Frye even dressed in tan when he wrote. It ensured an unspoiled writing experience. That's how Carl decided he would rationalize this barren room. He would keep the walls distraction-free, but he wouldn't wear the tan shirt. Once his mother told him that earth tones made his face look pallid.

Carl and Keith stood outside of Glen's Taproom. Carl cupped his hands and peered into one of the two windows on the storefront. "It's got a two-to-three."

"A two-to-three?" Keith said. "We need more x and less y, a five-to-one or a seven-to-two." Keith had devised a rating system for bars, expressed as a simple ratio of x-to-y (where x equaled the number of people sitting at the bar at noon and y equaled the number of windows). So Glen's Taproom rated a two-to-three, two people at the bar and three windows.

Keith looked out of place in Aggieville, the retail and entertainment district of Manhattan, Kansas. He stood six-foot-two in his standard glaring-white lab coat among the standard lot of college town fare: bars, salons, pizza places, small bookstores, and more bars.

"How about Buffalo Wild Wings?" Carl asked.

"Please. No chains. I don't want it to be some arbitrary place." He opened his arms and then clapped his hands together. "All right. I'm taking you straight to my favorite bar."

Carl nodded. "As long as it's not a Biology bar. I've always been uncomfortable eating lunch around strange biologists," he said, "except you, of course."

A moment later they arrived in front of a bright red door. The sign hanging over featured a disturbing depiction of a clown's face with glazed over eyes and a simple half-smile on his face. Below, in a whimsical, jumbled typeface blazed the words "The Lethargic Clown (Bar and Tables)."

Carl's eyes burned and his nostrils constricted at the harsh smell of fresh bleach and aged beer, and did he detect also a hint of peppermint? The blackened windows let in no daylight, so Carl had to struggle to make out the décor. The best definition he could come up with was "Circus/Western." The tables and chairs, crafted out of a collection of old barrels and wagon wheels, filled the expanse between the door and the bar. Orange and blue striped walls garishly represented the circus half of the theme. The Lethargic Clown was huge and unstylish, the way New York bars weren't. Carl felt as far away from the other Manhattan as he could possibly be.

A ringmaster appeared behind the bar: five-five, he wore a red jacket with black lapels, a white ruffled tuxedo shirt, and red bowtie. Two homemade buttons flanked his chest: "Hello to all the friends I've yet to meet" and "My name is Sparky." He had a hook for a right hand, which grasped a bottle of Fat Tire. In his normal left hand, he held a can of Pabst Blue Ribbon. "A Flat Tire for the new-comer," he said placing the beer before Carl, "and a Pabst for the regular." Sparky exuded a scent, equal parts Aqua Velva and sweat. He opened the bottle and the can with his hook. He handed them each a large menu decorated like a circus tent.

A miniature head-to-toe cutout of Sparky popped up grasping a big bass drum when they opened the menus. In the center of the drum appeared "Today's Prix Fixe: cheese platter, spaghetti, dessert. Drink special: pitchers of Long Island iced tea."

Sparky awkwardly wrote down their choices with a pen clamped in his hook. After he went in back, Carl asked, "What's the story with his hand?"

"Lost it on a train," Keith said.

"I guess that makes as much sense as anything in this place," Carl said. "This is my first two-to-zero."

Sparky brought out a platter with crackers and fruit on it. A bowl with yellow crumbles in it sat in the center.

"What is this?"

"Cheese rubble," he said.

Keith handed the plate back. "I've known this guy for fifteen years. He's cool. Bring out the good stuff."

Sparky's face clouded over and he nodded. He went into the kitchen, pausing to give Carl an appraising look through the round glass window in the swinging door.

"Rosalie told me you were the only one Frye talked to at that reception thing yesterday," Keith said. "Must've been hard to have a conversation with you genuflecting before him."

"Yeah, yeah. I figured my life wasn't working out so well, I might as well try someone else's."

Sparky returned with a mini wheel of soft white cheese.

"There you go. Eat some of that."

Carl put some on a cracker. The flavor danced on his tongue, a perfect combination of richness, sourness, and creaminess. He had never tasted anything quite like it. "This is great cheese."

"You can't get this just anywhere. It's made from un-pasteurized milk."

Carl placed a hand at the base of his neck, spanning his collarbones from thumb to fingertips. "Is this edible? Am I going to die?"

Keith shook his head. "Calm down. It's not poison. I performed my own tests."

"Tests?"

"Liquefy a little cheese in some water, add it to solid matter in a Petri dish, incubate, and see what grows."

"Teeming with bacteria, I'm sure."

"Of course. But it was the good kind," Keith said. "A lot better than the stuff I found on that bulk hamburger you buy. Now there was a scary collection of bugs. Could this stuff make you sick? Possibly. I wouldn't give it to the very young, the very old, or a pregnant woman, but I'd give it to you. You've had one life. A pretty good one from what I could tell. This second is a bonus."

"Let me tell you a story about my time at Ogilvy and Standpipe."

"I love stories that begin that way."

"As a consultant at Ogilvy they paid me an eighty-thousand-dollar salary a year out of college. Seven years go by. Instead of being a member on a team, I help a partner lead one. A couple years later I become a partner, make six figures. I move from the Kansas City office to New York. Living in Manhattan. Great apartment. Small, but great."

"Yeah, shit. Who needs all that?"

"Now, five years go by. I wake up one day and I realize that the most important thing to me was getting a contract on a six-month consulting gig. Then I started noticing the toll it took, me not caring about other things. The nadir came when the wife comes home to tell me she's having an affair, with a Director of Human Resources for Christ's sake." He shrugged. "Suddenly I felt like I was getting money to be a different kind of person, to play a role."

"Clearly you operate on a different plane of Maslow's Hierarchy. I'm the guy whose doctoral thesis, which holds my entire future in its pages, is called *Observed Fluctuations in Nutritional Content of Milk Due to Differences in Age at First Calving*."

Carl straightened his posture. "That's the kind of thing I want to do."

"Write about milk?"

"No, do something I'm passionate about. The other stuff is just clutter."

Sparky interrupted them with their lunches. "Save room after all this. We have a chocolate molten brownie cake

10

a la mode with a piece of apple pie on the side. I call it 'Operation Dessert Storm,'" he said. "All you care to eat!"

Kansas State had long ago changed its last name from Agricultural College to University. The campus, it seemed to Carl, remained in denial of this fact. For evidence, he only had to point out the Dairy Barn that sat at the center of the campus. Made of limestone, the front of the building still looked like a real barn, though decades had passed since anyone had milked anything in it.

In the Abingdon Square Park near his apartment in New York, it looked like the grass had sprung up around the trees. But here, on the edge of the prairie, grass came first, trees second. Not a single tree appeared to have grown from a seed in its current location. Carl imagined some landscaper selecting a species and strategically placing groves next to the appropriate campus building. Locusts here. Dogwoods there. Oaks over there.

Because the English Department faculty had their offices in the English/Counseling Services building, Carl assumed his classes would take place there. In fact, none did– all the upper-level English classes were scattered across campus, as if some low-level administrator selected facilities with a wall map and some darts. Carl perused the schedule, challenging himself to identify a connection between a class's subject matter and the building that hosted it. He came up with only two: Hirschman's Studies in Romantic Fiction (in the Chemistry Building) and Professor Fabresi's Poststructuralist Feminist Theory (held in Dykstra Hall).

Call Hall contained the offices for Animal Sciences and Industry, and looked a lot like an elementary school built in the '70s–low slung, flat roof, pink brick, and small windows. Carl didn't find a match between Frye's Fiction-Writing Workshop and this building until he saw the glass cases in the entryway labeled "Artwork Associated with the Poultry

Industry." It sounded just like something Frye would have written.

For the first time in years, Carl sat in one of those combination chair/writing surfaces. He slid his briefcase in the wire basket underneath. The seats formed a rough circle in the room, and Carl had selected one off to the side.

No one showed until three minutes before the scheduled start of class when a young Asian woman floated in. She wore her long black hair in a ponytail sticking out the back of a Wildcats baseball cap. She smiled at Carl. "Hi," she said. "I like your shirt." She sat next to him.

Carl wore a plain black T-shirt. "Thanks." Perhaps he had nailed at least the upper half of his wardrobe. More students filtered in. He vaguely recognized some from the reception. One of them, a bald guy in a white T-shirt with a gold earring, stood just inside the doorway and stared at Carl. When he folded his arms he looked like an emaciated Mr. Clean.

"Before we start, I want to know how the hell you," Mr. Clean said, pointing at Carl, "are gonna grade me in creative writing. It's all subjective, dude."

"I'm sorry, I'm not the teacher," Carl said. The girl in the ball cap scooted her chair away slightly. "I'm a grad student, just out of the working world..."

Mr. Clean held up his hands, "Dude, I don't need your life story."

Ten silent minutes elapsed. Mr. Clean passed the time reading an X-Men comic he produced from his back pocket. Another person trudged in and took a seat. About thirty years old, he had a black permed mullet and a sleeveless shirt that curtly and obscenely declared that *American Idol* and the Rothschild family were ruining society.

Mr. Clean stood up and put his comic away, accosting the newcomer. "You the teacher?"

"Yeah, sit down and shut your cake hole," the Republican-hater said. Everyone laughed, especially Mr. Clean.

The laughter died when Frye entered wearing a pair of long basketball shorts and a Celtics T-shirt, carrying nothing but a book. He dragged a podium to one side of the circle, opened the book, and began to read.

Carl recognized the passage from the end of Frye's book *Again with the Voortmans*, a sequel to his first book. While finding very little commercial success, this book had helped shape Carl's last two years of college.

The book centered on Ben Voortman, a third-generation horse trainer at Del Mar racetrack in San Diego. In the particular scene that Frye read to them, Voortman walked through a darkened tunnel leading from the stables to the parking lot. Carl opened his briefcase and pulled out his Kindle. He powered it up and searched to find the passage.

Voortman looked left. The shadowy camouflage of trees shifted in a light breeze, momentarily throwing dingy moonlight on some low moving figures. Above the nuzzling leaves came the whisper of satin brushing on satin. He saw a flash of round spectacles in front of him, and he knew they had surrounded him.

"Don't try to run, Voortman," the man in front of him said. "This will go easier if you cooperate, it will."

Ben Voortman had experience dealing with evil jockeys. When jockeys go rogue, they're like the mafia, he thought. They don't leave people alive to testify.

"Go to hell, shorty." Damned if these fuckers were going to get me without a fight, *he thought. "You're going to let me go. I'll walk to my car, go home, grab a plate out of my cabinets without using a stool, and I'm going to eat a steak that I can cut myself, without the help of my mother, and then I am going to have sex with my tall wife. Chew on that, runts."*

They came at him at once, leaping onto his back, biting his ankles, pulling his hair.

Carl loved the attitude of the piece, its irreverence. Frye's characters ignored political correctness that had infected most of the books Carl had read. Frye's work had an edge, an explosive rebelliousness that conflicted directly with the texts he read for his business classes.

He had recently written in his journal that reading Frye's book again helped him realize that writing fiction represented the diametric opposite of auditing the ledgers that made up a business's books. Carl had read that book the summer after his sophomore year and added a creative writing course every semester that followed. From then on, he split his life between writing and business, attacking each with equal vigor. During the walk from the business building at the northern end of campus to his English classes at the southern end, he kicked out thoughts of supply curves, pro formas, and receivables, to make room for character, plot, and language. Friday nights meant gin and discussions of post-post-modernism. Saturdays brought beer and pre-dictions of how liberating Kuwait would affect interest rates. Carl made no attempt to get his two groups of friends together, and neither side ever asked about the other.

In the middle of Frye's reading, another student entered the class. The guy's face had an unnatural flatness, accentuated by an enormous protruding beak. It looked as if someone had put both his feet on either side of the face for leverage while violently stretching out the nose. The guy with the beak did not immediately take his seat, choosing rather to flit between the rows of students, mildly accosting those he knew with a hair-tousling.

Carl's father had a name for people like this guy. He would call him a *Flanesser*, or flan-eater. No precise definition for what made a person a *Flanesser* existed. Krauthammers just knew one when they saw one.

"Sorry, Professor Frye," he said. "I had a couple of things to take care of for the EGSA." Then, though no one asked, he added toward the class, "That's the English Graduate Students Association. I'm the president." He looked around the room to see what sort of effect this revelation had on his audience.

"*Were* the president, Don," Frye said.

"I–huh?"

"You were the president of the EGSA. As the faculty sponsor of the EGSA, I can impeach you. Interrupt my

14

reading like that again and I'll find a way to have you kicked completely out of the university."

The *Flanesser* sunk in his chair and said nothing more. Frye continued reading.

"'It's your last quarter mile, Voortman," the tallest jockey whinnied, wielding the long yellow prod he was about to touch to Ben's temple.

Voortman did not pray, only thanking a secular anonymous power for sparing him from torture, and that he'd safely sent his family to San Francisco. Right there on the sidewalk, years after the Rosenbergs and Bob Dylan, came Ben Voortman's turn to go electric."

Carl moved to applaud but didn't when he saw no one else would've joined in. Frye closed the book and sat down with a self-satisfied smirk. Mr. Clean held up his hand.

"You don't have to hold up your hand in my class," Frye said. "Just say what's on your mind."

"Are you the teacher?" he asked.

In the name of efficiency, Carl thought it best to schedule his classes back-to-back on Tuesdays and Thursdays, and therefore selected Dr. Susan Hirschman's class based solely on its convenient time: an hour and a half after the conclusion of Frye's class. In between, Carl sat at a picnic table under an elm tree to read his notes from Frye's class.

Frye had said the class would be half writing exercises and half workshop. "This is where your peers, who know less about writing than you think you do, will critique your work," he had said. "This will prepare you for the lifetime of rejection letters that awaits you."

He had also reeled off a list of subjects and story types he wouldn't allow in his classroom: "No stories about dying grandparents, favorite pets, maturing teens ala Holden Caulfield, incest, or suicide, unless you can find a plausible way to write a story about all of those subjects at once: something like the story of a maturing teen coping with the

15

suicide of a pet who had been inappropriately touched by a dying grandparent. I'll read something like that." He completely forbade any fantasy. "I've seen enough *Twilight* knockoffs to choke a werewolf." At the end of class Frye gave them their first writing assignment: make a timeline of your life.

Sitting at the picnic table, Carl spread out his paper, lined up his pencils, and stared at a blank page of notebook paper. He drew a horizontal line a third of the way across the paper to represent his life through college. The next third would represent his life with Elizabeth and as an accountant, split evenly between Kansas City and New York. The endpoint represented his life now. He made little ticks in the line, labeling them with things like "began walking" and "braces removed" and "married." Important things happened to Carl Krauthammer during his prime years—that is, during the years when his age was a prime number. He had events for ages one, two, three, five, seven, eleven, and on up to thirty-seven.

Only when he came to the task of translating the timeline into an engaging passage of prose did he notice how warm the afternoon had become. Heat distorted the cars in the parking lot behind Waters Hall. No wind blew through the trees, and that made the lawnmower off to the north even louder. Above a green mesh trashcan by his table, seven or eight bees fought over the remains of a melted ice cream cone.

After an hour, he simply couldn't make his suburban upbringing and years at Ogilvy & Standpipe sound compelling. The papers had already printed everything interesting about that, and who wanted to hear the boring details about his failed marriage anyway? He leaned over to retrieve a pencil that had rolled off the end of the table and straightened in time to hear the splat of bird shit landing right in the center of his timeline, obscuring everything on the paper except the beginning *(Born)* and the last two entries *(Moved to Manhattan (NY), Moved to Manhattan (KS).*

"I can't teach you how to be a writer," Frye had said. "I can give you the tools of the craft, I can load up your

16

writer's toolbox, but it's up to you to live the writer's life. And that doesn't mean becoming a heroin addict, or an alcoholic. Or rather, it's not *just* doing those things." He paused for the scattered laughter to quiet down. "It's about writing as a way to digest the world around you, a way to embrace and make sense of all the chaos. That part cannot be taught. That you must learn for yourself."

The timeline, with the fresh splotch on it, gave Frye's words resonance. The life Carl had left held less interest to him than the life he now embraced. He wondered if he could use the symbolism of the shat-upon timeline to brighten his first writing assignment. But he gathered up his papers and threw the one with the befouled timeline into the trashcan. The bees briefly swarmed before resettling on the ice cream slag. After some consideration, he decided he wouldn't use the bird shit as symbolism. Too contrived.

Dr. Susan Hirschman's class shared little things with Professor Frye's, namely a few of the same students: Mr. Clean and a sullen undergrad with a ratty "Vote for Pedro" T-shirt. The differences proved more striking. Instead of a Celtics jersey, she wore a light grey cotton shirt. Rather than reading about murderous jockeys, she explained her detailed syllabus. Instead of a dictatorial list of *verboten* subject matter, she demonstrated the online system used for turning in assignments and conducting online discussions.

Carl knew of nothing sexier than competent meeting facilitation, and that's exactly what Professor Susan Hirschman did. You could tell it mostly through her com-posure. She moved smoothly through all the items on her agenda. Questions didn't faze her. Quite to the contrary, they allowed for her to segue to the next subject. The class did get off topic when the *Flanesser* entered the classroom.

"Hello, Don. Take a seat please," Dr. Hirschman said.

He walked through all five rows of seats and finally said to Dr. Hirschman, "I was late because I had to speak to

17

Julian Frye." He looked around the room, but no one met his eye. As Hirschman started up again, running through the historical context of the Romantic Era, the *Flanesser* listened for a few minutes, chuckled over a few text messages on his phone, and then turned to Mr. Clean. "You know, we'll be working together soon enough, Frye and me. I think he fired me as president of the EGSA because he's going to ask me to be his Research Assistant. Word is he's writing again." When Mr. Clean didn't react, the *Flanesser* turned to Carl. Carl's extreme distaste for the guy must've shown on his face, because when Don turned to look at him, he appeared startled and immediately turned back around in his seat. *Flanesser.*

*

Dr. Susan Hirschman also had office hours immediately after class, so Carl decided to visit. He remembered the positive impact a good first meeting with the professor could have.

Her narrow windowless office had pale pink cinderblock walls. An enormous wooden bookshelf crowded the room, its sagging shelves crammed full. She had shoved her desk - too large for the office - into the corner up against the far wall. Three women breastfeeding babies sat on a narrow couch along the wall directly opposite of the bookshelves. He didn't look long, but he did notice that they all stared straight ahead with a collective expression of resignation.

Susan spoke on her cell phone, extending an index finger to indicate she would only be a minute. "Just don't cave," she said.

On the shelves Carl recognized a few Romantic-period novels, including Shelley's *Frankenstein* and Wollstonecraft's *Maria*. On the end closest to her desk he noticed a thick, well-thumbed paperback, *The Womanly Art of Breastfeeding*. An issue of *Pedagogy* magazine lay on the desk. At first, he thought the headline said "Our Swimsuit Issue" on the cover, but really it said "Our Syllogism Issue."

"I know formula's easier," Dr. Hirschman said. "But it is not cheaper, and it is not better for your little angel. Think about her and be strong. Okay, Brianna, good-bye."

She hung up and said to the women on the couch. "We might lose Brianna." The women shook their heads.

"I can't talk for very long, Carl. I didn't expect anyone to come to office hours on the first day."

"What's going on here?" he asked. "Some kind of club?"

"It's a support group I started, a not-for-profit. Is this your first breastfeeding workshop?"

"Yes," Carl said. "It appears you're getting your message across." The breastfeeding women did not change their expressions, even as all three switched their infants to the other breast under small baby blankets.

"I'm also doing some research for an article on breastfeeding. I have this great idea revolving around the sym-bolism of breastfeeding in a few Romantic novels. Some of the works have interesting things to say about the immune-logical and nutritional effects on breastfed babies, things that medical establishment of the day hadn't yet proven. I'm really struggling with the science. I need some research help before I approach any journal with this."

"My roommate was just talking about this kind of thing the other day. With cow's milk, but it can't be that different." Everyone frowned at him from the couch. "No offense ladies."

Carl had been in Manhattan two weeks and he hadn't grilled anything. That meant he hadn't christened his new place. Carl always broke in his homes by grilling. He had even slow smoked a salmon on the terrace outside of his New York apartment before the super ever figured out where the smoke was coming from. After each of his moves, the inaugural charring of flesh signified the beginning of the "settling in" phase. He'd found his favorite bar and had made a couple of friends. Hell, he'd even eaten the super-secret local cheese.

Carl cleaned off the main cooking grate with a wire brush from the barbeque toolset he'd brought from New York. That and the kettle were among the few things he had taken from the apartment. The kit had everything: a spatula, tongs, a large knife, a two-pronged fork, a marinating brush, salt, and pepper. All gleaming stainless steel, the kit came packed into a silver briefcase that looked like one where a James Bond villain might keep a disassembled sniper's rifle.

He got the grill ready. He couldn't afford the kind of ribs he liked to cook. Instead he would prepare a couple of hamburgers he'd bought at Ray's Apple Market. The super-secret local cheese reminded him of what Keith had said about all the bad bacteria in ground beef. He decided to cook the burgers medium well. He found it counter-intuitive that raw milk cheese was supposedly safer to eat than something that he would char over open flame.

He noticed with disgust that the trip from New York had knocked off a fleck of paint from the top of the kettle. The chip looked vaguely like Australia. A spot of orange rust had already appeared near Brisbane. He would have to work on it with steel wool and primer. He thought he had some Weber Red touch-up paint somewhere in his things he had kept in the apartment building's storage.

The lighter fluid soaked into the neat pile of charcoal. Most people wanted to go ahead and light it, but Carl knew if you didn't wait, the lighter fluid would burn off and not catch most of the briquettes. In this moment of reflection, with the metallic smell of Gulf Odorless Lighter Fluid in his nostrils, Manhattan, Kansas, felt right. It had the laid-back vibrancy of a college town, a strong community of artists, and plenty of beef. He looked forward to getting to know the place.

Keith walked his bike up from the side of the house. He pulled a pair of small white buds from his ears.

"You ride your bike listening to an iPod? And doesn't your lab coat get caught in the chain?"

"Yes, mother." Keith sat down on a lounger across the patio. He had his eyes closed, his chin tucked down close to his chest. The extra flesh from his neck bulged out to the sides, giving him an inflated look. He said, "I just finished the meeting you set up with Susan Hirschman."

The corners of the charcoal had turned grey, signaling they had caught. Carl walked over and sat down. "Excellent! Did you two talk of breasts?"

"Only in the name of scholarly pursuit. She showed me one of the journals she wants to target. It has articles about all sorts of passionate things, like duels, love-struck landed gentry, and women having sex out of wedlock. But these are academics–they write in a clinical way, and it loses a lot in the dissection. So much so that I think they could use it to test potential erection drugs–if you can get a hard-on reading issues of *Eighteenth Century Literature* they know they have a winner."

"As long as they adjust for any English doctoral candidates in the experiment group."

Keith smiled but didn't laugh. He sat up on the lounger and shielded his eyes from the sun. "So, when you chatted Hirschman up, you tell her you're still married?"

"No, Elizabeth didn't come up," Carl said, brushing a fly off his shorts.

"You know we need a nickname for her," Keith said.

"For Hirschman?"

"No, for Elizabeth."

Carl rolled his eyes. As long as he could remember, Keith would go through the same set of actions after a breakup. First he would mourn, listening to a mix tape of depressing music and lying on his bed. Carl knew Keith had made emotional progress when he abandoned the tapes and began telling Carl about his ex-girlfriends and their sexual peccadilloes. The whole two-day process came to a close when Keith would settle on a degrading nickname for the woman. Carl still remembered many of them, most notably PhoneStank, Feeb, Pickles, and Hambone. And yet Keith still wondered how come none of his relationships ever progressed

21

anywhere close to marriage. Actually, Carl knew that wasn't true. Keith had an uncannily accurate self-image. He once admitted that the reason he came up with the nicknames was to put some distance between him and his exes. Carl believed it too, because Keith always reserved the vilest names for the women who broke up with him first. "I need to listen to the mix tape," Carl said.

"It's a playlist now. I have it upstairs if you want it."

"I don't want to hear your suggestions for her nickname, Keith. I'm sure they would be very nasty."

He laid down and closed his eyes. "Come on, Carl. You know *I* can't give her a nickname. You have to do that. Besides, I don't know any of her sexual predilections."

"I hope I don't need a nickname for her. We're going to sell the apartment in New York, and each of us will move on with our respective lives." After a moment Carl said, "Ex-Elizabeth."

"Ex-Elizabeth? As her nickname? But that doesn't make sense. She's still Elizabeth."

"The task has fallen to me," Carl said, "and I have decided that we shall refer to her as Ex-Elizabeth."

Chapter 2
The Outside Inn

After a couple weeks of writing exercises, Frye finally asked for volunteers to write a story for the class to critique. Carl signed up in the first group, meaning he had two days to write a short five-page story containing a setting and a situation unfamiliar to the author. So, he picked a town at random from a map of Riley County. He selected Ogden, Kansas, eight miles from Manhattan. He knew nothing of the town.

A small knot of buildings, some made of brick, some of cinderblock, made up downtown Ogden, among them a hardware store, a vacant warehouse, two beer bars, and the burned-out shell of a fire station. He saw no people, but from the three cars parked in front of Susie and Tom's Outside Inn, Carl deemed that life did exist in Ogden. As he crossed the street he noticed that two of the cars sat on blocks and the third had no doors. Strips of headliner list-lessly flapped in the light breeze.

He spent half an hour as the Outside Inn's only customer, eating stale pretzels, drinking 3.2% beer, and talking to Susie. She was about sixty years old with grey hair pulled back tightly into a bun. She reminded Carl of Aunt Bee, a perfect comparison if only Aunt Bee had chain-smoked and wore a dirty apron that read, "Don't Ask Me 4 Shit."

They exchanged small talk, and Carl prodded her about some of the characters who lived in the town. She couldn't think of any, but as he learned, she had just bought the place three months before.

"Well, tell me your story," he said. "How'd you come to be the owner?"

"Oh, you make it sound like I own an Applebee's or something. This place didn't cost as much as you might think," she said, waving a menthol cigarette around the single room that made up the Outside Inn. Stacking chairs covered in matted red velvet surrounded tabletops of blistered and peeling veneer.

23

"It was Tom's dream to own a bar. We planned to retire here. Moved from Blue Springs to get our piece." As she spoke a small curl of smoke accompanied her words and rose toward the defunct Smokeeter that hung unplugged over her head. "Spent a whole month cleaning the place and redecorating."

Carl glanced at the beer posters and Christmas lights lining the walls. He reached into his pocket and pulled out a small steno pad.

"After a few weeks, Tom passed."

"Sorry to hear that," he said.

"We weren't officially married or anything, maybe common law married. Do they have that in Kansas? Anyway, I don't know if I'll get to keep the place."

"Can I borrow a pen?"

She cocked her head, looking at the pad. "You a reporter or cop or something?"

"No," Carl smiled. "I'm a writer."

"A writer?"

"Well I hope to be. I'm a student."

"Oh, good luck to you." She stubbed out her cigarette. "I'm closing up."

"I'm sorry?"

"And *I'm* closing up." She took Carl's half-finished beer and tossed it into a large plastic lined trashcan. It shattered against another bottle. "Yep, that's one advantage of being the sole owner, you can do whatever the fuck you want. I want to close up."

"Oh, okay. What do I owe you?"

"Free beer for writers today," she said.

"I don't mind paying, but thanks! Here can I give you a buck?"

She refused and Carl left. He heard her bolt the door behind him. That's when he saw The Scene: A former Applebee's executive moves to Ogden and tries using his corporate handbook on a true neighborhood bar and grill. Carl's ideas for stories came to him first as a single situation created in limbo. It might represent the beginning of a story, the middle, or the end. The story would come later, as he filled in characters and their motivations, but always The Scene appeared first.

"Who has positive comments?" Frye asked.

No one spoke for a few moments. Carl wrote some non-sensical words on a page in his notebook, unwilling to make eye contact with anyone. He noted his wrinkled shorts looked as if he'd slept in them. A nervous carbonation roiled in his stomach, similar to that which overcame him before annual employee reviews.

Carl had labored over this story the class was about to discuss. His characters had complete resumes and family trees to back them up. He had obsessed over the setting, even returning to Ogden to make sure he had placed the street sign correctly at the intersection of Riley and North Walnut.

"I think the author is working hard," the Asian woman said, "to avoid passive voice."

Other students nodded but no one else said anything.

Mr. Clean cleared his throat and everyone looked at him. The top of his head reddened. He sat upright in his chair and riffled through his copy. "I liked the idea the author had for his story." He coughed. "I like it when an author takes risks, because even when he falls right on his ass, at least he can say he tried."

"For Christ's sake, did you like the story or not?" Frye asked.

Mr. Clean took a deep breath. "I liked the character of the woman who owns the little bar and restaurant, and the parts with the executive that she hires are actually very funny."

The Asian woman held up her hand. "I thought the author did a great job of making us feel something. So often in today's society, stories don't make us feel anything."

"What the hell does that mean?" Frye took off his glasses and ran both hands, fingers splayed, through his hair.

"One thing to remember, people," he said, "is to make sure your comments mean something. The Author can't benefit from comments that don't mean anything. Do you understand that?" Mostly the class nodded.

The positive comments gained both momentum and the specificity requested by Frye.

Carl tried to capture them all using the Zagat notetaking method, noting that people appreciated his "great use of setting" and thought his "realistic characters" were "well-portrayed." The "interesting integration" of the defunct Smokeeter "echoed the conflict between the old and the new."

There came a pause when everyone had said his or her piece, and it was Frye's turn to talk. Frye leaned forward.

"So, it's all great? Nothing's wrong? The thing with a story is, it either works or it doesn't, and this one doesn't," Frye said.

Carl transcribed the words verbatim.

"I noticed that too," the Asian woman said.

Carl insisted that the customary in-person story discussion with Frye take place as soon as possible, so they met in the classroom soon after the other students had filed out. The conference consisted of Frye repeating his assertion that the story "didn't work." With that he grabbed his book and prepared to leave.

"That's it?" Carl asked. "Do I get specific comments at some point, maybe on my manuscript?"

Frye exhaled an exasperated sigh and riffled through the pages of his book until he pulled out a dog-eared copy of Carl's story. "Write something worth talking about and I'll have more to say."

After Frye left, Carl found the manuscript had no comments on it. The only mark was a single coffee ring.

While his first attempt had proven lackluster, was his writing completely without value? It reminded him of Ex-Elizabeth. The scene he recalled took place soon after Carl had started working with her at Ogilvy & Standpipe, before they dated. She asked him into her office after reviewing a new business PowerPoint Carl created. She paced the length of the boardroom, hands clasped behind her back, looking very much like a high school principal in an After School Special.

"Your presentation lacks a certain polish," she said, her voice slowly rising. "The *way* you express yourself, the words you use, that's all fine. It's just that *what* you're ex-pressing, the meat of your presentation, kind of, well, frankly, sucks." She started to detail some of the defi-ciencies but stopped herself. "It sounds like a lecture. It's overwritten. These are business people, not literature inter-preters. Throw some clip art in there or something.

"What you've learned thus far, your education, the crap you got out of your M.B.A., it's a foundation. It's nothing—treat it as such. The concrete, the base, like any foundation, is nothing without a building on top. Teach them something, but for God's sake, you have to sell them. We're not doing this for their edification. Sure, no building, no skyscraper, no towering, solid thing can exist without that foundation, it's just that the building is the thing. That's what we're after." Her breath came out in a whoosh. "Want to go get some sushi?"

People like Ex-Elizabeth had ruined the architecture metaphor in business through overuse. However, Carl had drawn inspiration from that particular rant. Indeed, it applied to his writing. Most of the things he wrote felt stuck at the foundation stage. But hadn't he come to Manhattan so his favorite author could teach him? If Carl had nothing to learn he wouldn't need to be here. He'd have no excuse to work with Frye. No, Carl would build his writing to great heights, and the achievement would come from acknowledging how much he'd constructed from the foundation.

He would have to take another tack to get Frye's attention and eventually become his Research Assistant. He needed a more coherent plan. He needed a Progress Report!

27

The Ogilvy & Standpipe Project Status Report had three columns. The left of the form held a current project goal, the middle had space to describe the progress made toward that goal, and the right had room for a list of action items required for achievement. He took the black pen (blue was reserved for revisions) and wrote his name in the project manager blank. He named the project "Carl Krauthammer."

Prioritization provides a context in which the process owner can make decisions on issues that may not serve all goals. Only significant marketplace changes would ever justify reprioritization. He wrote, "1. Cultivate a working relationship with Jules Frye." He immediately crossed it out. That was a tactic, not a goal. As much as he admired Frye, working with him wouldn't represent a true end. What did he hope to gain from working with Frye? He wanted "to become Jules Frye's peer." In parentheses, he wrote the metrics by which he would measure his progress toward this goal: "to have a national personality mention Carl Krauthammer as a writer of Frye's caliber" and "to be respected by Jules Frye."

On to the second column–had he made any progress toward this goal's achievement? He'd moved to Manhattan. He'd met Frye, made an impression. While he hadn't shown significant advancement toward the goal, it made him feel better to acknowledge he had made progress. He added a few action items: "Continue to garner Frye's notice (talk to Rosalie about serving on EGSA). *Lead* him to deduce that the synergy of working with Carl would *lead* Frye toward something Frye wants." Those stark words intimidated Carl, but he could do those things. He had done them with clients– he could do it with Frye.

Carl hoped his working relationship with Julian Frye would live up to his expectations. They would write together, Carl providing research and maybe inspiration for Frye's comeback masterpiece, Frye giving Carl advice on writing and living the writer's life. Frye would be a Miyagi to Carl's Daniel-san.

Now with the priority goal fully described, Carl moved on to the second. He had embarked on a new life here in

Manhattan, and he didn't want to end up just relocating his past. He wrote, "2. Learn from Past Mistakes." This goal didn't look right, though. He would never have accepted something so vaguely worded from one of his subordinates at Ogilvy & Standpipe. It also lacked objective measurability. He replaced it with "2. Do the right thing for close relationships." Better, but such a binary goal resisted in-cremental progress. He kept it for the moment until he could come up with something better. He left the progress column blank and wrote, "Form some close relationships" under action items. In small letters, above that action item he inserted the words "Get divorce."

He felt encouraged. He had defined a clear path to success and had made progress along that path. He attached the progress report to the magnetic white board next to his desk.

Rosalie sat at the main desk in the English department faculty offices marking up a manuscript. The page she worked on looked mortally wounded–a mass of red ink with complex arrows, scratched out paragraphs, and angry scribbles in the margins. "Hi, Carl," she said. "I'm swamped. What do you need?"

"I'm sorry to interrupt you, but I need to find some way to get involved in the department. I know that the English Graduate Student Association might be a little short-handed."

"The applications are right there," she said, pointing to an empty inbox.

He looked around the desk, seeing no sheets of paper anywhere, just lots of neatly stacked folders. He opened the top folder closest to the empty inbox. Her right hand shot out and closed the folder.

"That's *mine!*" she barked.

"Yikes," Carl said, recoiling. "If this is you on Tuesday, what're you like on Monday?"

"I'm off caffeine," she said.

29

"If your withdrawal correlates to the amount of coffee you used to drink, remind me to short Starbucks in my IRA."

She scowled. "Hell, I don't know what happened to the applications." She started lifting folders and looking inside envelopes. "I'm so buried here." She threw her pen down on to the manuscript.

"What are you working on?"

She tipped her head toward the door to Dr. Grey's office, whispering, "I'm editing his book," she said. Then in a voice near screaming she added, "which is a fucking mess!"

"Can I borrow a pen?" Carl asked.

"So," she said as he filled out the form she gave him, "you're trying to kiss some ass via the EGSA? Keith told me you were trying to hook up with Frye."

"Hook up?"

"I just mean that you want be his Research Assistant. Word is he's working again now that he and Dr. Hirschman broke up. You trying to hook up with her, too?"

"Hook up?" he asked again.

"In this case I mean sex." Apparently, Keith told Rosalie everything.

When she saw he was done, she said, "I've got a feeling you're going to get this EGSA gig. Frye wants to get the group moving." She crossed her fingers and held them up by her face. "Plus, you're the only one to apply. Good luck, Carl!"

A terse email from Rosalie notified Carl he had been accepted as a member of the EGSA. Carl looked forward to the first meeting, though he did harbor some reservations about agreeing to join without even really knowing the organization's purpose. Hopefully he hadn't signed on to extremist group that would require him to lob Molotov cocktails outside of World Trade Organization meetings. The group consisted of Carl, Mr. Clean, the guy in the ancient Vote for Pedro T-shirt, and a female lit major whose numerous sneezes sounded like a librarian's "Shush!" They met in a shabby student lounge on the second floor of the English/ Counseling Services building, everyone sprawled out on their own couch or in a recliner with footrest extended.

According to the EGSA bylaws, the Vice President ran the meetings, but Mr. Clean said that The *Flanesser* usually handled this. Apparently, this usurpation had forced the previous V.P. to quit. Carl expressed no surprise. Frye never showed up. Even without his disruptive influence, the meeting was a mess. It took place on Monday morning, with no agenda or end time.

They spent two hours on old business, including a lengthy discussion about what should go on the back of that year's EGSA T-shirts. It would have gone a little longer, but Carl cut off debate by moving that they vote on Mr. Clean's design. The issue was suddenly settled: the back would read, "Frankenstein was the creator, not the monster." The committee agreed it had the right mix of humor and condescension. No one had any official new business. They spoke about the department's associate professors, complained about the tenured ones, and universally proclaimed they could do a better job than either group. Eventually the entire meeting descended into an argument over whose schedule left them less free time. By the end, Carl determined he would rather endure an Amway recruiting presentation than go through another meeting like that. So, for the next meeting, he took it upon himself to do some extensive advanced planning. He prepared an agenda, emailed in advance to all the participants. He sent them links to sites explaining parliamentary procedure. He notified them that he would squelch conversation topics outside of their stated mission.

Carl noted how the current members of the EGSA reacted to their newfound efficiency. Sullen Pedro no longer lay down on his couch. The Shush-Sneezer sat upright in her recliner and took meaningful notes on the proceedings. When Carl adjourned the meeting, everyone buzzed with the intoxicating effects of slight forward progress. The meeting lasted just sixty minutes.

While even he didn't consider it a home run, he'd led enough teams to know that singles and doubles represented a more reliable, though less dramatic, way to victory. His efforts at streamlining had actually made a difference for the other people in the class. They all said they were busy–he had enabled them to work more efficiently.

These advances wouldn't have impressed Ex-Elizabeth. The types of things that affected her fell more along political lines, things that allowed her to benefit directly as an individual. She couldn't care less how much time Carl had saved his fellow committee members. She would suggest Carl spend time on activities that benefited himself. Without Frye there to see his trudging progress toward greater efficacy, his efforts lacked any direct benefit. But Frye would have to show up one day, right?

Ex-Elizabeth inherited her attitude from her father's side of the family, the Austens. A gang of influential objectivists, generations of Austens had entwined their history with that of the state of Kansas, from her recently deceased grandfather, Douglas Austen, Mayor of Tonganoxie, to her dad, Stephen Austen, former state senator. Her dark hair and large blue eyes came from her mom, Victoria Austen, who had parlayed her looks and married name into her second term as Governor of Kansas. Carl always thought that by studying the Austens' genome, geneticists could easily identify the markers for charisma and the mental capacity to instantly calculate the political implications of any action years into the future. Only Ex-Elizabeth's sister, Mary Austen Tawfee, worked outside politics or traditional business, picking television instead. She worked for her husband as the producer of the regional television show, *Bill Tawfee, the Tastemaker of Topeka.*

Ex-Elizabeth approached every situation with the deadly combination of her politics and psychology. The gravity of the situation had no bearing on the amount of gusto with which she attacked an issue. It didn't matter whether she was talking the pet store into taking back an "unhousetrainable" puppy, convincing the lawn guy to move some furniture into the garage, or persuading her grand-father's doctor to conduct a few more tests.

Upper level management at Ogilvy called Ex-Elizabeth "The Natural." Once she identified an under-performing account, she would have lunch with the business owner. They would chat, nothing more than small talk, and then Ex-Elizabeth would go to work. She would take in each verbal cue and facial tic, and instantly pinpoint what business problems weighed on him or her most. She called it "identifying what caused them the most pain." It might be human resources, fluctuating cash flow, or a high tax burden. Then she and Carl would devise a package of services to relieve that pain. It happened over and over again. When Ex-Elizabeth explained the impact their services could have on the client's business, a moment would come, signaled by the appearance of an expression on the client's face. The look of dumbstruck admiration meant the client would sign up for the proposed service offered right then.

Carl could only think of one time when The Natural had clumsily delivered some information without care of the impact it might have. That was when she had told him she was leaving him to pursue a relationship with the HR Director of one of their clients.

She hadn't cared how Carl received that information.

33

Chapter 3
The Bland Fiction Scholarship

In the East, college athletic facilities had names. He'd been to plenty of events for client entertainment purposes at places like the Carrier Dome, Agganis Arena, even the Corey Ford Rugby Clubhouse at Dartmouth.

No wealthy philanthropist had yet died and left enough money to have K-State's stadium named after him, unlike the namesake of Fred Bramlage Coliseum next door, where the basketball team played. Though Carl felt the name KSU Football Stadium was bad, it sounded better than the lugubrious name of the structure that used to hold the football games: Memorial Stadium, generically dedicated to dead people everywhere.

Carl followed the directions he held in his hand at the bottom of Rosalie's "exclusive" email invitation to the tailgate party before the Kansas State vs. Kansas game. He wore a K-State T-shirt. The only article of purple clothing he had ever owned, it featured the Powercat, a stylized version of a wildcat in profile. Carl envisioned English professors and distinguished alums all wearing purple, standing around the back of a customized van, swilling—what would they swill? Certainly not keg beer. Wine? Smirnoff Ice? Whisky? WWFD: What Would Frye Drink?

Would they talk about the uncertain future of K-State's football program or the rise in the popularity of nonfiction? Perhaps some astute GTA would draw a postmodern connection between the two. He had to go to find out. It might be good for him politically to attend, even though Frye probably wouldn't be there. This event smacked of everything Jules Frye probably despised: an official department party, stale food, and a few people he would never choose to see in a social setting. In fact, Carl really knew nothing about the party. It just might be fun, he thought. At the very least he might get to chat up Dr. Hirschman.

The white tent in the parking lot looked more like it should house a small circus instead of an English department tailgate. He followed a bicycle rack fence to the tent's entrance, guarded by a chubby bouncer in a yellow security vest holding a clipboard.

"What's your name, Chester?" he said, scratching between the fat rolls of his neck with his pen.

"Carl Krauthammer."

"Is that with a C or a K?" The vest, a size too small, struggled to cover his T-shirt, which read "Campus Security: Keeping Order with a Smile."

Carl answered, "Which, Carl or Krauthammer?"

"Huh?"

Carl just shook his head and looked at the list to search for his name. The bouncer quickly clutched the clipboard to his chest with his left hand while his right moved toward the nightstick that hung from his belt.

"Easy does it," he said. "How do I know you're not just going to find a name on this list and tell me that's your name and then 'It's free food and booze for Chester.'" He screwed his face up and leaned forward, pointing. "I been on this beat for four years, paying my dues. Next year it's a promotion. The year after that they give me a gun. I'm not letting you screw any of that up."

Carl laughed. "Who's going to crash an English department party?"

"This is Forrest Bland's party." Although the bouncer released his grip on the clipboard, he was careful to keep it from Carl's view. He looked over the list again, this time with a section of his tongue showing from the corner of his mouth.

Forrest Bland? What the hell was that guy doing here?

"Here's your name, Kraut," the bouncer said, then adding, "hammer." The bouncer peeled back a triangular section of the tent. "Entray voo, Chester. You got lucky... this time."

Carl entered to the applause and laughter of two hundred people. It smelled stuffy, a mix of beer breath and barbeque. The crowd faced away from the entrance toward an older man standing in front of a band setup, speaking into

35

a microphone. He wore a white T-shirt crisscrossed with the sleeves of a purple sweater tied around his neck.

Carl ordered a beer from the bar and turned to watch the man, whom he recognized as Forrest Bland, II.

"Before the band," Bland said as the group quieted down. "I said, before the band Der Kommissar starts playing, I want to recognize one more person here," he said. "You may have never heard of him before." Bland moved the microphone stand to one side and leaned forward to hear something from the crowd. He straightened and spoke with his lips touching the mike, "Jules, if you'd just write another book, they would all know who you are."

Everyone laughed.

He continued, "Here is a real sports fan's sports fan, and a pretty damned good writer. We are lucky to have him here at Kansas State. The small gift that my foundation has given to the university, and the gifts we hope are to come, are due to this man. Please put your hands together for Jules Frye."

Frye raised his hand and gave a cursory wave to the politely clapping crowd.

Bland leaned forward and said, "Say a few words, Jules." He extended the microphone to Frye.

"Barring Alzheimer's, I will never forget this moment."

Carl laughed. The crowd groaned in a ritualized display of academic political correctness.

It momentarily put Bland off his prepared speech. With one line, Frye had managed to throw sand in the eyes of Forrest Bland, II.

"All right," Bland said, "we have Call Hall ice cream, there's plenty of food, and yes, Jules, lots to drink. So enjoy yourselves and let's beat the shit–sorry, Chancellor Schroeder. Let's beat the heck out of the Jayhawks!" This brought the applause level up, and Bland stepped down into the crowd.

Carl snaked through the crowd. He had to see how Frye interacted with Bland.

Two streams of thought conjoined in his brain. Here Forrest Bland, a person from Carl's former accountant life,

36

collided with his new venture. He had trouble cramming both lives in his head at the same time. He scanned the crowd—some were eating cheese chunks off Styrofoam plates, others drinking wine or beer from clear plastic cups.

From twenty feet away, he spotted a knot of people by the riser. Frye and Bland stood at its center, chatting in hushed tones. Dr. Grey and Professor Susan Hirschman flanked them but did not appear to be a part of the other conversation. Carl walked up as Frye and Bland reached a lull.

Frye had his head thrown back, trying to free a stubborn ice cube from the cup hovering over his mouth. "Somebody get a Physics professor over here," he said. With a harsh slap on the bottom of the cup the cube came free and dropped in his mouth.

Everyone turned to look at Carl. He greeted each face with a smile or a nod.

Hirschman's dangling owl earrings drew Carl's gaze, which led to her delicate jawline, which led to her perfect chin, her lips, her nose, and, ultimately, her eyes. She focused on Bland.

Frye gestured to Carl with his empty cup. He shifted the ice cube to his right cheek and said, "Forrest Bland, I'd like you to meet one of our graduate students with a writing emphasis, Carl Krauthammer."

Dr. Grey brightened. "Carl is just the kind of person we're hoping our program will attract in greater numbers, Mr. Bland." His small glasses had no frames, just two discs attached to gold temple pieces that burrowed into the hair on either side of his head. They reinforced his resemblance to John Denver and gave his eyes a constant look of magnified incredulity.

Bland had a firm grip, and the shake lasted longer than Carl expected. "Nice to meet you Carl."

"Nice to see you."

Bland looked to Grey. "What makes him so special? Does he pay his tuition in cash?"

Grey and Hirschman chuckled. Frye bit into his ice cube.

"He comes from the business world," Dr. Grey said. "From the other Manhattan."

"Really?" Bland asked. "You must be related to Elizabeth Austen-Krauthammer?"

From his peripheral vision Carl saw Dr. Hirschman glance his way. "Yes, she's my ex-wife, well, soon to be ex."

Bland bit into a pork rib then said around the mouthful, "Very talented woman. Seems to know what you need before you need it."

Carl wondered when Bland would have learned so much about Ex-Elizabeth. "Of course, that must not have been *your* experience."

"I could go on and on about that situation," Carl said. "But this is a celebration of the creative writing program, right?"

Bland smiled before spitting some gristle into his napkin. "So, what do you write?"

"I have this idea for a novel rolling around. You might not like it. It skewers corporate America."

"Interesting," Bland said. He brought his drink to his lips and lowered it without taking a sip.

"I hope so. It's about people in the trenches at a mid-sized company, cube farmers mostly." Carl squeezed his empty beer cup between his hands, alternately rolling it from fingers to palm. "It would be comparable to your acquisitions arm in New York. Comparable in every way, except perhaps for the incompetent Director of Human Resources in my story. The HR guy is the foil."

Frye may have picked up on the bitterness because he arched his eyebrows and grinned. Bland did not, and furthermore gave no indication that he made the connection to his own Director of Human Resources. Instead he smiled and took a drink this time around. "God damn, that's something that needs making fun of." He glanced from Frye to Grey. "I mean that's something of which fun needs to be made. Did I wrangle that preposition back into line boys?"

"You did, at the expense of intelligibility," Frye said. They all laughed. Carl wondered if perhaps he had misread

38

the conflict between Frye and Bland. They seemed almost chummy.

"Sounds like you know something about corporate life," Bland said to Carl.

"I worked for Ogilvy & Standpipe in New York," Carl said. "I handled the Heartland Dairy deal for the Sellars."

"Of course, with Elizabeth," he said, appearing finally to have put Carl in context. To bring the others up to speed, he continued, "We acquired the Heartland Dairy earlier this year. It's turned out to be quite lucrative for us." He raised his glass as if making a toast. "Excellent work."

"Thank you," Carl said between his teeth.

Frye turned to whisper something to Dr. Hirshman, but she appeared not to hear, watching Carl as he tried to drink from his empty beer.

"At any rate, the kind of novels we have out there in the market now about business are all written by liberal dip-shits whose business knowledge extends no farther than their hatred of Wal-Mart."

"Carl has a good portfolio. He's here for some polish, some mentoring," Grey said.

"Lots of polish," Frye said.

Carl frowned. Why did he have to say that here? Was he trying to kiss Bland's ass?

Bland nodded. "Well, you're in good hands here. I hope you'll consider submitting something for my scholarship this semester. Open to any college student in Kansas."

Carl started to respond but Frye cut in, "If he does his work. Perhaps we should have sicced Grey on him, get the basics in line and then I could help where talent comes in."

Everyone looked at Dr. Grey, whose expression never changed from a mild smile. "Perhaps you could take my 'Anatomy of Creative Writing' class next semester, Carl. I can't think of any writer who wouldn't benefit from a re-fresher on the basics once in a while."

"Once these two make you a great writer, you can finish that HR Director novel. We hope to cultivate some young talent for West Egg Press," Bland said.

Carl hadn't known that Bland's West Egg Holdings had a publication arm, but it didn't surprise him. The Blands were big on diversification. "Thank you. I look forward to learning everything I can in the meantime."

After a moment of silence, Dr. Hirschman said, "Mr. Bland, has your foundation completed its giving for this year?"

"You should be warned, Forrest," Frye said. "Dr. Hirschman is a lactivist."

"A what?"

"I have a breast-feeding advocacy group I work with, and I would think that as a company that makes baby formula…" At that point, the band started playing "Girls Just Wanna Have Fun." Bland motioned to his ears and shrugged.

The group dissipated. Bland and Frye headed to West Egg's skybox suite in the stadium.

Bland's company, West Egg Holdings, represented the holy grail of Carl's tenure at Ogilvy. The company had all the earmarks of a perfect cash cow for Carl and Ex-Elizabeth's team. The Blands had operated a venture capital fund before forming West Egg Holdings, a conglomeration of thirteen unrelated companies: dairies, food processing, transportation, small publishing imprints (think on-the-cheap travel guides), and a website dealing in low-end sofa paintings. Companies like Nestle and PET Milk outsourced some of their food processing and transportation needs to West Egg. The valuation of all the companies hovered around a billion dollars. The company relentlessly pursued acquisitions that increased its reach in the Midwest.

Carl and Elizabeth's goal was to broker the Heartland Dairy deal for the Sellars, then exploit that connection as a possible inroad to doing work for West Egg Holdings. Larger corporations like Archer Daniels Midland always sniffed around and proposed tender offers for various West Egg operations. Bland and his father fielded all of these inquests personally. Ex-Elizabeth diagnosed this constant demand on their time and resources as the source of considerable pain, best alleviated by Carl's team. She thought the sweetheart terms with which West Egg acquired Heartland

Dairy deserved some *quid pro quo*. She even dreamed they might offer to permanently hire them from Ogilvy & Standpipe - not unheard of in consulting relation-ships. She had practically negotiated stock options and benefit packages in her mind, but before they materialized, Elizabeth left him, and Carl left the company.

Dr. Hirschman led Carl through the crowd to a table far from Der Kommissar, where they shared a plate of raw vegetables. She wore a purple K-State jersey with a plunging v-neck. Her eyes adopted some of the color of her shirt, warming up the blue, where it had the effect of softening her whole face, smoothing out the angles of her nose and the points at the corners of her mouth.

"You know your way around important people," Hirschman said.

"Bah."

"I think you made an impression. You'll be a ringer for that scholarship if you kiss ass a little bit."

Carl said, "That might be hard for me to do. Could I rely on the quality of my writing?"

"I'm sure it'll have to hold its own, but this won't hurt," she said.

"What's he doing here? What does he have to do with the English Department?"

"He was an English major here, before he transferred to Baker. Just before you walked up he was telling us how he felt he owed all his success to being able to communicate clearly," Hirschman said. "Smacks of B.S. to me, but now he's got this West Egg Press thing. He buys books from larger publishing houses, older best sellers, mostly. Bought a couple of Frye's books and reissued them as hardbacks. Then they sell them directly to Costco and Sam's Club."

"Sounds like a great business model."

"I need to be able to use words like 'business model,'" she said, "if I'm ever going to get his charitable foundation to give up some money. The formula mongers say on their ads, breast milk is best, but why not try our formula?' The bastards. Did you see how Bland reacted when I brought it up? He couldn't get away fast enough."

"Where does all that come from, the breastfeeding stuff?"

"I just think it's best for babies to be breastfed. Haven't you seen the articles, all of the studies?"

Carl shrugged. "Guess I figured I'd think about that after I had a baby."

"Anyway, you handled him beautifully."

"I wasn't trying to handle anyone. It's a tailgate party."

"I could tell Julian thought you did a good job, too." She stabbed a broccoli floret. "When the time comes I'd be happy to help however I can. I've never judged a writing competition before, nor do I have any pull with Bland." She stared blankly at her plate. "And I'm not a creative writing professor. Actually, I'd probably be of no help to you at all." She brightened and touched his hand. "But I'm a hell of a lot of fun on a date."

"Yes, you Romantic-Period experts always are." She had kept her hand on his for an extra moment, or perhaps it just felt like she had.

Before he quite thought it through, Carl said, "There's a party Friday night; perhaps we can go and I'll see for myself how much fun you are." His ears reddened and he quickly stuffed two baby carrots in his mouth, afraid to look her in the face.

She continued as if she hadn't heard the last part. "I'm so swamped with the research on the article I'm writing with Keith. We have this deadline a week from Monday—we may be working Friday night."

"But Keith's the one having the party."

She laughed. "In that case, I guess I'm in."

Carl hadn't placed exercise high on his priorities with all the reading he had to do, but he enjoyed riding Keith's bike through campus. The day was warm for early September. A few renegade trees had already changed to a slightly yellow-tinged green, but it didn't feel like any specific season, a limbo between the cut clover smell of summer and the wet leaf smell of autumn. One of his professors, Dr. Fabresi, referred to it as Native American Summer.

He headed down Mid-Campus Drive past Weber Hall. The university's livestock arena dominated the building's exterior like a bulbous polyp. The arena held cattle shows and mysteriously named demonstrations like "Breeding Soundness Examinations for Rams." Carl acknowledged that no matter how much Frye wanted to raise the status of the department, they would never put on an event that could draw enough students or visitors to fill up a place like that. His bitterness abated, though, when he recalled the shit-smell that had assaulted his nose when curiosity had driven him inside the place. The ram examiners could keep Weber Hall to themselves.

When he returned home he met Rosalie heading out the front door.

"Well, well, well!" she said. "Look who it is. Mr. B.M. On Campus."

"I don't care for that name."

"No denying, you are the shit around here. You're all anybody is talking about." She counted off his accomplishments on her fingers. "You know Forrest Bland, you're hooking up with Dr. Hirschman, and you're running the EGSA. Speaking of, you want to kiss two asses with one pucker? Hold those EGSA meetings in Dickens Hall. Dr. Grey is trying to raise the status of the English department."

"What difference would it make where we hold those meetings?"

"He and Frye have been talking about moving the department in a swankier building. Actually, you probably don't have to kiss Frye's ass anymore, since you two will be working together."

"Huh?"

43

"I'm just guessing about Frye. He called me and asked how he could get in contact with you. Said he wanted to talk to you."

Jules Frye lived out where the streets didn't warrant signs. Carl thought Elm Hollow Corner might be a quaint little town, replete with brick streets and maybe a courthouse square. Instead, it resembled more of an intersection. He continued north on an unmarked street that had to be Frye's street. It was the only street.

As he drove, the trees flanking the road parted and smooth green prairie spread out for miles on each side. With no wind to stir the grass, the gentle slopes obscured their true scale–they could just as easily have been small moss-covered rocks in a stream or mile-wide hills.

The street tried to stay paved for a mile or so, but then the patches of asphalt gave way until none remained. As he approached the crest of a small hump in the landscape, the hood of the car gently aligned with the horizon, and Carl felt suddenly like an intruder. The grass below grudgingly supported him–the cloudless sky glowered at him. He increased his speed.

He was twenty minutes early–a condition Carl called "Manhattan Lag." After a month in town he still left himself too much time to get places, as if he still had to negotiate with subways and cabs in New York. He pulled over before reaching Frye's house and closed his eyes to visualize a successful meeting. This tactic came from a short webinar entitled, "Show Me the Money! Visualize Your Way to Financial Freedom," created by Ogilvy & Standpipe. Ex-Elizabeth had bundled it with another self-help treasure, the vintage CD series *Negotiate Your Way to Happiness the McKenzie Brackman Way* (Featuring the voices of your favorite *L.A. Law* characters). Her grandfather, Douglas Austen, had left it to her in his will.

44

She had demanded he watch the Webinar on their second wedding anniversary after Carl failed to negotiate an upgrade to their suite at a Vermont bed and breakfast. The webinar taught him two simple techniques needed to achieve financial freedom. The first, visualization, took up four slides, but basically boiled down to imagining how a conversation might go, all the way until you seal the deal. The second technique had proved the most valuable for Carl: make sure you explicitly ask for what you want. They called it "asking for the order." Apparently, Ogilvy & Standpipe internal audits showed that employing both methods increased success rates over eighteen percent. But to Carl, the issue was binary - you either achieved freedom or you didn't. Eighteen percent closer to freedom meant you remained in servitude. Still, he had seen benefits to using the techniques. He did not, however, get anything out of the *L.A. Law* CDs because the last time he looked in the set's case, the first one was missing.

The meeting progressed in his mind. Carl could practically hear Professor Frye saying he *had* to have Carl as his research assistant. He saw himself not as a fawning groupie but as a self-confident student hoping to gain knowledge. Carl opened his eyes and picked up his Blackberry from the passenger seat, revealing the ration of herbal supplements he'd bought at the gas station. Labeled "Brain Boost", the packet contained ginkgo biloba, St. John's Wort, oriental ginseng, and one pill with a shit-ton of caffeine. He'd purchased them on a whim, figuring he could use any advantage he could find. However, he'd forgotten to take them the prescribed thirty minutes before his meeting. Now he might not achieve Optimal Mental Clarity and Alertness™ until after he met with Frye. He swallowed them with a swig of Mountain Dew and opened the browser on his phone.

He selected the bookmark for Wikipedia and re-read the entry on Frye, some of which he had contributed:

Born in October of 1957 in Michigan. Graduated from Lahser High School in Bloomfield Hills, Michigan. B.A. 1981 in English from University of Michigan, M.F.A. in English from Indiana University, rodeo star 1998-1999 until

45

he broke his hip in Strong City, Kansas. Teaching at Kansas State 2004 to present. He published four books The Voortman Trifecta *(1988),* Faulty Cradles *(1995),* Again with the Voortmans *(1996), and* The Atomic T-Bones *(2001).* Trifecta *sold two and a half million copies, and each subsequent book dwindled in popularity from there.*

Carl had read all of them and had a first edition of *Faulty Cradles* in a box in storage in New York. He started the car and recited the rest of the bio in his mind. Frye loves basketball, especially the Celtics and the Pacers. He used to appear on the sidelines of the Pacers games until he moved to Manhattan. In 1988, he appeared on *Bill Tawfee: The Tastemaker of Topeka.* Married in 1997, divorced in 1998.

As he pulled in the long driveway he added one more item to the bio: Jules Frye collected lawn jockeys. Frye had lined his driveway with ten of the little men, all repainted to be Caucasian, leaning forward and grinning, right arm clutching rings or lanterns. The figures crowded up next to the stone house. He had no fences, a freshly dug hole in the middle of the yard, and a BMW in the open garage.

Just as Carl got out of his car, a shirtless Frye appeared from around the corner of the house pushing a wheelbarrow containing some yard tools. Frye's glasses had tinted themselves to eighty-five percent black. Two stumpy mixed breed dogs accompanied him. They noticed Carl, and ran up to bark. The one with longer fur started growling and snarling.

"Goddamn it, Taint," Frye said, a cigarette dangling between his lips. "Shut up. You scare no one. Get lost." The second dog sniffed and urinated on the closest lawn jockey. "Merkin! We've been through this. Don't befoul the statuary."

Frye freed a cigarette lighter from inside the waistband of the plaid boxers that showed above his cutoff shorts. He lit his cigarette and shook Carl's hand.

"Thanks for coming out. Too many people bothering me at my office."

A short burst of unvisualized words came out of Carl, "I'm a fan of yours, a big fan. I own all of your books."

"So you're the one who bought *Again With the Voortmans.* Thanks." Frye looked out over the expanse of his front yard that had no jockeys on it. "And here I didn't think anyone in that class had read a single one of my books, let alone liked any of them. Why didn't you say anything?"

"I've referenced your work in the class."

"I just took that for ass-kissing." Frye leaned over to pick up the handles of the wheelbarrow when something in his navel caught his glance. "Now what the hell?" He dug it out and put his glasses up on top his head to examine it closer. "Do you get the feeling that things visit you, that stuff goes on while you sleep? And the only trace, the proof of their occurrence is the stuff you discover in your navel?" He held a piece of pink lint out between them. "I don't own anything that color."

Carl laughed. "One time I found a thread knotted around my second toe when I took my sock off." He pointed to the lint. "As a matter of fact, the thread was that very color."

Frye closed one eye and focused from the lint to Carl's face. "It's a sign. That makes us *compadres.*" Then he smiled, letting the lint drift to the ground, where Merkin sniffed and eventually ate it.

"Hope you don't mind if I do a little work while we talk," Frye said. "It's something I've been putting off."

"Sure. I mean no, I don't mind." Carl followed Frye toward the hole in the front yard. It was rectangular, almost like a small grave. Frye kneeled at its edge and reached down to the bottom, about two feet. "Bland tells me you two have a past."

"We do," Carl said.

"He's pretty impressed with you. He said you're the kind of student the creative writing program ought to–he used the word *target.* I told him creative writing programs *attract*, snipers target."

"It does sound aggressive."

Frye gingerly dug around the perimeter of a two-foot square something wrapped in black plastic.

"I buried this a year ago," he said.

"What is it?"

He cleared the last bit of dirt off the top with his hands. "Notes for my latest book. I've decided to bring it back from the dead."

Carl bent down to help him pull it out of the hole. The box, or whatever it was, did not weigh more than five or six pounds. Frye removed duct tape and plastic to reveal a cooler that could hold twelve beers. He brushed off some dirt with the whiskbroom, and wiped it down with a bandana. So Frye would be writing again. Carl felt a peculiar needling sensetion at the base of his skull. It intensified and spread from his scalp to all over his body. It signaled the attainment of Optimal Mental Clarity and Alertness®.

Frye opened the cooler and averted his face from the air released. He gasped, waving the sour smell away. Then he pulled a stack of papers from the cooler.

Carl moistened his lower lip with his tongue. "I'd like to be your Research Assistant on that book." He pointed to the papers in Frye's hands. "I want to learn firsthand about the writer's life."

Frye smiled. "Well, Goddamn! I knew you'd do it." He whacked the papers on his thigh, raising a billow of light dust. "Bland didn't think you would. He said, 'That guy will never ask for it, you'll have to offer the assistantship to him.' But I knew you'd do it."

"Bland? What does Bland have to do with it?"

"His family foundation is ready to place a new large grant at a university in Kansas. I'd like to think we have an in here at Kansas State, since Forrest II is an alum. I'd like to get that money earmarked for Creative Writing. I'm also hoping to publish my book through his new press. Bringing in that kind of money and getting another book published, these are the best things in my quest for tenure."

"How can you not have tenure with four books published?"

Frye began shoveling dirt back in the hole and appeared not to hear. "Yes, you can be my Research Assistant," he said. "It'll have to be informal. That is, I can't pay you."

Carl did need money, but that was a temporary situation, until he sold the apartment in New York. He wouldn't have to wait too long for that to happen, and then he could get out from under the loan, which Ex-Elizabeth was making payments on as part of their separation agreement. "No problem," he said.

"Great, Carl. You start today. Fill in that hole." Frye handed him the shovel and went back in the house. When Carl was done, the dirt didn't come close to filling up to ground level.

Chapter 4
UR Raw

Dr. Susan Hirschman's house, a pale blue split level, overlooked a rectangle of grass called Pioneer Park, a tribute to the rugged men and women who begrudgingly founded Manhattan after their riverboat ran aground on a nearby sandbar. Carl sensed order here–her lawn distinguished itself from the neighbors' in its weed-less homogeneity. As Carl walked up the front steps, he could see through the glass of the door. Inside Susan kissed a young man briefly on the cheek. She spotted Carl over the man's shoulder with a slight look of panic. She turned the man around with her hands on his shoulders and gave him a playful push toward the door. She went up the inside staircase as the guy came outside. He looked about twenty, wearing a black T-shirt and black pants. In one arm, he carried two empty glass milk bottles.

"*Bonjour*. She said to go on in," the guy said, jerking his head toward the door. "There's a beer in the fridge." He studied Carl's face a minute. "Don't worry, *Monsieur*, she's known me since I was very young."

Carl watched the man get in a minivan and drive off without fastening his seatbelt. The car roared off down the road, the sound of its rusted emissions system finally yielded to the late afternoon rustling of leaves.

Inside the house, she'd painted the walls of each room in rich deep colors: navy blue in the entry and up the stairs, burgundy in the dining room to the left, forest green in the living room to the right. The hardwoods had blanched, slightly past due for a refinish. Music seeped from a boom box: Lyle Lovett. A vanilla-scented candle burned somewhere.

She entered the room. "Don't stand up," she said. "I'm still not ready." She kissed him on the cheek the same way she had kissed the younger guy. She picked up her purse from the coffee table and pulled out a tube of lipstick.

"All right, I gotta ask. Who was the guy?"

She spoke over her shoulder as she headed back up the stairs. "Oh him. He's my milkman."

"Your milkman?" She had a milkman? It sounded like a scene in a porn movie. He stood up and headed for the bookshelves that lined one of the walls. The first shelf Carl looked at clearly held the personal enrichment section, because there he saw *Chicken Soup for the Volunteer's Soul: Stories to Celebrate the Spirit of Courage, Caring, and Community; Co-Dependent No More: Why You Need Therapy Even Though He's the One With the Problem;* and *Why Does He Do That: Inside the Minds of Angry and Controlling Men.* He picked up the co-dependent book and looked inside the cover. There, he saw with relief it did not belong to Susan but to someone named Suzanne Sherman.

But still, she had borrowed it. Either she has issues, Carl thought, or she's only dated guys who do. He made his way through a swinging door into a yellow kitchen and opened the fridge. On the top shelf sat a stack of three round cheese boxes. The only marks on them at all appeared where someone had hastily written a cryptic code in orange grease pencil: "UR *Brie de Mieux, lait cru,* 28 d." Next to them were two full milk bottles, also with no formal labeling. He picked one up. The glass felt warm. It had "UR: Raw" written on its side.

"I'm your milkman," he said aloud, followed by a "walka walka wah wah" guitar: the universal adult film soundtrack. He found a Bud Light on one of the shelves of the door and popped it open. Stale. While he couldn't find the born-on date, he did eventually place the beer's age thanks to a logo on the side, "Bud Light, Proud Sponsor of the Olympic Winter Games in Torino." So she had warm milk and stale beer.

Carl didn't know they even had milkmen anymore. This one drove a van with windows, clearly unrefrigerated. So he was an *unsafe* milkman. Was he an ex-husband? Perhaps it was part of their divorce settlement that he would have to deliver milk for the rest of his life in lieu of alimony. Yet, he looked too young for that. Perhaps a young, angry, controlling man. But why would you kiss an angry and controlling man

51

on the cheek? Carl would share no woman with an angry and controlling milkman. He poured the beer out and tossed the can into the recycling bin. On a shelf Carl noticed a framed picture of a very young woman in a hospital gown holding a baby. He looked closely. He saw Susan's eyes, but the complexion looked paler, and the hair color was different, dark red.

Dr. Susan Hirschman cleared her throat from the doorway. She wore a low-cut pink T-shirt and jeans and had curled her hair. The effect of the "going out" version of Susan was quite positive. She wore a small gold necklace with a single diamond, which tastefully drew Carl's attention to her neck. He hadn't noticed her neck–slim, smooth and perfectly proportioned. How had he never noticed her neck?

Her right hand went to the necklace. She took the diamond in her hand and moved it back and forth on its chain. "I can't sleep with you until the semester is over," she said. She smoothed the pink T-shirt just below her left breast and looked back up with sparkling eyes. "Let's go to dinner."

President McKinley (his mother apparently liked the sound of "President" as a first name) claimed to weigh the same as when he was the third string quarterback in 1998, the year K-State lost to Purdue in the Builders Square Alamo Bowl. Carl learned everything about President McKinley from the mounted articles in the foyer of his restaurant, The White House Supper Club in downtown Manhattan.

Though his statistics for the game amounted to one attempt and zero completions, Wildcat fans attribute his one-play substitution to giving Michael Bishop, starting quarterback, the time he needed to recover from a stinger suffered on his throwing arm. That recovery time helped Bishop lead the team to come back from a ten-point deficit with only 6:44 to play. Even though the 'Cats eventually lost the game, McKinley combined his performance and a B.S. in Animal Sciences (concentration: livestock) to garner the support of some enthusiastic alumni who eventually underwrote The White House Supper Club. Carl's budget allowed one nice meal per semester. Susan had told him it was the best place in Manhattan, and he wanted to try it.

Across the restaurant Carl watched McKinley, a large African American man regaling an older couple with a story that, judging by the gesticulations, involved a forward pass. Carl decided it was the incomplete one he'd thrown four years earlier. How many times had President McKinley told that story? The man could have weighed what he did in college if, as Carl had heard, fat weighs less than muscle. Someone had placed his head, covered with a short scrub of black hair, directly atop his shoulders, rendering any need for a neck superfluous. His brown suit appeared tailored for him.

Susan walked up to the hostess station and spoke quietly to the woman there, who leafed through a notebook and emphatically shook her head, indicating that all the tables were taken.

A slight, stern woman who looked like she weighed what she did in 1998 glared at Susan. A brass nameplate on the hostess station read "Lady McKinley."

Carl approached the women and said, "Is there really nothing you can do? I mean, look at all the tables."

"You are aware of a common practice called 'making a reservation?'" Lady McKinley asked. "Those are reserved."

Carl nodded. "That is the standard procedure, especially on a football weekend. But I just found out that it's a special occasion," he said. "This woman just told me I have something very exciting to look forward to after finals."

Susan elbowed him in the ribs.

Eventually Lady McKinley promised them a small two-top in an hour. Keith's party didn't start until nine, so they had time to wait. They decided to walk around until their table was ready. It was early and there weren't many people on the street.

Lately, the evenings had started cooling off. They paused at the open door to a small taproom. Inside a large party of male students sat at a few tables pushed together. There were plastic cups and pitchers in various states of fullness covering the tabletop. They could hear the men talking about the next day's game.

"If we don't beat McNeese State, I'll literally kiss your ass," the largest one said. "We'll score fifty points."

Another said, "Will you suck *me* if we don't score fifty points?"

"Hand job, maybe."

Susan blew a laugh out of her nose.

They kept walking. "Charming," Carl said.

"Oh, that guy's all right. He's in one of my undergrad classes." A breeze kicked up and Susan shivered. She drew a little closer to Carl and put her arm through his.

Her close proximity startled him at first. It was a move Ex-Elizabeth never would have made. She didn't approve of Public Displays of Affection, so no handholding, no arms around the waist, and certainly nothing beyond an air kiss. He recalled only one time when she broke this rule, the first time their team at Ogilvy & Standpipe beat out the others for the largest increase in business. Her impromptu kiss led to their first date.

"So," Susan said, after a brief silence, "about your marriage."

Carl coughed. "Yes, about that."

She waited for him to respond further, but he felt uncomfortable. He needed a specific question. "What do you want to know?"

"Whatever you want to tell me about it." She looked straight ahead.

Did she want to know how they met? Why they're splitting up? Which were their favorite sexual positions? "It got to the point where I thought we should part ways."

She nodded.

"This was *after* she'd moved out and had taken up with another guy." He'd surprised her. He could tell by her laughter. "I'd been putting in a lot of twelve and thirteen hour days, trying to help broker a deal between my client and

54

Forrest Bland's Dairy. It was a tough time for us. We were trying to have a baby, too. It scares me to think that I wished for something so hard that I now see would have been a horrible mistake. Thank God that never happened."

"You don't want kids?" she asked.

Jesus, Carl thought, it's early for this conversation. "No, I just mean, that I didn't want to be involved with her forever, you know, constantly have to deal with her forever."

"My sister? She's the one you saw in that picture in my kitchen? Her ex never came to visit or anything. She was lucky, but I'm not so sure it's best for the kid."

They stopped at the windows for Barrack Brothers, a clothing store divided into Lady Barrack and Man Barrack. Carl saw some interesting shirts, but nothing he deemed worth the money. Susan looked into the window at a black sport coat on a mannequin. "Do you think that's possible, to excise someone out of your life? Someone who was so deeply woven into your past? Pretend they never existed?"

Carl considered that beyond a few curt emails, he and Ex-Elizabeth hadn't communicated since he arrived in Kansas. "I do. I mean, you notice the hole left behind." He pulled his jacket tighter around his shoulders. "But you stretch the rest and eventually the gap gets sewn shut. Or better yet, you patch it over with something."

"I'm not so sure you can do it so easily. I fear you're never free of someone who's played an intimate role in your life." She clearly wanted to know where Carl stood with Ex-Elizabeth.

"I don't know about that," he said. "This is really the first time I've tried. I could be wrong." Why did he have to obfuscate?

"There was a guy. I was so young. He was so influential. It practically amounted to abuse the way he presided over the formation of so many of my beliefs."

Carl thought she must refer to the angry and controlling guy. He had to come clean, to leave no doubt. Her honesty deserved reciprocation. "I'm not divorced yet."

"I know that," she said, looking into his eyes. "But what does it mean? Might that hole have some more fraying to do?"

"Perhaps. And, so you know, I hate clothing metaphors."

She pulled his arm to draw their faces closer together. She kissed him on the cheek right by his ear.

Once they reached Crum's Beauty College they crossed the street and headed back down in the opposite direction. They passed Amelia's Home Ambiance and suddenly found themselves right in front of Finn's Pub.

"Should we get a drink?" he asked.

Before she answered, the door burst open and Jules Frye came out with another man. He said, "I'll kiss *your* ass if Pynchon's next book isn't a bestseller." He stopped when he saw Susan and Carl. He looked back and forth between them before his face cracked into a grin, the dimple in his chin deepened. "I'll be damned. My two favorite people." His eyes looked dull, like he'd been in the bar for a while. "Well, I heard all the Rosalies, but until I saw it myself–"

"The Rosalies?" Carl asked.

"Ah, I tend to forget," Frye said, "Carl's a *student* here, isn't he, Susan?" His breath smelled of beer and CornNuts. "Those are rumors initiated by Rosalie. Quite virulent, they usually only take half an hour to spread through the department. In this case I think it took less time."

Carl studied Frye's face. The mouth and the raised eyebrows registered a good-natured wryness, like all he was doing was giving Susan trouble. But then he sized Carl up, a quick head-to-toe inventory. His eyebrows rose a little higher. Frye was jealous.

Frye held the door open. "Come on back in. I'll stay for one more now that I have some interesting folks to speak to."

Susan spoke quickly. "That's not necessary, Jules. Our table should be ready at the White House."

"The White House?" he said, his face transitioning into a sloe-eyed grin. "You must be celebrating something. Perhaps Carl's new research assistantship with me?"

Susan glanced at Carl, looking surprised. "I hadn't heard that Rosalie."

"I planned to tell you at dinner tonight, but yes, Professor Frye has accepted me as his research assistant."

She spoke to Frye. "Just make sure you don't ruin him, eh, Jules?"

"Goodnight, Krauthammer. See you next week." Frye pushed between them and continued down the sidewalk.

Carl appreciated the White House Supper Club, despite the continued rude treatment from Lady McKinley. Their dinner conversation passed easily, starting with small talk about *Frankenstein*, the book they had just finished in her class. She made some remarks about an article she'd read in a journal about Dr. Frankenstein's lab as a womb metaphor. Carl thought it a stretch, but Susan said she hadn't decided what she thought. After dessert Carl asked Susan about the ruin comment she'd made to Frye earlier, and she demurred, conceding only that it was an inside joke.

After dinner, they didn't stay together long. She left Keith's party soon after, saying she had to get up early to edit the initial treatment of the journal article. They kissed briefly on her front porch. Carl got the impression that neither of them thought anything further should happen that night. He headed back to the party to help Keith and company finish off the keg.

Dickens Hall was the kind of charming four-story building of textured yellow limestone that screams "college campus." The tenement effect produced by window air conditioners protruding from each set of windows melted away the moment Carl saw the two-story arched entrance-way. A plaque just inside the front door revealed the building's namesake as Albert Dickens, "faithful servant of the Horticulture Department, 1899-1930."

Besides a Philosophy class on Thursdays, and now the EGSA meeting on Mondays, nothing else occurred in the room, according to a schedule taped to the door. Some deteriorating bookshelves flanked a small window that held an ancient Kenmore window unit. There were no chairs around the table.

He stepped back out and looked down the hall. Three students at the far end watched him and then pretended to have a conversation, all of them speaking at the same time. He eventually found some chairs, crammed in a classroom across the hall. He could hear hushed laughter coming from the end of the hall.

"That was a good one, guys," Carl said to them. "You really got me."

He thought he heard one of them say, "Weiner!" They laughed a little louder and then scurried through a doorway. As he arranged the chairs around the table, he felt better about going a little overboard on the EGSA meetings. Even though he had gained the favor of Frye and Hirschman, the group needed him. They had no leadership. He couldn't abandon them just when they were about to begin work on the Spring English Event (item two on the New Business portion of Carl's agenda). Besides, he took pride in the gentle and continuing progress they had made. With the chairs in place, the room looked perfectly uncomfortable and conducive to a quick meeting. Carl hadn't even bothered wheeling in a chair for The *Flanesser* or Frye.

Old business moved along quickly, with only six minutes spent on Mr. Clean worrying that he hadn't asked enough people's opinion on the Frankenstein shirts. They discussed a social event for the end of the semester that the Shush-Sneezer offered to "own" after a short argument. After the meeting concluded in under an hour (a new record), Carl received a text message.

A couple wanted the apartment in New York.

Carl headed to sign the sale papers at the Law Offices of Boris, Heckerson, Thune, and Thune, located in a suburb of Kansas City, about two hours east of Manhattan. The lobby felt out of date. The carpet pile was a little too deep, and dulled brass showed through the worn places on the gold-plated doorknobs and light fixtures. A curt paralegal named Tom greeted Carl at the front desk. Tom had the face of someone who perpetually smelled something foul. He led Carl to a large oak door with an engraved plastic plaque on it that read, "Private Meeting Room #2."

"I don't have a lot of time, so please hurry up with your pleasantries," Tom said.

"Pleasantries?"

He tilted his head toward the door. "*She* said it had been a while for you two. Just open the door when you're done and I'll bring the papers in."

"She?" Carl wondered why a pedestrian legal procedure suddenly felt like a conjugal visit.

Tom left him there in front of the door. Carl opened the door slowly. Ex-Elizabeth sat on a sofa upholstered in paint drips and splatters, facing the opposite wall and talking on her cell phone.

She wore a pinstripe jacket over a deep blue turtleneck. It was still feminine but all business. She nodded at something the other person said. Then she performed the Sequence of Gestures–the left index finger tucks a strand of her black hair behind the left ear, then her thumb traces her jaw-line, and finally her left hand settles into a loose fist in front of her chin, as if it's a blow gun, ready to fire a dart at the opposite wall.

How many times had he seen her do that gesture at work, even when talking to clients with a phone squeezed between head and shoulder? The Sequence of Gestures meant she had shifted into sales mode.

"Let's do this damn thing and get it over with. I have an appointment."

When he continued past the threshold she aimed her glance at him, as if determining the threat level of a thrown object. Then without saying goodbye she poked a button on her phone and dropped it into her purse. She stood and gave Carl a hug, the first since they had split. He smelled cigarettes

59

under her perfume. "Carl, the broker in New York says we have a deal. I pulled the credit report and everything about the buyer looks legit. Even the appraisal came in on the high side. Can you believe it? In *this* market!"

He didn't like any of it. The surprise visit, the great news, the sudden familiarity—as if no time had passed since the last time he saw her. The memory of that moment briefly flashed in his mind. She sat on a bar stool at the counter in the kitchen popping bubble wrap while he sat on the floor packing up a set of wine glasses that had belonged to his parents. Neither of them had spoken, leaving the crackling plastic between her fingers as the only sound.

Here, now, this was a noisy intrusion. In response, he thought he should turn to catch the door with his foot before it closed and say, "Let's do this damn thing and get it over with. I have an appointment." Instead he moved his foot too late and missed the door, saying, "Let's have an appointment."

"Right to business?" She took his hand and led him to the sofa. "Sorry for the impersonal setting. I have some great news and I hope a great opportunity for you," she said.

"An opportunity?" It was getting worse.

"I've been working with Terry Cotter, remember him from Ogilvy?" She again completed the Sequence of Gestures–hair, jaw, blowgun. "And Lorraine Laird. We're starting our own consulting firm."

"Great," Carl said.

"So what do you think?"

"Great," he repeated.

"We started out targeting unsophisticated small businesses, you know, mom and pop shops that might be ripe for a buyout. Low-hanging fruit."

Carl leaned back, his head against the sofa. "What is it, Elizabeth? Why do you need me?"

"Now see? I love this about you, always have. You cut right to it. You know these people from Ogilvy. None of them have any face time experience with clients. They can't lead an execution effort for a large client," she said.

"Sounds like a terrific team," Carl said.

Selective hearing was engaged. "I'm so close to landing a large client. You're going to flip your shit when you hear who it is. West Egg Holdings. We're going to be working for Forrest Bland. I'd love to have you involved. It'll be a no-brainer for them if we come in as a unified team." She scooted her leg close to his. "We can get some testimonials from Heartland Dairy about how you handled their sale."

"I'd be afraid of what they might say," Carl said.

Elizabeth clapped her hands on the top of her thighs. "My little charmingly naive Carl. Again with the overactive conscience?" She shook her head and looked at the only artwork in the room, a Nagel print of a woman with shoulder pads, bright red lipstick, and pale fingers tipped with red fingernails grasping a champagne glass. "Still obsessing over the little things. You did your job. So you held back a little information. That's what you had to do to get more sales."

"You're not making me feel any better."

"Bland never would have purchased Heartland Dairy from the Sellars without your involvement."

Carl moved his hands to his temples. "God don't say *that*."

"You know it's true. That deal would have never happened if you hadn't told them to take an all-cash deal."

He knew that, he just didn't like acknowledging it. It was a classic conflict of interest for Carl to work for the Sellars in that transaction, because his team also worked toward getting business from Forrest Bland's West Egg Holdings. Carl had written up a brief for the Sellars that stated what he thought they should demand as part of the deal, including some stock, cash, and job offers with a healthy severance package. Without those things, Bland could cut them out and leave them behind. That's exactly how it played out, because Carl never gave them his brief. He held it back because he wanted to do Bland a favor.

"Ultimately, your job was to look out for Ogilvy & Standpipe," she said. "You can't balance everybody's needs. You didn't get compensated based on how the Sellars fared in the aftermath of the deal, only on the deal itself. You worked your ass off on that deal." She turned and leaned directly over him, her hair falling on either side of his face. "It'd be fun to do it again. We can get our dream back."

She shifted slightly so that one of her breasts brushed up against his forearm. He thought she'd given up the dream. She was, after all, the one who left *him*. He realized he had begun to get an erection. He breathed deeply, and reached up to tuck her hair behind her left ear.

She closed her eyes at his touch.

He said, "I'm not sure that dream exists anymore."

Her eyes snapped open. "Bland remembers. He knows how much that deal helped his company."

Carl put his hand on her shoulders, and with all the strength his abs could muster sat upright and gently pushed her back. "When you said 'our dream' I thought you meant our marriage."

"I meant that, too, Carl, of course. Ultimately, I mean the dream of our lives. You have to have the money stuff squared away first and then the personal stuff follows naturally."

"Naturally," he said. "I already have this other thing going in Manhattan. My writing. I don't have time to start a business with you."

She started on a rapid variation of the Sequence of Gestures, but midway through it sputtered out. "I'm not asking you to do that. Just lend your name and credentials. Then consult with Cotter and Laird. Get them up to speed. This is real money, Carl. You know Ogilvy made a million dollars in the Heartland sale. A million! What'd you get as a partner for your billable hours? Almost fourteen thousand?"

"Yes, and at your counsel we poured it into that apartment instead of shoring up our 401k."

"We're going to get every penny out of it, Carl. This kind of money doesn't come easily to writers. You're being overly romantic about it."

"Fake pride?"

"I'm just looking out for you," she said, her voicing turning sweet. "What can you get as a writer? Realistically, what's the *best* you can hope for?"

"I have to believe I'm capable of writing something great."

Elizabeth smirked. "What, you think you're the next Dan Brown?"

She could always find what caused him the most pain and exploit it. She leaned back slightly as if she knew she'd gone too far, then forward again, as if it was too much trouble to go back now.

"Thanks for the opportunity, Elizabeth, but I have other things going on. In the meantime, keep that dream alive."

Her face hardened. She stood and tugged the bottom of her jacket. "Yeah, great." She snapped her purse off the floor and left the room. He heard her exchange some hushed words with Tom.

Carl sat on the sofa for a few more moments. He felt like he could fall asleep right there. He closed his eyes and repeated to himself that he'd made the only sane decision, that he'd chosen the right direction for his life, if not for his finances. But that wasn't exactly true. He'd already made the decision to align life and career, to join their outcome.

When he left Private Meeting Room #2, he didn't see Elizabeth. Instead he found Tom standing in a cubicle, stuffing papers into a briefcase.

"I guess your pleasantries weren't so pleasant," Tom said.

"A side show," Carl said. "Where are the papers? Where do I sign?"

"Papers?" he asked. "The lady told me the deal was off and there would be no sale. She said I should send the bill for our services to your Kansas address."

63

Chapter 5
Ground Rules

Carl rode Keith's bike south along 11th Street past the Manhattan City Park Pool. He hopped the curb and rode on grass to cut the corner leading west on Poyntz. When he passed between two trees he saw one of Manhattan's few roadside attractions. It was the thirty-foot statue of Johnny Kaw, the Kansas version of Paul Bunyan. Johnny had a more jaundiced complexion than Paul and carried an enormous scythe instead of an axe. When he saw the statue the first time he drove through town, Carl found it kitschy. The man looked absurd with his bright yellow skin, sculpted mullet, and his oversized "K" belt buckle. The statue was especially amusing when approached from the northeast, as Carl did. The handle of Johnny's scythe, the same yellow color as his skin, appeared to protrude directly from his crotch–a perpetual erection for the state's tallest wheat farmer.

However, the statue lost some of its playfulness when considered along with the town's nickname of the Little Apple. It was as if every self-expression of the town demanded you compare it to another place. We're like New York, only small. We're like Minnesota–only Johnny is better endowed than Paul.

After living in the town for a while, seeing its physical beauty, getting to know the people, and enjoying how simple it was to live there, he felt the town deserved a better self-image. It didn't need a Johnny Kaw to attract people. It didn't need comparisons to other places. So far, he thought, Manhattan was putting on a good face all by itself.

Carl walked his bike past Johnny Kaw and along Poyntz when he saw Susan and the Milkman, in a car turning left on Poyntz from 12th Street. He knew it was her car when he saw the bumper stickers. "Human Milk for Human Babies" one said, punctuated by La Leche League's rudimentary icon of a woman cradling a baby at her breast. The other proclaimed, "Well-behaved women rarely make history."

Susan had told Carl she needed to go to Emporia to help a friend who had lost her husband. Of course, seeing them like this did not prove that the Milkman had accompanied her on her overnight trip. But it did point to a relationship beyond dairy products, and that caused some jealousy. He pedaled down the sidewalk as if to follow, but the car immediately drove out of range. Was he over-thinking the whole thing? Were Carl and Susan even officially dating? They had barely even kissed once.

And what about Ex-Elizabeth? Did she really want to get back together? This line of thought led nowhere. He decided to focus on something else. Instead he visualized his first research meeting with Frye.

Frye's desk overpowered the room, a thick oak slab designed for two people sitting across from each other. Someone must have assembled it in there because it wouldn't have fit through the door. At eighty square feet, the room provided just enough space for someone to get around the desk to browse the contents of a small bookshelf, or gaze out the only window, which overlooked a dumpster. The branches of a maple tree extended large bouquets of leaves above the window, blocking any sunlight. The walls featured dog-eared posters of Frye's readings and workshops, none dated after 1997. A quick visual inspection delineated three distinct groups of debris: departmental memos, unopened utility bills, and past issues of *The Sporting News*. A scratched metal folding chair sat wedged in a corner between the empty trash can and Frye's seat. Carl moved to sit in the folding chair but instead decided on the one at the desk, facing Frye's. He struggled not to straighten the piles of papers and files on the acre of desktop. Frye hadn't yet arrived in his office.

Carl opened his briefcase and removed The Frye Clipping File. The file's growth had coincided with Carl's hopes of leaving his job. He had a departure point, he knew what he would leave, but he had no clear destination until

65

he'd read a few blog posts written by Frye. From the posts, Carl gathered that Frye had moved to Manhattan as part of "an artist immigration to central Kansas." In 2006, Frye had appeared in articles and junket interviews with reporters for online magazines and a few newspapers. In 2009 he had started a Twitter stream describing life in Manhattan. His quotes glowed with descriptions of the town's cultural landscape. Fiction writers, poets, sculptors, even fiber artists had converged on "The Li'l Apple." Carl snapped off the rubber band and began peeling through the jagged stack of printouts.

Frye entered with a few pieces of mail, his briefcase, and a Styrofoam container of food. It smelled like some kind of meat - corned beef hash maybe? His expression changed to mild shock when he saw Carl.

"What is that?" Frye said, pointing at the file. "Did you get that off my desk?"

"These are some clippings I assembled over the years. I was just reading your blog post describing the Li'l Apple Elite," Carl said.

"I have never referred to this town as the…" he said, narrowing his eyes and flaring his nostrils, "Li'l Apple." Frye put his glasses on top of his head and bent to resume looking over a baseball box score. Carl saw that the hair on the crown of Frye's head had thinned considerably. He noted with relief that Frye hadn't tried to comb it over or obscure it in any way.

While the Big Apple boasted a deep concentration of artists, Carl's job and lifestyle there left no time for him to explore it. The size of the New York art community intimidated him. The Li'l Apple offered an opportunity to mingle with a more manageable group of artists.

He found a printout of Frye's Twitter stream and held it aloft with a flourish. He read aloud, "'Learn more about the Li'l Apple Elite in my blog post.' Then here on your blog post," Carl said, "'On Wednesday nights we gather at a local watering hole. We shall call our roundtable the Li'l Apple Elite.'" Carl laid the papers in front of Frye on the desk.

Frye straightened and held the papers at arm's length.

Carl remembered how he had felt when he had first read Frye's posts. Here was a place, halfway across the country, where men in fedoras and women with unshaven armpits conversed over coffee, in the morning, and beer, late at night. They spoke about politics, debated local architecture, and lamented the poor souls who failed to acknowledge that God was dead. Carl thought those discussions sounded a lot more exciting than sitting at Sbarro with a bunch of guys in khaki pants debating the prospects for the Mets offense that summer.

"I have never Twatted nor blogged," he said, letting the paper flutter down on top of the food container, where it immediately soaked up a round grease spot.

Carl grabbed it. "But it has your name on it and your picture."

"It was the Chamber of Commerce of Manhattan. They paid me to be their shill as soon as I moved here." He returned to his box score.

Carl picked up the article and the paper bent, hanging limply in his hand. "They paid you to write this?"

"No, I think someone at the Chamber wrote it," Frye said. "But they paid me. Two thousand more than the Chamber of Lawrence was going to pay."

Carl laid the article back in the file. He bent up one corner of the stack with his thumb and let the pages fall one-by-one, as if shuffling a deck of cards. He thought back on his decision to come to Manhattan. Of course, he hadn't based it entirely on one article about a group of people getting drunk and arguing politics. No, he had come to work with the man sitting before him.

Carl unpacked his laptop, turned it on, and plugged it into a jack on the floor under the desk.

He aligned his mechanical pencils, a small tube of 0.7 mm HB leads, and an eraser refill. Then he folded his hands on the desk before him. The smell of corned beef filled the room.

"The EGSA is going well," Carl said.

"Oh."

"I've whipped those meetings into shape."

"Uh huh."

"Regarding this assistantship, I'd like to know what your expectations are."

"Expectations?" When Carl nodded, Frye continued. "I expect you to research the topics and incidents I provide."

Carl grimaced. "But I'll get to read your stuff, right? See how you've incorporated my research?" He wanted to see the writing process in action, how a bit of prose formed from a snatch of research. "How can I help you if I can't look at how my research appears in the final piece? What if something's not exactly accurate the way you incorporate it?"

Frye rubbed his earlobe. "Do you know why I'm not going to let you read my book? I only let agents and editors read my stuff before it's published. You're neither," he said. "Besides, it deals with real people, here in Manhattan. I've never written about a place while still living there."

Carl leaned forward. "That makes a difference?"

Frye began eating his corned beef. He said between bites, "I buried the notes from this book a year ago while I was dating your Dr. Hirschman."

My Dr. Hirschman, Carl thought.

"I let her read it. She knew some of the people I'd based my characters on, and she told me to stop writing it. 'No good would come of it,' she told me. And so, I stopped writing a book based on someone else's opinion of it. It's a mistake I won't repeat."

Carl wondered why Frye had taken Susan's opinion to heart. Had they been that close? Had they fallen in love? After a year and a half of dating it was possible they had. But Carl saw something else in the way Frye held his slight frown as he kept eating. Perhaps he still loved her.

Frye opened his briefcase and pulled out the stack of papers he had recovered from his front yard. "She felt so strongly about it that she wanted me to destroy these notes. I told her I had. When she found out I buried them instead, she dumped me." He tossed the papers across the desk. They

68

smelled of decomposing leaves, overpowering the corned beef.

"That's quite a story. But I don't operate as much on…" Carl paused to get his emphasis right, "*emotion* as she does."

Frye waved a hash-laden fork at Carl. "Emotional or not, I'm not leaving myself vulnerable to that sort of thing again. No one reads the book, and no one tells her about it or the kind of research you're doing for me."

"You don't have to worry about Susan and me. I don't think we're really that close."

"You looked close the other night."

He thought of her and her milkman. "I think she is seeing someone else."

Frye belched, closed the container of hash, and threw it in the trash. "That doesn't sound like someone who operates on emotion."

"She told me she had to go out of town yesterday," Carl said, "and then I saw her coming back in town with some guy."

Frye looked surprised. "No kidding? I think she would be upfront with you about something like that. She sure as hell didn't mince words when she dumped me."

"Was she dating someone else?"

"I don't think so. I'd have to check with Rosalie, but I don't think she's dated anyone since me. Until you, I mean. I just wonder if she's a little afraid of her partner's success. Like it might eventually eclipse her relationship with the person."

Carl nodded. This was what he'd wanted. Shooting the shit with Frye–and about the same woman. Somehow Carl had achieved his visualization. He had ingratiated himself with this man. He felt he should try to negotiate a little while his stock was up. "How about if you let me read the galleys, before they go to print? I don't want to have to wait until the book is published to find out how much I contributed."

"I have to write the damn thing first." He pointed to the musty pile of notes. "Read this first batch and we'll meet again next week."

That night Carl tried to make sense of the earthy documents. They were scattered printouts culled from Lexis-Nexis (Drake, J. 1993, May 14. Wreck investigation concludes with no conclusion. *The Wichita Eagle*, pp 1A, 7A), questions on torn pages from a spiral notebook ("Possible motives for an inside job"), and cryptic phrases etched on cardboard coasters from the Manhattan Project Brewery ("Sparky left a whole life behind"). It was going to take some work reverse-engineering Frye's book.

Keith gave Carl a list of cool things to do around Manhattan, reprinted from *K-Stater Magazine*. Carl looked it over until attraction number ninety-nine seized his attention. He simply had to see the K-State Agronomy Department Weed Garden. He set up a tour and soon found himself standing in a dense waist-high thicket. Were it not for the small placards labeling each living specimen, Carl would've thought he stood on any untended patch of Kansas ground.

He listened to the tour guide, a squat woman wearing a pair of oversized glasses and an undersized T-shirt that read, "Agronomy Students Do It In The Dirt."

"Now I give you the common pokeweed," the tour guide said in a voice rendered inflectionless by too much repetition. "It's distinguished by its rapid growth and poisonous leaves. Those who supported James K. Polk for president wore common pokeweed stems on their clothes."

The small dark green plant and the role it played in getting our eleventh president elected didn't hold Carl's attention. His mind jumped around, alighting first on the EGSA and the strides he'd made with the group since taking over. He had given an order and discipline to the group

70

without pissing them off. He instituted Robert's Rules for Parliamentary Procedure without fomenting a mutiny. The EGSA led, inexplicably, to thoughts of Susan, then to sex, then to sex with Susan. While he did not like the idea of waiting until the end of the semester, he had grown accustomed to such gaps in intimacy ranging from 234 to 248 days throughout his life. He had identified this statistical quirk in an Advanced Excel class. During a boring discussion of creating formulas in pivot tables, Carl created a spreadsheet depiction of his sex history. He entered data on his six relationships that had resulted in sexual activity. While he didn't always remember dates (except for those surrounding holidays) or even the number of times (except for the record-breaking three in one afternoon), he estimated as well as he could. He saw nothing revealing in this initial collection of data, except the fact that he had unprotected sex on the British holiday of Boxing Day every year between 1990 and 1995.

"That brings us to white snakeroot," the guide continued. "If eaten, a toxin in this little number can poison cows and the milk they produce." She shifted forward on her toes and waved an arm over the small plot of white flowers. "Legend has it that Abraham Lincoln's mother died by drinking milk from cows that had eaten snakeroot." Apparently, she had decided the only way to connect weeds with an audience was to relate them to a president.

The data on his sexual activity had remained parochial until he added information on his relationships. The graphs showed no activity in the initial weeks of a relationship, followed by a drastic up-tick during the second quarter, which then reached a plateau, and eventually slowed to nothing near the end. Without exception, a gap of approximately eight months separated one relationship's final sexual activity from the initial activity of the next. He had termed the whole phenomenon the Krauthammer Alternating Sexual Mesa (KASM).

"Lambsquarters is a terrible nuisance for corn and soybean farmers. Its tenacity is unmatched. But, historians know it for a different reason."

His expected end-of-semester coitus fit perfectly within the standard KASM, totaling a projected 240 days since his last sexual event with Elizabeth. The anomaly here was the short period between his breakup with Ex-Elizabeth and his first date with Susan. This meant that he would go nearly two quarters of dating Susan with no sex, the longest drought of his career. He thought he could handle it with a mix of research, writing, and masturbation.

Back on the Weed Garden tour, the guide asked a question. "I said, does anyone here know why history remembers lambsquarters?"

Carl, as the only person on the tour, shook his head, unwilling to hazard a guess at the presidential tie-in.

"It's famous as the first weed actually eaten in the White House. That's right. President Jimmy Carter requested it and had it for dinner in 1978. Apparently, it goes well with peanuts!"

Chapter 6
A New Hand for Sparky

None of the red meat dishes appealed to Carl so he had the Grand Mal Caesar Salad with Chicken. It suffered in Sparky's absence. All of the ingredients were there, but it lacked a certain…

"Zip?" Keith asked.

"Yes." Carl said. "It lacks zip."

"That's Sophia," he said, indicating the woman behind the bar. Sophia's hair appeared to have once been blonde. Since then it had developed a calico appearance. She rimmed her green eyes with thick eyeliner and applied too much blue eye shadow. Keith continued, "She's a physical therapist."

"And as everyone knows physical therapists can't make a decent chicken Caesar."

Keith laughed. "She and Sparky have lived together since soon after the accident."

"Where is Sparky?" Keith asked when Sophia came closer.

"He's in back getting ready to show off his new hand. He just got back from Wichita an hour ago. Cripes, he had that coat hanger, or some worthless facsimile on the end of his arm for eighteen years." She shook her head as if she needed to let it sink in. "He'll not only be able to write with it, he'll do things people with mortal hands can't do."

"Then you'll be a very happy woman." Keith said.

She slapped him on the forearm. "I hadn't thought of that!" Someone hailed her from down the bar.

"You know how he lost his hand? It's an interesting story, actually. It'll tell you something about Manhattan, too."

Carl knew what was coming but he wouldn't let on. He'd researched Sparky's train accident for Frye for almost two weeks. Keith confirmed a lot of what he already knew. Sparky used to run a train as an engineer. In 1987, he was running a freight train from Kansas City to San Diego, and it derailed near Manhattan.

"He wasn't hurt bad, not life-threatening. Mangled up his arm pretty good. A couple of weeks later he lost his hand," Keith said, cutting his hamburger in half. "At first he stayed because he couldn't afford to leave. He was waiting on insurance money that never came. They said he was driving that train drunk."

"Was there some doubt about him being drunk?" Carl asked. "I assume they did a breathalyzer."

Sophia burst back into their conversation. "He drank that whiskey *after* the accident and before the ambulance arrived. To calm his nerves." She tapped her index finger on the bar in front of her. "Someone derailed that train on purpose."

"The legal investigation concluded that it was simply an accident. But West Egg was the company that operated the train and owned the cargo. West Egg's insurance company kept up a private investigation for years, trying to see if it was an inside job, some kind of insurance fraud."

This was what Carl wanted to hear. Here was the unofficial version of the story, the conspiracy theory that the articles he read only alluded to. This was some added value he could give Frye.

"Anyway, he left his old life behind and never left Manhattan." Keith said. "The people around here kind of adopted him."

"Adopted him?" Sophia sneered. "For the love of Pete, you make it sound like he's helpless."

"Don't get your panties in a bunch. I meant that he was immediately accepted in town by people wanting to help him out."

Carl sensed this was the point where fact left off and urban legend took over. "So, he makes enough money here at the bar to buy a new hand and have it attached?"

Sophia grabbed a Fat Tire for Carl and two Pabsts—one for Keith and one for herself. "No. He breaks even. Keeps the place open to give the clean-up guy a place to work."

"Every year on the anniversary of the accident, some mystery person leaves money on his back porch," Keith said.

This was all new information to Carl. "So who's leaving the money?" Carl asked.

When Sophia didn't answer, Keith did. "If you think the derailment was no accident, you assume it's those responsible."

Sophia slammed her can down on the bar. "No one knows who's leaving the money. And who gives a spit? That's private. It's a good deed and good deeds tend to go away if you look them in the mouth." She tossed her head back and emptied the rest of her beer. She blew her nose into a wadded Kleenex and replaced it in her sleeve.

Sparky burst out of the kitchen, his right arm and new hand raised.

He had upgraded his jacket to one with a red sparkly rhinestone collar. He saluted Sophia, who whooped. The applause quieted down. The tip of his tongue showed between his lips as he concentrated on the hand. He bent each finger independently to touch its tip to that of his thumb. He went from index to pinkie and back again. Carl cheered along with the rest of the crowd.

He walked over to Sophia and kissed her on the cheek. She grabbed the new hand in hers and kissed the palm. He raised and lowered his eyebrows and winked at her. Then he grabbed a pepper grinder from the bar and held it over Carl's salad. Sparky held the small grinder vertically in his left hand, and grabbed the turning part on top with his plastic hand. It looked like a real hand grasping a doorknob. With a faint whirring, the right hand twisted and didn't stop, revolving at the wrist 360 degrees. Pepper scattered over the salad. He stopped and held the right hand up in front of their faces, where he let it spin around again, back of hand to palm to back of hand.

"I give you my new hand." Sparky said.

Carl tasted the salad. "Now that's what I call zip!"

75

Twenty minutes later Carl grabbed a pen and headed to the bathroom to scribble down everything he had heard and seen.

"Now I know you're a writer, Krauthammer." It was Frye, standing at the urinal. "Taking notes in a goddamn bar pisser. I don't do that anymore. Perhaps I should."

"I got some great information about Sparky tonight. I could run it by you."

"Actually, I am here with some friends," he said, and then he brightened. "There's a painter, a guy who works in plaster, another guy, Ray. He handles all the big stage productions at the school."

"So the Li'l Apple Elites do exist," Carl said.

"Yes, they do." Frye washed his hands and dried them on a paper towel. "I gotta say something to someone, but then why don't you come on over and join us."

So it wasn't all made up by some intern at the Chamber. Carl always had interesting conversations with Keith, but this group would operate at a higher level. This meeting would represent the first step in Carl's transformation from student to artist. He hadn't eaten enough food to compensate for the suddenly elevated production of acid in his stomach. He took two deep breaths and remembered the guidelines from his various visualizations of the scene. He must not express his moderately conservative leanings at the first meeting. Listen and learn. Hear what they think on various issues. Answer only if asked, but don't hesitate to talk. Nod a lot. Be funny.

"The visualizations will serve you well, young Skywalker," Carl said to the mirror. At the bar, he explained the situation to Keith. "This is huge," he said.

Keith finished his beer. "If you say so. I'll be right here having my plebeian thoughts. Then maybe take in a few more of Sparky's tricks."

Carl grabbed his beer and headed off in search of the Elite. He saw Frye talking to another professor, leaning way over the person.

Frye must've sensed Carl hovering behind him because he stood up. "They're over there by the popcorn machine,"

76

Frye said, pointing at the very back of the bar. "Terry, Ray and Don. I'll be over in a few."

Three men sat huddled together, talking across a rectangular table. One of them, with paint-splattered coveralls and cap said "Bullcrap." All three turned to look up at Carl as he approached them.

"Hi, Julian Frye suggested I come over."

Terry, Ray, and the painter, who turned out not to be Don, a man, but Dawn, a muscular woman, nodded. Ray held his beer in the remaining two fingers of his right hand. They all had PBRs. Damn it. Beer hadn't appeared in his visualizations.

Dawn continued their conversation. "Like I say, it's bull crap because it seems like the Wildcats never have a team that can shoot *and* run a consistent zone."

Ray, apparently the self-designated narrator of the group, said, "There's nothing sexier than a woman who knows her hoops."

"May I join you?" Carl asked.

"As long as you're buying the next round. They're talking basketball. I'm a football man myself, but we talked about that last Wednesday."

Carl introduced himself.

Terry extended a tanned hand with dabs of dried white and grey plaster smeared on it. More dry plaster smudges covered his neck and one ear. He had black hair with grey flecks in it. His chin revealed a day's experiment in growing a Vandyke.

"So, tell me about your work," Carl said. "Your medium is plaster?"

"Mud and tape, yeah." Terry pointed at Dawn, who said something about unnecessary fouls. "I do all the prep for her."

"Interesting," Carl said. "So you'll do a piece and she'll paint it? I don't know a whole lot about that. I didn't realize people worked together like that."

"Oh yeah, you have to specialize nowadays. I'm working up at the Beach Museum. They've redone their lobby, and somebody punched a hole in the wall moving the old artwork out."

"I'd love to see that."

"Really? If you're that interested you can come up any time. We'll be there for another week or so."

At this point Frye returned to the table. He clapped Carl on the back and laughed. "Well, Carl, what do you think of the Li'l Apple Elite?"

"I think they're great. Terry was just telling me about the exhibit in the lobby up at the Beach Museum. Have you seen it?"

Frye looked at Carl then at Terry. "Exhibit?"

"I was just telling Carl that somebody punched a hole in one of the walls with a sculpture or something. I'm patching the hole and mudding the wall so she can paint it."

"Wait," said Carl, sitting back in his chair. "You're not artists?"

Frye beamed. "Hell, yes they're artists. When they're done you'll never know the hole was there."

Since Susan's trip to Emporia with her Milkman, she and Carl had reached a plateau in their relationship where they did chores together. He termed it the "Errand Stage" in his journal. They would wash her car, do his laundry, or maybe weed the landscaping around her house. They'd reached the stage early, he observed, an arrival he attributed to his lack of discretionary capital. While this phase of their relationship offered them more time together, Susan spent an increasing amount of it in a contemplative mood.

One night on his way to the bathroom at the Lethargic Clown, he saw into a back room where a man dressed in black unloaded wheels of cheese, all marked with "UR" in red stencil. When the guy turned around to have Sparky sign for the delivery, Carl could see it was Susan's Milkman.

The Milkman had pulled the empty dolly behind him and came through the doors. He stopped short when it appeared he would collide with Carl. They exchanged greetings. Before he passed, he stopped Carl to say, "I wanted to thank you, *mon ami*. She's lucky to have a friend like you right now." He smiled and left through the back door.

"*Friend?*" Carl wished he'd said, "We run errands together, Dairy Boy!"

A week or so later, Susan offered to buy him dinner in Aggieville, so Carl walked to meet her. His initial comparison of the area to a movie set of a small town in the 1950s had begun to change. Shops that had eluded his notice now took to the foreground, like Scaly Dave's Herp Shack, SOS Music, and Twisted Apple Tattoo. He knew which places the English department frequented. The faculty met at Radina's Coffeehouse more than they did on campus, Richard Russo once read at Auntie Mae's Parlor, and everyone went to the Rock-a-Belly Deli before and after any department event. He knew that the neon-encrusted theater at the end of Mora Street actually housed a bookstore. He knew where he could eat for less than five bucks (the Pita Pit), and at what time you had to get to Kite's to comfortably watch an away football game. He did not, however, suspect that a place called Hibachi Hut served Cajun food.

"All this time I thought they served kebobs," he said, looking over his menu at Susan.

She closed her menu and inhaled as if preparing to initiate an important conversation.

Carl leaned forward, but she just exhaled and looked at the wines by the glass on the table tent. He wondered if she wanted to discuss her feelings for him, contrasted with those she felt for her Milkman. Did bringing it up make him sound too aggressive or jealous? He thought so. Instead, he interrupted the silence. "I guess I'm going to have to get a part-time job. I haven't worked in the service sector since I was an undergrad."

"But you've had a career. You were partner at a large company."

"Somehow, I don't think that qualifies as experience to the eighteen-year-old manager at Arby's," he said. "I should go to Twisted Apple and have the word 'Overqualified' put on my forehead."

"Perhaps 'Overthinking' would be better."

He resettled himself in his chair. "Is everything all right?"

"Of course," she said, not looking up from her menu.

He took a couple of Sweet'n Low packets that had gotten mixed up with the Equal and put them back in place. "Since you went out of town you've been quiet. Some might even say distracted."

She sighed. "Others might bear with me, observing that I am clearly dealing with personal issues."

"It's him, isn't it?"

She kept her gaze on the placemat. "I could tell you knew about him," she said.

"Sometimes it seems like I can't get away from the guy. It's as if he's taunting me."

She whispered, "He's haunting you, too?"

"Taunting," he said. "*Tuh*. Taunting." Her confused expression angered him. Of course he knew about him. Had she forgotten the Milkman left her house as Carl arrived for their first date? This was crazy. With Ex-Elizabeth, his oblivion had kept him happy until she revealed her affair. In this case he knew about the guy all along. Neither oblivion nor foreknowledge held an advantage. They both sucked.

"Then you know it was a long time ago that we were involved. Many, many years."

"Can't be too long ago, unless you like dating little boys."

She cocked her head at Carl. "I have no idea what that means."

He prepared to leave, not willing to drag this out any longer. He sat upright and put his hands on the chair's arms. "Just please don't make a fool of me in this whole thing. Just let me tell Frye before he hears it from Rosalie that you prefer to be with this other guy instead of me."

Then she laughed. It issued from her as a peculiar bark. Her face betrayed no humor, just a baffled horror. "Carl, he died. Just over a week ago."

"Died?" Carl said, a little louder than he had intended. "I just saw him delivering Camembert or some shit at the Lethargic Clown."

She put her hands over her face and made a sound that could be either laughing or crying. When she removed her hands from her face, she said, "My husband is not the milkman. He was fifty-eight. We were married when I was eighteen. It's not something that I like telling people."

Carl thought back to their conversation at the White House Supper Club. "You mentioned him once before," he said. "I'm sorry I got so worked up over a misunderstanding."

"It's funny because that night we talked of cutting people out of your life. And here's this guy, my ex. I hadn't seen or heard from him in fifteen years and then he dies. And instead of being out of my life forever, he leaves me money," she said. "I mean, what the hell?"

"Are you okay?"

"I'm not even sad, just surprised." She looked as if she might cry. She took the straw out of her water and tapped the end on her paper placemat. Small drops soaked in. "Anyway, I wanted to ask you to help me. This full disclosure thing I'm trying here? I've come close to some serious relationships since my marriage, and each one was undone by something I should have disclosed. I want to do it right this time. It's going to take some work on my part." She put the straw in her mouth like a sprig of grass. "Just, please, bear with me."

"Sure, yes." Carl's ears burned. He was embarrassed for jumping to so many jealous conclusions. "Full disclosure sounds good. I'm not a fan of relationship surprises."

"Thanks. I owe you one."

Later, he dropped her off and they kissed, this time longer and more sensually than before. On his way home, he realized they hadn't discussed the Milkman at all.

In between classes and errand-dates with Susan, Carl would sit across from Frye and poke around on his computer for anything having to do with Sparky's train accident. Frye kept his promise not to let Carl read any of his stuff. As things moved ahead, the piles of debris on Frye's desk grew in volume and complexity. One Thursday afternoon Carl offered to straighten it out, but Frye refused.

"Say this slushy were to spill," he said, indicating the thirty-two-ounce cup from Dara's Fast Lane. "It might very well take out a semester of English department memos, but it would never be able to stain the top of this antique desk."

"I prefer their milkshakes."

"Not me," Frye said. "Lactose intolerant."

"A pity. What flavor is that?"

"It's purple-flavored. I prefer red," Frye said. "It's the red slushy at 3:00 a.m. that keeps me in Manhattan." Frye slid the straw in and out of his lid, a method of stirring that emitted a hoarse moan. "These and the Konza keep me here."

Carl scrolled through some LexisNexis search results. "What, the prairie? I haven't made it out there yet."

Frye's straw stopped abruptly. "Put your computer away. It's Thursday. It's lunchtime. We're going right now."

Carl looked from the computer to Frye and back. "I've driven by it. And I'm trying to get deeper into this research."

"Later. We're doing the Konza."

Carl had to move a pile of trash from the front to the back so he could sit in the passenger seat. Claw marks scored the leather of the seat, and dog-nose prints fogged the window. Carl could see blue clouds behind the car whenever Frye accelerated from a stoplight. They headed out of Manhattan on 177 and turned off onto a two-lane heading south. Out his window, Carl watched a creek flirt with the road, coming close, then veering away across a plowed field planted with winter wheat, only to nuzzle up close again a quarter mile later. Why was Frye taking him out here? They had work to do.

They left the road and turned into a small gravel parking lot, edged by golden grass over six feet tall. A small wooden sign jutted out of the ground with "Trail" routed into it. Frye explained that although the Nature Conservancy owned the thirteen square miles that made up the Konza, the university cared for it, studying its ecosystem.

"When they recruited me, they brought me out here. They knew I had affection for the Flint Hills, having lived in Strong City. At this end of the prairie," he said, "I don't know, seems like things are more *exposed*."

Carl understood what Frye meant. Here the earth's skin was pulled too thin to keep its flinty layer concealed. It made for a bleak view, the spare soil and scrubby vegetation revealing pitted rocks. It felt barren.

"Bluestem grass, that's most of what you see here. Goes through thirty different color variations: grey in the winter, charred black in the spring after they burn it off, then bright green as it sprouts, dark green, dusky blue, back to grey by now. You need the 128 Crayola box to describe all of the variations."

They moved on, walking up a gentle slope where the crushed limestone path looked superimposed over the grass.

"Ever been scuba diving, Krauthammer?"

"Nope."

"When I went diving in Belize, on my honeymoon, the bottom of the ocean looked just like this. The exact same contour."

Carl looked over the limestone-capped hills, struggling to imagine them rendered in the deep blues of the ocean. "What are you doing here?" Carl asked. "What are you doing in the middle of Kansas?"

Frye looked east. "I use writing to make sense of the world, to find my place in it. I got a reputation for fouling my own nest by exposing something about the places I've lived. My ex said she couldn't tell if I really considered our relationship character research. She said my work showed an unhealthy selectivity, that I was too picky about who I was nice to."

"Just what I might expect from a self-described misanthrope." Carl could see the influence of the people around him in the characters who populated his books. They had few positive qualities, which were always overshadowed by their scheming.

"My old agent, back when he called me, would start with, 'What's happening in fly-over country?' You probably ran into plenty of those people in New York."

Carl nodded.

"The tolerant liberal aesthete who summers in Napa, autumns in Nantucket, and makes an annual spring trip to La Jolla. Anyone can see the beauty in those places. Oahu or the Grand Canyon, or flying over New York City at night? You don't have to think to appreciate the beauty of those places. Here, you have to work at it. It takes an active, advanced intellect to find beauty in grass and sky."

"You like the landscape here, but teaching? I would think you would be writing fulltime."

"I'm writing now, but I don't know if it will ever get published. I don't have an active contract right now. I think I have a good story, but it feels like it's missing something in the third act. I'm hoping your research will provide it, but right now I don't have it. I need to eat." He finished his slushy and set the cup to his side.

Frye's answers made sense. They explained why he wanted to raise the department's stature and get tenure. But his lack of confidence felt out-of-character. Who was this person who'd decided to settle down in Kansas, who mistrusted his talent, who not only wanted to teach, but wanted tenure? Perhaps he was experiencing the uncertainty of coming off a period of low productivity, and it scared him.

By the time they left, Carl decided that's all it was and filed it away. He threw the slushy cup in the trash by the

84

parking lot, wondering if he would get mentioned in the acknowledgements of Frye's book.

Chapter 7
With Apologies to Harriet Tubman

Carl kept all his writing tools in a coffee mug on his desk. One side of the mug had the jumbled-letter logo of the Financial Accounting Standards Board. As he turned the cup to look for a red marker, he revealed the organization's slogan, "We mind the GAAP." He had a mouse pad that said the same thing, but he had banished it to a box in the basement.

He uncapped the marker and held it over the words "Kinko's/FedEx" on the white board. He crossed it off. He'd found out the opportunity was for a night position, and Carl had learned years ago that people over twenty-nine do better on a normal sleep schedule. He'd tried living that way while doing the due diligence for the Heartland Dairy sale: work at the office until three in the morning, doze fitfully for three hours, workout, and repeat. His body had settled into a crazed state of sleep deprivation highlighted by adrenaline rushes, irregular meals, and angry outbursts over things like fast food condiments.

He used to sneak away from the office for catnaps during the day, but back then he and Elizabeth were trying to have a baby. Often the catnap times coincided with the "optimal hours for conception." At her request, they would have sex over his lunch break (she insisted he eat light), or after his workout (he must shower), or in the middle of the night when he got home (she asked that he brush his teeth). But then, the sex stopped abruptly. Carl attributed its cessation to a merciful short-term change in ovulation patterns.

His experience without sleep made the nighttime Kinko's job a non-starter. The other position was for a server at Glen's Taproom. Keith called it "Glen's Tapeworm" out of disgust for its over-served collegiate clientele.

Glen sat across the bar from Carl. He was an older, barrel-chested man of sixty, with tufts of white hair protruding from his nostrils. "I had an English major in here one time. A bartender," the older man said, leaning over the resume on his forearms, a red beer in reach.

"Great. One thing about English majors..." Carl began.

"She sucked," the owner said. "Taught me a little something about the people who come in here, though. Something I didn't know in fifteen years of owning this place."

"What's that?" Carl asked.

"That the students who come in here don't give two shits about the *Canterbury Tales*."

He read the resume a few moments longer, his lips moving slightly. "An English major and a man. Hmm," he said.

Carl slouched forward in his chair slightly. Why had he come? He had no experience in the bar or restaurant business. He wasn't even qualified to bus tables.

"What the fuck does this mean you 'consulted on an LBO of Heartland Dairy?'" he said in a voice so loud it provoked a thin whine from his hearing aid.

"Leveraged buyout," Carl said. He reached for his resume. "Look maybe..."

"I know what a leveraged buyout is." The manager snapped the paper up to his chest and glared at Carl, one white tuft advancing and retreating with each incensed breath. "What I mean is whose side were you on?"

"Heartland Dairy. From that experience, I learned a lot about small business..."

The man threw the resume back at Carl before he could finish. "I remember that deal. Happened in Wichita?"

"You're familiar with..."

"You're asking me to hire someone who negotiated a leveraged buyout with ninety eight percent debt and two percent cash based on a multiple of one times annual earnings?" He rubbed his eyes with both hands and shook his head. "I don't think so. You guys got ripped off. You should have gone for stock."

The interview terminated.

Back in his apartment, Carl crossed "Glen's" off the list. Unqualified to broker deals, unqualified to bartend, unqualified to bus tables. At least he took some comfort in knowing he was qualified to help Julian Frye finish his third act. He just wouldn't get paid for it.

Why couldn't Ex-Elizabeth just agree to sell the apartment? Illiquid capital was such a waste. Just like kissing your sister.

The Battle for Dickens Hall had slowly intensified. One week the enemies of the EGSA had removed all the bolts holding the tabletop to its base. The next week, they left a bag of dissected rodents from the Biology Department.

As Carl headed to another week's meeting, he spied two people crouching behind the balustrade of a small stone balcony over the arched doorway of Dickens Hall. He sidestepped behind a tree. They were either snipers from the Statistics Lab or the Philosophy guys, ready to drop a Looney Toons anvil on the EGSA members as they entered. They had a trash can between them, and one held a hose that ran into it from one of the second floor windows behind the balcony. They suddenly crouched lower, having spotted someone coming. The one holding the hose dropped it and it snaked back and forth at their feet, soaking swaths of their pants with each pass.

Carl followed their line of sight and saw Mr. Clean walking toward the door. They got the nozzle of the hose turned off, and each grabbed a handle to lift the trashcan. Carl stepped out from behind the tree and yelled to Mr. Clean. He stopped and turned around, standing directly where they would be able to dump the trash can. Carl yelled louder. Instead of moving, he began fishing through his backpack. The two guys struggled with the trashcan as its weight shifted and some water sloshed over onto their feet. They lifted it higher, to get it over the balustrade.

Carl again yelled to get away from the door, but instead Mr. Clean held up one of the EGSA T-shirts they'd ordered. Above him one of the handles broke off the trash can, and the guy on the other side couldn't support all the weight. The trash can spilled onto his partner, completely drenching him. Water ran off the balcony and harmlessly out of two small gaps in the stone serving as downspouts.

Down below, Mr. Clean turned the shirt around to show the back, "Frankenstein was THE CREATOR."

Mr. Clean blamed the unintended emphasis on the caps lock key as he filled out the form on the website. He apologized through most of the time allotted for old business. Even though he had made the mistake, the T-shirt company gave him a ten percent discount.

As they came to terms with fifty T-shirts to sell that made the EGSA sound like some kind of fringe religious group, someone knocked on the door. The Shush-Sneezer opened it, and two men dressed all in black entered. Clearly dressed to intimidate, these men didn't look like guys from Statistics or Philosophy. They looked like models.

The one on the left, an African American with light blue eyes, said, "We have a message."

He put a stack of paper bowls and plastic spoons on the table.

Carl saw Mr. Clean mouth the words "Free ice cream" to the Shush-Sneezer.

The other visitor, a blonde with pronounced cheekbones, set an insulated paper sack next to the bowls. "This is for you, Carl Krauthammer." He eyed the others before looking back at Carl.

"It's up to you if you want to share."

The two men nodded and left the room.

Carl tentatively opened the sack, in case it contained a rabid ferret from the animal testing. He peeked in and took out a cardboard pint container. He found it filled with vanilla ice cream. On the underside of the lid was written, "Carl K. Call UR to set up an interview" in black grease pencil.

89

Carl had never gone into a job interview so blind before. He had spent time trying to research the company but found nothing relevant. UR didn't appear in the phone book. A search for UR on the web only found the ancient town at the mouths of the Tigris and the Euphrates. He read a few of those pages just in case the dairy had taken its name from the ancient Mesopotamian capital city. Finally, he called Susan to get her Milkman's name and number, which she recited from memory.

After Carl introduced himself on the phone, the man recognized him as "the one Susan called about" and suggested they meet that night at the dairy.

Flanked by the dueling blackness of River Pond on one side and River Pond State Park on the other, Spillway Marina Road led to the perfect place to see stars and planets at their brightest. Carl looked up through his sunroof but saw no stars, just the soggy overcoat of an early autumn night. Following the directions, he turned on Dyer road, veered right, and passed a "No Outlet" sign.

He came to an unmarked gate with a small attendant booth. A flickering blue fluorescent bar lit the empty box. As Carl got closer a figure popped up, dressed in the vaguely police officer-looking uniform common to security personnel. The man rapped the light fixture with his knuckle to make it glow solidly.

The guard shined a flashlight in Carl's eyes as soon as he pulled up. "This area's restricted, Chester. State your name."

"Carl Krauthammer."

He grunted and pointed the light away from Carl's face and onto a clipboard. The light reflected off the paper. Despite the burned-in flashlight image in his field of vision, Carl managed to get a better look at the guard.

"I remember you," Carl said, "from the Bland tailgate."

The man shined the light back in Carl's face.

"You with the university?" his voice had acquired a thin, sharp tone. "Because I just do this on my own. I'm freelancing. There's nothing in my contract that says I can't freelance."

"I don't have anything to do with the university, except I am a student there. I'm here to see a guy named Ocean?" That was the name Susan had given him.

"I guess I believe you, Chester, but that tailgate act needs some work. Didn't fool me for a second."

"Denny, it's Ocean," a voice said over a two-way radio. The guard put the flashlight under his arm and pushed a button on the bulky microphone clipped near his shoulder.

"This is Denny," he said, tilting his head toward the mike.

"I'm expecting a guy named Ca–"

Denny interrupted. "Mr. Ocean, please. Protocol clearly states that you confirm I have my earpiece in before saying the name of an expected guest so that it is not overheard. Stand by please, over." He took a moment to remove a small earpiece from a pocket on his uniform shirt. He unraveled the wire and put it in his ear. "I'm secured now, sir. Tell me the name."

The volume was so high on the earpiece that Carl heard his name.

"Roger that, thank you sir." Denny looked at his watch. "New orders as of twenty-one thirty. I will let you know if I see this person. Denny out." He took the earpiece out and let it dangle over his shoulder. "Now Chester, what did you say your name was?"

Ocean sat at the head of a large black boardroom table, leaning back, hands clasped. His index fingers formed a steeple under his chin. If pressed to come up with a single adjective to describe Ocean, Carl would say healthy. He looked slightly tan with a long face, the top marked by a shock of dirty blond hair, the bottom distinguished by a pointy chin.

He wore small angular spectacles, very stylish, giving him the look of an eyeglass model, those attractive men and women who only wore the frames because someone paid them to. On the table lay a fountain pen on two overturned sheets of paper.

Ocean rotated in his chair, a motion accompanied by a repetitious squeak. Carl looked around the room. By the door was a small table, with a plate, a pitcher, two crystal goblets and a small cheese knife. The plate held a PacMan-shaped wheel of cheese, and the pitcher contained milk. The entire left wall consisted of a huge World War II poster featuring an anthropomorphized globe cupping its hand to its ear under the words "Keep mum, the world has ears." The opposite wall had a framed two-way mirror. Beyond the obvious paranoia they tended to provoke, Carl found something indelicate in the fact that they never truly looked like real mirrors. They never fooled anyone. Carl thought that even people who had never seen an episode of *24* knew this kind of mirror.

Was that possibly the key to its purpose? Was the point not to see how people act when they're unobserved, but rather how they act when they *know* they're observed? And who wanted to watch him during this interview? Perhaps the head of UR HR? Carl preferred to dismiss thoughts of what he didn't know during the interview, because that can erode confidence. He did know he sat on the grounds of a dairy, or at least a business that used a dairy as a front, and Carl knew dairies.

"Tell me what you know about our business, Carl," Ocean said in the calm voice of someone who knows what's on the other side of the glass.

Carl straightened. An adrenaline rush sapped the saliva from his mouth, leaving a tinny film over his tongue. "I know the basics. Depending on your specialty, you have equipment costs..,"

Ocean cut him off with a raised hand. "Your resume proves you've seen cows get milked. I don't mean the dairy industry in general. I want to know," he said, pointing with both hands at the conference table, "what you know about *our* business."

92

The tipping point arrived, the moment where the applicant reveals he has performed no research on the company, proving himself to be a lazy no-good applicant. His instinct suggested that he lie, but he figured he'd get the job or not based only on honest responses. It's hard to bullshit the milkman sitting right across from you. "To be frank," Carl said, "I know a lot about the dairy business, having represented a dairy in a sale. I learned a lot more after the deal, but I don't know a whole lot about this particular business. I know nothing really."

"Really?" Ocean said, looking surprised. "You didn't ask any of our customers about our products? You didn't ask Susan?"

Carl rose in his seat and pulled his pant legs from the knees to get the wrinkles out. He should have asked Susan. "No. I did look UR up on the Internet but only got a bunch of sites about Mesopotamia." When Ocean said nothing Carl added, "Which I didn't think had anything to do with your organization."

"You might be surprised. But first?" Ocean said. He stood and walked the length of the table with his hand on the sheets of paper, dragging them until they were in front of Carl. "Would you mind signing this standard NDA?"

"You want me to sign a non-disclosure agreement before we talk about Mesopotamia?"

Ocean laughed as he circled to the small table. "We're going to discuss a little business in this meeting, and there are aspects I don't want released." He picked up the pitcher of milk. It had begun to separate since their meeting began, so he stirred it with a glass stirrer he found on the table.

Carl wanted to know what UR stood for. And he might just figure out how close Susan and Ocean were. He turned over the sheets of paper. He signed them both, folding one up and putting it in his pocket.

"Most people forget to take their copy," Ocean said. "Impressive." He held the pitcher up to the light. Satisfied with whatever milkmen look for, he filled the two goblets. He

93

handed one to Carl. With his own glass raised he said, "To Mesopotamia."

Carl raised his glass and gambled with the only information he had. "One of the earliest civilizations to domesticate animals," he said, "like cows."

"Excellent research," he said. "Now, *á votre santé*." They drank the milk.

This milk was warm, and Carl had expected it to be cold. It had lumps in it, globs of heavier milk. Carl liked its rooted, earthy flavor. The unexpected temperature, texture, and flavor combined to produce a pleasant experience.

"Whole milk just out of the cow," Ocean said, licking off the remnants of a creamy moustache.

"Just out of the cow today," Carl said, draining his goblet. Like drinking pudding, he thought.

"Just out of the cow ten minutes ago," Ocean said. "*Délicieux!*"

"I take it you use the shorter, higher-temperature pasteurization? They used the thirty-minute variety at the Heartland Dairy. That must explain the different taste."

"Here we run a simple business, Carl—no unnecessary expenses or effort wasted. And a better product for it. Heat kills off all the nutritional benefits. We don't pasteurize at all. Camembert?"

"I just drank unpasteurized milk?"

"Yes, pre-Pasteur. We call it *lait cru*, raw milk. Comes from a grass-fed cow," Ocean said as he poured himself another goblet-full. "It's technically legal for me to serve milk to you like this, but the KDA can make up its own rules if they ever find out about me." He took a pull from the glass. "But it was worth the risk because you just did your body a tremendous favor, my man. Seventeen enzymes your body needs—*pardonnez-moi*—enzymes and good bacteria your body *requires* to maintain excellent health."

Carl stared as the raw milk slowly ran slowly down the sides to the bottom of the goblet. He imagined it doing the same inside his body, coating his throat and pooling in his stomach. "So all of the dairies out there who pasteurize, they're just wasting their money? Why do they need to pasteurize and you don't?"

"Because my business operates outside the law," Ocean said.

Carl trusted his body would eventually dispose of the evidence that filmed in his throat.

"Civil disobedience, *mon ami*. We disobey the law because people deserve the nutritional benefits of this milk. And not just the people who would see a sign for fresh milk and stop by. No, they deserve to get it delivered to their homes. And we age our soft cheeses for just thirty days, also illegal. But these arbitrary rules, these whims of the state attorney general are morally wrong," Ocean said. "And they keep people from the great flavor of unadulterated dairy products."

"*Incroyable*," Carl said, summoning undergraduate French II. "It *keeps* people from getting e-coli, lysteria, and tuberculosis." He knew these things because the Sellars had told him.

"You've fallen victim to lies and propaganda that flow out of the Bovine Industrial Complex."

Carl shook his head.

"When handled safely and cleanly, with grass-fed, healthy cows, people don't get sick from unpasteurized milk." He held up the pitcher. "Five vitamins, primarily A, C, and D, twelve minerals, including calcium, none of it fortified. Twice as much nutrition as in homogenized pasteurized milk." Getting no response, he continued. "It's one of the healthiest things you can drink. I've been drinking the stuff since I was a kid. My whole family does."

Carl tried not to look angry. He visualized crossing "Milkmen in Black" off his white board at home.

"All right," Ocean said. He looked at the mirror and shrugged to the person on the other side. He moved to sit in the seat right next to Carl. "We sell our products to a rotating group of 513 customers the day of or day after it comes out of the cow. I get people who drive all the way from Kansas

City. I ship to fourteen states." He modulated his voice into the rasp of a co-conspirator.

"They pay us double what corporate grocery store milk and cheese costs, and I'm sure our overhead is lower. We're thinking of adding yogurt. Triple digit growth in every one of the past five quarters. Right now, we pull in 450,000 dollars gross a year."

"From 500 customers? Holy shit," Carl said. Those numbers doubled the per customer sales of Heartland Dairy.

"Upstanding citizens, our customers. These are closet rebels. They wouldn't dream of breaking the law in any other aspect of their life."

"They pay double?" Carl asked.

"All because we don't pasteurize it, and we deliver. We're considering a proposal with a group of hippies out of Emporia to provide raw fruit juices, wheat grass, and a whole line of black market produce."

These numbers sounded good, but definitely not *incroyable*. This guy had garnered Carl's interest. He got a tingly feeling in his upper extremities, a feeling he hadn't had for a number of months. "What about all of the government permits and fees?"

"I have a special strategy for avoiding that. I don't have any permits and I don't pay any fees."

"Your business is totally illegal?"

"I prefer a *Laissez Faire* approach in my state government. They don't know I exist, and no one tells them." Ocean took his copy of the NDA and folded it in quarters.

"What's your profit margin?" Carl asked.

"I don't have that information. That's the problem. I know you wanted to work delivery, but when I saw your resume, it fit perfectly with our immediate need for someone to get our finances in order. I have detailed information on how much we bring in, but I'm afraid to take out a significant salary without knowing how much the company can afford. I need meaningful numbers–a real accounting system. We've grown too much from when I had two cows and three customers, one of whom was my mother. How can I structure a partnership with the hippies if I don't know my profit margin on each half-gallon I sell? I'll pay you forty-five an hour cash for accounts payable and accounts receivable."

Forty-five was more than the other jobs he'd looked at, but far from the one-hundred-eighty-five he used to bill. And there would be no taxes. It was a simple operation, simpler even than Heartland Dairy in size, and probably in processing expenses as well.

"Let me think about it for a day or two. It's a risk," Carl said.

"Everything's a risk. You walk down the sidewalk on campus, an anvil could fall on your head."

"But this is a calculated risk, not a risk from some random force," Carl said. "You know the ways you could be shut down, and the penalties."

"These things needn't concern me if I never get caught," Ocean said. It sounded just like something Carl's first boss at Ogilvy would've said. "Can I answer any other questions?" Ocean asked.

"What's UR stand for?"

A man entered the room. It was the African-American who had delivered the ice cream to Carl during the EGSA meeting. He held a cheese box. He said, "Yeah, tell him what it means, Ocean."

"It came from back when I first started. It was a conceit that a seventeen-year-old would think was funny."

"Uh huh, *funny,*" the man said. "Tell him."

"Udderground Railroad," Ocean said. "Now I just call it 'UR,'" he pronounced it *er*.

"You know, like the Mesopotamian city." Ocean stood and clapped Carl on the shoulder. "If you accept, you can start this week. We'll deprogram you on your first day."

Carl sat with a frozen expression as the word deprogram bored into his head. First, he pictured Patty Hearst robbing a bank with the S.L.A. Then he saw Laurence Olivier approaching Dustin Hoffman with a dentist's drill. Finally, he saw Powers Boothe playing Jim Jones in the TV movie from the 1980s, raising a glass of milk.

A few days later, Carl went to the English/Counseling Services building to find out if the records from the Kansas Bureau of Investigation had arrived from the archive. When he stopped by Rosalie's desk he saw her sitting back in her chair, biting her pinkie nail and glaring at a thick coil-bound manuscript.

"Hi Rosalie," Carl said. No answer. "Did I get a Fed Ex from the State of Kansas?"

When she didn't respond again, Carl noticed she looked wan and somewhat thinner than she was even a week ago. She pulled most of her long black hair back into a ponytail, but strands hung over her face. She looked from the manuscript to Carl's face, showing no expression and registering no recognition.

"It's done," she finally said. "Now it's done."

He leaned forward to read the title page: *Half-Life Horniness: Sex in Contemporary Apocalyptic Literature and Film.*

"Grey's book. Congratulations. It's really done?"

"What do you mean by that? What could I have possible left undone? Perhaps the annotated bibliography?" She opened the manuscript and flipped frantically through the pages to find it. "Nope, didn't forget. See? There it is. You were wrong. Wrong wrong wrong." She sat back and then jerked forward. "Maybe the fourth chapter, you say? Perhaps you think I didn't incorporate all of the edits that Professor Grey added last night at three in the morning." Again she looked through the pages. "Nope, got that. too. See here it says 'penis' and not 'phallus.'"

Carl looked and nodded. "Yes, it does say that. It seems to really be all done."

She started looking for something on her desk. With increasing rapidity, she looked under the manuscript, through each in-box, and in the drawers of her desk. "Where's my fucking nicotine gum?" She held up a cardboard FedEx envelope addressed to Carl. "And what the hell is this? Get it off my desk."

Carl zipped open the envelope and took out the file. He looked through the first pages as he made his way up the steps. Susan stopped a few steps up from him, distracting him from the file. He snapped the folder shut and moved in to hug her.

They heard someone coming down the stairs and separated.

"Do you have lunch plans?" she asked him.

"I can't," he said. "I have to go through this research for Frye."

"You never told me what kind of a book he's writing."

He tucked the folder farther up into his armpit. "I don't even know what kind of book it is. He's keeping that to himself." Enough of that was true that he didn't feel bad holding back the rest.

"Keeping it from his research assistant? What kind of stuff are you researching?"

"Various stuff. Old accidents. You know Jules, finding connections. What are you going to do, the man's a post-modernist? But I think I'm really going to like working with your, with your, Milkman," he said. "How do you know him exactly?"

Carl thought he saw her face lose color. "He's - he's my Ocean, my nephew," she said. "Better get going." She moved down a few stairs.

"Are we still on for dinner?"

"Sure," she said over her shoulder.

Carl stood on the steps for a moment, listening to the clack of her heels fade away.

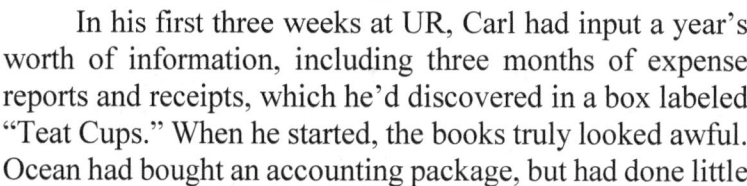

In his first three weeks at UR, Carl had input a year's worth of information, including three months of expense reports and receipts, which he'd discovered in a box labeled "Teat Cups." When he started, the books truly looked awful. Ocean had bought an accounting package, but had done little more than protect his files with a password: "RU-486." The company was a mess, too. Not operationally nor profit-wise. The problem with UR was conceptual. Carl considered it ridiculous that Ocean had started a business that required so much secrecy. As an expense line item on the budget, security looked even more fool-headed, skimming off two-thirds of the dairy's potential profit with things like overtime salaries for late-night deliveries, shipping through third parties, and all the surveillance equipment. But every business had a blind spot. He had learned that this rubric particularly applied to the small, family-owned companies, which he had specialized in at Ogilvy & Standpipe. Some hired a family friend who sat in a side office, drawing a salary for no work at all. Others retained something nostalgic in their product line that cost too much to produce and had lost its potential for sales growth long ago. But he knew those entrepreneurs who founded their companies on untenable premises had the biggest problems. It took effort to convince that person that his blind spot would someday ruin everything.

One afternoon, after completing the UR's first accurate balance sheet, Carl discovered he could work with a sense of detachment. When he looked objectively at UR's central conceptual challenge, he no longer took it on as his problem to solve. Instead he wondered how he might work it into a story. The UR had the potential for conflict, high stakes, and unique situations. It stood out markedly from the other things he and his fellow students had previously written. It drew upon small businesses and Ocean's dairy; two things Carl knew. And that represented a dilemma. Ocean would object to the writing of any story involving the dairy. He would probably consider it a breach of confidence. Carl couldn't logically disagree.

After he emailed the balance sheet to Ocean, he stopped in where the Milkmen in Black packed up the bottles from the afternoon milking. He watched the bottles rising and falling on the filler, a stainless steel contraption that handled four bottles at a time, each at various stages of the process. Empty bottles on small individual platforms rotated to the different stations on the machine. The machine filled each bottle, placed a cap on it, and then an arm came down to heat seal the cap. The moving bottles and the machine's rhythmic pneumatic hiss mesmerized him. That's when The Image appeared in his mind–a grown man drinking from a baby bottle, pursing his stubble-covered face to suck the plastic nipple. What did it mean? What could he make it mean?

He rolled down his window as his car reached the bumble bee-striped gate. Denny dozed with his face smashed against the glass of his booth.

Carl honked and Denny stirred just enough to hit the button that raised the gate.

"Good night," Denny mumbled.

As he passed through the blackness of Spillway Marina Road, an idea about The Image began to coalesce. He thought it might provide the perfect way for him to write about the dairy.

When he got home, he looked at his schedule for the next day. Depending on who read it, any story inspired by the UR could jeopardize Ocean's entire business. He came up with multiple scenarios. Yet this idea had an irresistible quality. Everything lined up. He had never felt a story take on its own agency like this. He glanced at his new life Progress Report.

"1. To become Jules Frye's peer," it said, and below that, "2. Do the right thing for close relationships." He recalled one of the most important tenets of the Progress Report: Goals appear in order of their importance to the success of the overall project for circumstances just like this. It appeared no course of action would satisfy both goals. So, with the image of a man sucking on a bottle in his mind, Carl decided to write the story in the spirit of achieving his first goal.

101

Chapter 8
Fat Man and Little Boy

The story came quickly once he had a premise. It centered on a guy struggling with his boring job at a dairy, dreaming of how he'd do things differently if he had his own business. Yet each time his imagination soars, the reality of his familial responsibilities grounds it. As his wife returns to work after the birth of their son, he spends a couple of weeks at home with the baby, wondering if he should become a stay-at-home dad. But he clearly cannot handle the household. He struggles with the dietary requirements of his four-year-old daughter, whom his wife has raised as a vegetarian. He has problems defrosting the bags of breast milk without making them too hot or too cool. His daughter suggests he take a sip from her juice bottle. "It always helps me," she says.

He realizes he's driven himself into a rut. When frustration finally overtakes him, the house a mess, the baby screaming, he drinks out of his daughter's bottle. It tastes familiar, like something he had years before but gave up for some reason. A soothing calm spreads over his body. His daughter is right–it does help. He takes another drink, but it doesn't taste like juice. He opens the top and looks inside. He's been drinking his wife's breast milk.

"We'll start with Carl Krauthammer's story," Frye said. "Who has positive comments on *Breast of Show*?" The class looked down at their copies. The Asian woman thumbed through a few pages. Mr. Clean shook a pencil between his thumb and forefinger, attempting to make it look rubbery.

The guy with the permed mullet sat upright. "It was amazing that the author could come up with such a premise," he said. "A secret dairy that sells human breast milk for grownups to drink?"

"Amazing?" Frye asked.

"Because it's not only implausible, it's disgusting."

102

Mr. Clean said, "I was turned off by the sheer hubris of cramming so much plot into a short story. And the characters weren't like anyone in real life."

As Frye had taught him, Carl based his characters on real people. The wife was one of the people Susan had counseled as part of her La Leche League work. Lake, the dairy owner, was like Ocean. It was set in Indiana. He exaggerated reality and took it to an extreme, just as Frye suggested. Had he strayed too far from the believable? Apparently. Everyone hated it.

The Asian woman said, "I would have more positive things to say if I felt the story weren't attacking me personally, as a woman and as a vegetarian." After a pause she said, "Well, I eat fish."

"Who comes up with this stuff?" Sullen Pedro asked. "When Lake tries to recruit the vegan wet nurses to see if grain-fed milk tasted any different? That shit's whacked."

The positive portion of the workshop continued in this negative fashion for ten minutes, until the class had ravaged Carl's choices of character, theme, action, setting, and even his choice of typeface. After the comments tapered, Frye leaned forward. Carl shuffled his notes around and poised his pencil atop a new sheet of paper.

"You people are all full of shit," Frye said. "This story works."

The Asian woman thumbed through her copy of the story. "Despite some of the problems I had with it, I thought it did, too."

Frye spoke directly to Mr. Clean. "It does have believable characters. Frankly, I believe this guy Lake exists more than I believe you exist," he said. "Here's what Carl has done. He puts someone in a situation that's funny, bordering on implausible, I'll grant you, but then instead of getting more exaggerated, it gets more believable. You forget the in-sanity of the premise and get absorbed by this guy's dilemma. You feel his panic, the problems brought on by the double identity he has to keep up. And playing off the public's appetite for

103

anything with the word 'natural' slapped on it? That certainly didn't feel exaggerated. The title sucks, but overall, it works."

Carl drew a happy face on the paper.

Carl determined his conference with Frye would be a celebration. He headed to Library Discount Liquor. The beer they'd pour must say something more than Frye's usual PBR, so he splurged on local beer from the Manhattan Project Brewery. He grabbed a "Mixed Six" pack of the flagship beers, Fat Man Stout and Little Boy Lager. On impulse, he also purchased a pint of Woodford Reserve from the shelf behind the cashier.

Carl's car growled into the driveway behind Frye's silver BMW. Now out of the garage, it looked like an older three series, possibly a 2000, its wheels blackened with brake dust. He peered through the bubbling tint job to discern the trim package. One of Frye's dogs popped up right on the other side of the window, barking non-stop. Carl recoiled. As he backed up he stepped on the bony foot of Frye's other dog that had snuck up behind him. He windmilled the arm that didn't hold the sack of liquor, tottering for one terrifying moment until his body ultimately decided against falling.

Frye came out of the garage laughing. "What the shit, Krauthammer. You trying to kill my dogs?" The one in the car ran in circles on the seat, his barking rising to a frenzy, oblivious that the passenger-side door sat wide open.

"Shut it, Taint! He's no threat!" Frye said, his face close to the window. The dog did not shut it.

Carl bent down to assuage the other dog, but it just yelped again, as if struck, and ran into the garage.

Frye shook his head. "Poor Merkin. Beaten as a pup. Now she's afraid of anyone in dress shoes." They went inside and sat at the kitchen table, a handmade chunky affair. The scattering of chairs around it looked as if an intruding gunman had just interrupted a poker game there. The white Formica countertops covered darkly stained cabinets with mismatched pulls. Overall, it looked to Carl like the set of a volunteer theater production of a Neil Simon play. The effect extended to the painterly view of the prairie out the window, where he could see across an unlikely expanse of untouched landscape. The setting sun (or the hobbyist in charge of scenery) had applied a gradient to the mesas and blunt rolling hills, from deep green up close to a faded greenish amber in the distance.

Frye gathered two chairs and placed a bottle opener between them. "Congratulations on the story," he said. "Your characters really stood out - especially Lake, waiting for the authorities to crash in on him." Frye said, opening his stout. "Where do you get such ideas?"

Carl examined his lager's label, unsure what to say. With such an obvious question, and asked in such a condescending tone, Frye laid out his intentions. Here was the former love interest, plumbing to determine the depth of his replacement's new relationship. Perhaps Frye hoped to learn how deeply Susan had accepted Carl into her life. It was as if knowing about her nephew constituted a tipping point where Carl's relationship with Susan surpassed Frye's.

"Where does any writer get ideas?" Carl asked.

"It just seemed so quirky," he said, "compared to your previous work."

"No mystery. I just used the tools of observation you're always suggesting we sharpen."

"The situation with the dairy? You observed that?"

The sparring grew tiresome. "I'm working at the dairy with Susan's nephew."

"Susan's nephew," he said. "At the dairy."

Carl saw no sign of confusion or shock. He decided never to play Texas Hold 'Em with Jules Frye. Susan's relationship with Ocean was too close for him not to know about her nephew. Carl guessed that somewhere in this house was Frye's own signed Non-Disclosure Agreement.

105

After a moment Frye said, "What did Susan think of the story?"

This time Carl didn't bother with a ruse to cover his pause. He remembered that Susan had originally objected to Frye's novel about Sparky, the one he now wrote in secret from her. He recalled the words she had used, *No good would come of it.* In fact, Carl hadn't even mentioned the story to her. All along he had worried only about Ocean's response. "You think I should have shown it to her?"

"You should have a good reason if you haven't, considering the–let's call it tenderness–she has about the fictionalization of people she knows."

"It's just a story for the class. Her *tenderness*, at least to me, is completely reasonable when the fictionalization is designed to be published and read by thousands of people."

"So you wrote your story solely for your own edification?"

"I hope lots of people read my story, but I have no illusions that *The New Yorker* will call."

"I only ask that you consider telling her because I plan to submit this story to the Bland Fiction Contest."

Carl took a drink. "You think it's that good?"

"I do. You did everything right: tight, dramatic scenes, the story is odd yet completely believable, your characters sympathetic. You've made tremendous progress."

Damn! Frye didn't just think the story worked, he thought it *worked.*

"I'm headed over to Bland's place this afternoon. I could take it over and give it to him personally. I really think it will go over well with both Forrest Blands, junior and senior."

So Frye thought it exceeded the work of anyone else who might enter. This represented a bigger victory than Frye merely praising the story in class. To personally deliver it to Bland practically amounted to an endorsement. Then, if he won, no worrying about tuition for a whole year and the possibility of publication in a small journal. It sounded like *a lot* of good could come from this.

Carl said, "The question is, do you think Susan will object?"

"Does it matter if she objects?" He smiled. "Why should you forego your own success to protect someone's over-developed sense of what constitutes privacy?"

No shit, Carl thought. He cared what Susan thought. He valued her feelings. But this was progress. She wouldn't want to hamper that. "You're right," Carl said. "Let's enter the thing."

"That's the spirit," Frye said, tilting his beer toward Carl.

"I appreciate this."

"Hey," he said, swallowing, "it helps me in my bid for tenure. I've taken one of my students from the world of business, practically another planet, to a point where he can write a story that works. Bland just might award his scholar-ship to a student from Kansas State. Don't you corporate assholes call that a win-win?"

"Some might call it synergy." Carl grabbed the remain-ing beers under his arm and shook Frye's hand. "You want me to get a clean copy from my car?"

"Don't bother. I have mine from class," he said.

Driving to campus, Carl noted how his latest accom-plishments held greater significance because he achieved them on his own, not as a member of a team. He struggled to name the feeling. Not exactly victorious–that connoted an end rather than a waypoint from which new triumphs might extend. *Dominance* got closer, but that sounded as if his recent success had to come at someone else's expense. No, this was the plain old self-satisfaction of personal achievement.

It looked like he would earn straight A's for the semester, something he had never done as an undergrad. Though a week of classes remained, he had finished all the work, and the semester's conclusion stirred in him thoughts of sex with Susan. He thought of the KASM, how today's date might fit into the statistics, but he quickly dismissed such detailed musings when the words for the way he felt came to mind: excessive virility. Could one feel varying degrees of virility, or was it like being unique: Either you are or you aren't? What did it matter? He felt virile.

The afternoon sun and dark walls made Susan's dining room look smaller. She stood at the dining room table sorting laundry on its mismatched leaves. She folded something, a pair of panties, and shoved them under a shirt as he came around. He'd brought the leftover alcohol from his meeting with Frye and placed the sack on a stack of jeans. Susan had a sheet of Bounce stuck to her pant leg. She looked great, rendered sexy, Carl concluded, by what her long-sleeve T-shirt and pajama pants didn't reveal.

"Well, hello..." she said.

He dipped her back and they kissed deeply. He kneaded the muscles between her shoulder blades. She closed her eyes, her fingers slaloming the moguls of his vertebrae. His lips moved lightly over her cheek. Short exhalations puffed out of his nostrils. Along her jaw toward her neck he made out the faint smell of her perfume. She gasped when he kissed her neck. He kissed her mouth again. They both straightened up.

He whispered into her ear, "We never defined what constituted the end of the semester." He softly blew onto the nape of her neck. He felt her shiver. "But I've turned all of my projects in, and I don't want to wait any longer."

She opened her eyes and smiled at him. "Let's do it."

He cleared a bit of laundry off the table.

"Right here?" she asked.

He nodded. He'd never had sex anyplace other than on a couch or in a bed, but he wanted to try it right there. He lifted her up on the edge of an unsecured table leaf. He kept her from sliding off with one arm and put the other behind her to stop the leaf from whacking the back of her head.

"My hero," she said. "We should go someplace more stable?"

They fell onto the bed, Carl on top. She pushed her hips up toward his. He sat up astride her and she removed his sweatshirt. He reached down for her T-shirt, but she held it down at the bottom.

"Not yet," she said. She moved her hands up inside her shirt and removed her bra, *Flashdance*-style. This sudden coyness added to his excitement. She took his hands and placed them on her breasts up beneath the shirt. He felt her nipples harden under his thumbs.

He had moved things along so quickly he hadn't considered birth control. He sat up. "Shit. I'm unprepared."

"What does that mean? You appear prepared." She looked to his crotch and back.

"No condoms," he said.

She looked relieved. "I think I have one. In the bedside table." He leaned over, rooted in the drawer, and saw the blue wrapper of a Trojan. He pulled out a streamer of condoms, attached to each other with a light perforation.

They kept coming out of the drawer like belts of ammunition.

"Costco," she said.

He tore one off and set the rest of the strip aside. "One ought to do, as long as…" he said, examining one label, "extra large. Perfect." He untied the drawstring on her pajama pants and pulled them down. No underwear. They kissed, groped, and eventually broke the KASM. She never did remove her T-shirt.

In the bathroom, he peeled off his third condom of the afternoon and tossed it into the trash can with the others, sending up a sour waft. He looked at himself in the mirror as he washed his hands. Damn, I even look virile, he thought.

When he came out into the bedroom, she was gone. He lay back down on the bed, having to make a space among all the pillows. He stuck his feet under the twist of sheet and comforter.

109

She returned, still wearing only her T-shirt, carrying two bottles of the beer he'd brought. She handed him one of the stouts and took two sips of her lager before placing her bottle on the bedside table. She spread an arm and a leg across him, her head on his chest.

He did not remember feeling this energized after sex with Ex-Elizabeth. He couldn't recall three times with her in a week, let alone one day. The first time this afternoon he had been quick, finishing before Susan. But on the second and third times their pleasure coincided.

"It's been a while. Years?" she said.

"Not quite a year," he said. "Somewhere around eight months."

"I meant for me," she said.

"Ah," he said. Here with Susan, the loneliness of the KASM hiatus receded into memory. He had transitioned to a new life. Though he had yet to make any money from his writing, he now felt it would someday become his career. It would allow him to simplify many aspects of life: stress, politics, and people to depend on for his own success. Other aspects would expand: the public profile of his career, the personal investment he made in his work, and the pride he took in his accomplishments. What remained constant? He still required someone close to him, a friend or a lover, to acknowledge his success, recognize it, and appreciate the importance he placed on it.

He said to Susan, "I have something to tell you."

She pushed up on her elbows. "The post-coital revelation. Should I be afraid?"

"It's a good thing," he said. "My latest story, the last one for Frye's class? It worked. It was a success."

"I've been so busy with my book, I didn't even know you had written another story. You must feel neglected." She kissed him.

"No one could feel neglected after the last hour we've spent," he said. He could taste the lager on her lips.

"Tell me about it. Did the class rave? Of course they raved."

Carl wrinkled his forehead. "Well, Frye liked it. Loved it, in fact."

She nodded, eyebrows raised. "Uh huh."

"He thinks it's good enough to enter in the Bland Fiction Contest."

She sat all the way up and grabbed his shoulders. "That's a big deal. If I'd known all this I would have brought up the Woodford Reserve, but something about drinking whiskey in bed sounded untoward." She smoothed out a wrinkle in the sheets around Carl's feet. "I'm happy for you, Carl. You seem to get everything you want." She smiled but she kept her eyes on the sheet.

"I've never been happier."

She nodded. "I'm excited to read your story. What's it about?"

"I'll email it to you." Carl swallowed. "You'll like it."

"Of course. So what happens next? I know you well enough to see that Frye's approval isn't the ultimate goal."

He thought for a moment on that ultimate goal of being Julian Frye's peer, then resisted mentioning it. Framing his needs and desires in terms of Julian Frye might not work for Susan. "Right now," Carl said, "I prefer to focus on the short term successes."

"I'm all for how you act when you have a short-term success. Can't wait to see what we do when you reach a bigger goal."

Over the next three days, Carl didn't leave Susan's house. When they weren't sleeping together in full up-tick mode, she graded final projects. He made notes, trying to nail down a concept for another story. His next one might be about Manhattan. He wanted to capture the town, the feel of it. He struggled to describe it in a few different ways – eventually settling on a comparison to an oasis in the middle of all that grass. It wasn't great but it was a start until he could come up with The Image.

111

He journaled about Susan, mixing up his feelings of affection for her with some detailed ideas for a female character who kept her shirt on during sex. He had lots of ideas of the psychological underpinnings as to why a character might do that, but none as to why Susan continued to do so. Did it have to do with breastfeeding? Maybe she shielded them because she considered their main purpose was nourishment of a child. That might make her feel guilty that she received pleasure from them. Carl hadn't stopped trying to take off the various T-shirts, sweatshirts, and crop-tops she wore during intercourse, but he realized she had grown more adept at distracting him from the task, either by changing to an intriguing position they hadn't yet tried or sliding down to pleasure him orally. Most times he would forget he hadn't seen her breasts until sometime later in the day.

When they finally left the house, Susan headed to campus and Carl went shopping downtown before he had to meet Frye for lunch at the White House Supper Club. He bought some clothes, mainly black, a color he had determined his wardrobe lacked. He wore some of them out of the store, a black waffle-weave shirt and some black pants in a style he'd seen some classmates wearing.

They sat at a high bar table, near the window, and played chess until their food arrived.

"Krauthammer, you're looking good. Straight out of the Man Barrack Sunday circular."

Frye took the mustard bottle and turned over the bun top on his hamburger. He squeezed some pallid mustard-water onto the edge of his plate.

"And Dr. Hirschman? She positively floated through the department this morning."

Carl picked at his plate, relishing the curiosity he detected in Frye's voice.

"Are you going to tell me what's changed?" he asked. "I'll guess. She's proud of her man, of the writer he's become. You showed her your story? Don't leave me hanging. Am I right?"

"She hasn't had time to read any stories," Carl said, "since our relationship has intensified."

"Intensified," Frye said, cutting his burger in half. "In a good way?"

"In an exceedingly good way."

"Congratulations," he said.

"Just about everything I ever dreamed it could be."

"Just about? Something missing?"

"No," Carl said. "It's great. Better than anyone else, better than with my ex."

"You said, 'just about.' Come clean, Krauthammer."

"Isn't it a little untoward, us talking about Susan?"

"I have no idea what you mean. I don't use the word 'untoward.' Stop demurring."

Carl took a super-sized bite of his burger. This was a conversation Carl might have had with Keith just a few weeks earlier, but now he and Frye had progressed from the level of friends, not yet to that of colleagues, but to the precursory status of confidantes. "This is a strange thing to bring up," Carl said, "but you're the best person I can ask about this." He made sure all patrons and servers had moved out of earshot. "Is there something wrong with Susan's breasts?"

"What makes you ask?"

"She keeps her shirt on."

"Huh?"

"When we have sex, she keeps her shirt on."

Frye looked out the window, holding his hamburger. He hadn't yet taken a bite, as if this new information required some digestion before the food did. "I'll be goddamned," he finally said.

"Did she do that with you?"

"That's a new one on me. Interesting. Strange," he said. "Kinky."

"Well if she didn't do that with you, it must have something to do with me."

"Most certainly it has to do with you."

113

Great, Carl thought. Frye was going to rub this one in. He hadn't seen anything like this when she dated him, blah blah blah.

"It's got to be her tattoo."

"Nah, I know about her tattoo."

"You do?"

"I mean I know she has one. I've seen it, the top of it, peeking out of her bra."

"But you haven't seen it in full. You don't know what it is. Secrecy, mystery," he whispered, "drama." He took a bite of his burger and winked at Carl.

After lunch, Carl lingered for a moment in the bar, looking over the chessboard, trying to determine how Frye had beat him in their last game.

He ran into Rosalie on his way out.

"Look at you, Carl Krauthammer. Playing chess at the White House, spending time with Jules Frye, got a new lover, dressed in all black. At this rate, your transition to insufferable prick should be complete by Christmas Day."

Two weeks had passed since Carl mentioned the dairy story to Susan, and he had not let her read it yet. He could name three reasons why. First, he forgot to attach it to an email he sent her. Second, her research for her article kept her busy. Third, they spent most of their free time having sex.

He hadn't pushed her about reading it, never even asked her about it. His earlier reluctance to show it to her, now that he examined it, was ridiculous. She, among everyone, would get the humor, even if it did hit a little close to home. In fact, that might even make it funnier to her. They were close now. She would love his story.

The Friday before Christmas Break, on Frye's invitation, Carl attended a Holiday Cocktail Reception in the improperly named Hemisphere Room of the Hale Library.

With its half-circle floor, arched wall of windows, and domed ceiling, it was more like a quarter-sphere. Designed to hold parties much larger, the room was too big for the fifty people attending the reception and felt more like ten small parties with large expanses of carpet between them. Carl searched the crowd. He saw no other students. He'd made the right decision to wear a sport coat over his turtleneck.

Frye waved him over to the bar where he stood with Forrest Bland and an older man. Frye handed him a Woodford Reserve on the rocks.

"Forrest Bland, Sr.," Frye said to the older man, "I don't think you've met Carl Krauthammer."

"A pleasure, Mr. Bland." Carl shook his hand firmly.

"Call me Woody. Are you a professor here?"

"No, a student," Carl said. Up close, Woody looked like a photocopy of a photocopy of the younger Bland, with whiter hair, more deeply set blue eyes, and generally blurrier edges. He wore a sweater covered in bright swirls, like something from *The Cosby Show*. "I'm sure you know the story I wrote…"

"Hot crap," Woody said. "Look what just walked in!"

They all turned. Susan, wearing an austere black cocktail dress Carl had not seen before, slowly scanned the room. Carl took a drink and watched the men watching her approach. He kissed her on the cheek.

"I thought I gave the bouncer strict instructions: no literature types," Frye said. "Must be that dress."

"He's not alone," Woody said and introduced himself.

"He's a promising writer who also happens to have excellent taste in women," the younger Bland said. Then to Susan, he said, "Have we met?"

"Yes, I'm the one who always asks you to consider donating to Manhattan's 'Breast is Best' campaign. So far, you haven't."

"Pardon my son," Woody said. "He's always been more of a leg man."

115

Susan smiled into her wine glass. "Does that mean I can count on your more discriminating taste to release some funds from the family foundation?"

Woody handed her his card. "Call my secretary and we'll get something sent over. We could discuss it over lunch." Carl rolled his eyes.

"Thank you. We're really doing some great work encouraging breast feeding to Manhattan's..."

"I remember now," the younger Bland said. He swished a finger between Frye and Susan."You two used to date?"

"We did," Frye said. "Though I don't recall us ever looking quite as happy as these two."

Forrest nodded. "There is a certain glow."

"Who wouldn't glow with all of the attention Carl's latest story has received?" Frye asked.

Susan entwined her arm in Carl's. "It's funny, sometimes it almost feels like his successes are my successes."

"One of the signs of true love," Woody said. "Forrest's mother used to come with me to every awards ceremony, no matter how insignificant."

"So you've read *Breast of Show*, Susan?" Frye said.

"She's been so busy with her own writing project." Carl explained to the Blands. "She's working on a book."

"I hope to read it soon," Susan said. "From what I've heard it's something special." Her face showed Carl she did share his success.

"It is," Frye said. "Unusual characters, and a great set-up with the breast milk. Sounds like something right up your alley."

"Breast milk," Susan said.

"Excuse me, Carl. I didn't know that was your story." Woody said. "I hadn't connected the name. I'm taken with your story. Your situations are so well-conceived."

"Glad you liked it." Carl struggled to keep his excitement from showing.

Woody squared his shoulders toward Carl. "Where did you come up with that premise of the illegal dairy?"

116

He felt Susan's grip tighten on his bicep. She really was as excited as he was about the story's reception. "It's just an exaggeration, you know. Not anything realistic."

The younger Bland nodded. "I found it quite unique, me being a dairy man. You presented it in such a realistic and funny way. Right now, the frontrunner for the scholarship. Unofficially."

Carl wanted to see Frye's reaction, but it appeared he wasn't listening. Instead he tipped the top of his head toward Susan, indicating that Carl needed to look at her.

Susan's expression had changed to something Carl had trouble reading. Ostensibly she smiled, but her teeth were gritted, and little knobs of jaw muscle protruded below her ears. "Breast milk? An illegal dairy?" she said. "This sounds like something I need to read right away."

"Plenty of time for that, darling. We're at a party." Carl said, pulling her closer.

"No," she said, digging the heel of her hand into his kidney. "I think I need to read it right now. I just can't wait any longer to read your story. I feel out of place here not having done so."

To the other men she said, "Excuse me, you gentlemen have a nice evening." She put her wine down on the nearest table.

"You're going to read the story right now?" Carl said. "It can't wait a couple of hours?"

"I don't think it can wait another minute," she said.

"Susan," he hissed in her ear. "Don't go now, it looks strange."

She freed her arm from his grip and was halfway across the quarter-sphere before Carl caught up with her.

"This is a big deal for me. I need you here by my side."

"I really think it's time that I read your story. Come over after your party here."

"I'll do that. I'm anxious to hear how much you like it."

"Let's hope that anxiety is misplaced," she said and left.

117

Carl smiled when he returned to the group. "What can I say? She's that intent on reading my story. I guess it is true love."

"Was that what that was? True love?" Frye said to the Blands. "I would have said she looked pissed."

"It takes a certain amount of sensitivity to read her emotions," Carl said. "Must be why she and Frye split up," Carl said.

"Must be," Frye said, nodding.

"I'll have to side with Carl here," Woody said. "That's pure devotion you're seeing. Pure devotion."

Carl glanced back at the door, certain that devotion had probably not guided her.

He spent the next twenty minutes schmoozing with Frye and the Blands over hummus and the university catering department's standard crudités. They debated the details of his story, rating each element as to its relative believability. They really were interested in talking to him and hearing his thoughts on process and what he'd written.

Later, he looked through one of Susan's porch windows, watching her reading on the couch.

She still wore the black dress but she didn't have any shoes on. He admired her calves, folded up beside her. He expected her to laugh occasionally, but she didn't. His breath condensed on the glass, and he raised his arm to wipe it off. This movement caught her attention.

She shook her head at him, returning to the manuscript. When he entered she didn't look up from the story so he went into the kitchen. His stomach felt a little sour from the bourbon, so he poured himself a glass of UR milk. In the living room, he sank in a chair across from her. She did not acknowledge him, looking up from the printout only when he placed the glass of milk on the table. Finally, she finished, turning the last page over on the others face down on the coffee table. She stared at Carl. He saw the expression again, the grimace/smile he had trouble reading earlier.

"That is a great dress."

"Holy shit, Carl. How could you do this?"

"The breastfeeding thing? That's meant to be funny."

"No, not the breastfeeding thing. Did you have to make it an underground dairy in a college town?"

"What, don't you like it?" He now wondered how he could have misunderstood her expression. He now recognized the down-turned mouth corners and furrowed eyebrow as anger. So she didn't like him using Ocean's situation. "I didn't have to, but it fit in so well. This is not Ocean's story. I mean, in a broad stroke it is, but it's in a different town, the details of the dairy's operations bear no likeness to people living or dead. Really different. Ultimately it's a positive story about people who choose to do what Ocean does." Carl watched to see if any of this had an effect. It didn't look like it. "I'm arguing with myself. What's your issue here?"

She began fluffing her hair with her hand. "When you said you were taking Frye's advice on writing, I had no idea that extended to his proclivity to steal the stories of people close to him."

"Come on, Susan. That's what writers do. You take stuff from everything around you. The character in the book isn't Ocean. He's an amalgam of things. That's what makes a story work."

"You agree with Mr. Frye that thieving is the elusive quality that makes a story work?" She stopped messing with her hair, leaving half of it fluffed. "You're like Julian's proxy. Even though we broke up a year ago, I get to keep arguing with him."

He leaned up to the edge of his chair. "At the core, I'm looking for something real that people can relate to. Call it a higher truth."

"You can save that shit. You didn't think of how Ocean might react to having his dairy outed? He trusted you as his accountant."

"I'm no longer an accountant," he said. "Writers write about stuff they see around them. I set the story in an underground dairy ultimately because I thought it would make a great setting," he said. "And look at how it's being received. You heard Bland and his father. That's the part they liked the most. I think I made the right decision."

"Don't you understand how monstrous you sound?"

"Monstrous?" Carl asked. "What about how over-dramatic you sound? I will not have anyone tell me how or what to write."

"Except Frye," she said. "I do not pretend I can tell you what to write. I just can't believe that you would disregard what it means to let your story get to the Blands. They're dairy men, for God's sake." She put her hands on either side of her head, speaking to the ceiling. "It's such a Julian move, not a Carl move."

"I consider that a compliment because he is a better writer than I am. That means I'm learning from him."

"You're learning the wrong things from him, don't you see that? Did it never occur to you that the Blands might wonder, 'Where'd Carl get such an idea? Hmm. Maybe there is such a dairy here in town.' Think about it."

"Oh, please. Ocean is not selling human breast milk. You're taking things too literally. It's just a story."

She grabbed the story and wrung it in her hands. "For you it's just a story, but it's Ocean's living, for God's sake."

"Come on. Don't demean me or my work, especially for Ocean. You keep talking about him like he's not a joke."

That looked like it stung her. "What do you mean?"

"No owner of a *real* business has to hide what he does," he said. "No real business can keep everything a secret. Christ, he's operating straight out of a bad spy novel over there." He picked up his milk glass. "Don't get me wrong, I like Ocean..."

"You have so many wonderful ways of repaying him for what he's done for you."

"What he's done for me? I'm keeping the guy afloat over there at that train wreck of a dairy. Before I got in there he didn't even know which products made money and which ones cost him money. Sure, he shows the right instincts, but that's what makes it all the more ridiculous that he runs a business whose only possible exit strategies involve bankruptcy or a government shutdown. Eventually, everyone gets found out."

"And whose fault will that be if that happens because Bland starts snooping around? Because of what you did?" She turned her back to him. "I'm telling you, no good will come of it."

Carl sat back in his chair. So Frye was right. She even used the same words. Susan truly was afraid of her partner's success. Here she was, taking the side of a failure in this situation, refusing to even acknowledge that this story was a good thing for Carl.

"I thought you loved me," he said. "Yet you're subordinating my future to Ocean's." He continued when she did not turn to face him. "You think I should have foregone my own success to protect your nephew's illegal dairy? See how crazy that is? It makes no sense."

She kept her back to him. "But why not at least tell him what was coming so he could prepare?"

"Prepare how? He's a grown man. He's not my responsibility. What makes him yours?"

"I'm not answering that. I don't have to answer that," she said. She turned toward the kitchen.

He could feel his whole head turning red. He stood up, waving his finger at her back. "That's exactly what my wife said when I asked her who she was having her affair with."

He thought she might be crying. He could hear her breath become shallow. "All right, Carl." She went into the kitchen and returned holding the framed picture of her sister with her newborn baby. "In the interest of full disclosure, that's me," she said, pointing at the woman she had told him was her sister. "That's Ocean, my son," she said, pointing at the baby. "His father Ron Sherman is now dead. That makes him my responsibility."

He grabbed the frame from her. He sat down. Ocean was her son? How was that even possible? "Why didn't you tell me?" he asked. "Why all the mystery?"

"Don't do that. Don't make this all my fault." Now she had tears rimming her eyes. "I thought I could trust you to be discreet," she said. "The one thing I need from the people around me is their discretion."

"How can I be discreet with a truth I don't even know?" he asked.

"You should just go."

"No. I don't want to leave things this way."

"What way is that? With me knowing how you really are?" She threw his manuscript at him. It landed on the floor by his feet. "Run along back to Frye. You two belong together."

"Since we're finally really disclosing things this evening, the one thing I expect is that no one keep secrets from me. It's unbecoming." He put the frame down on the table and left, stepping on the crumpled paper.

Over the next few days, Carl resisted any notions he might have to call Susan. She had not told him the truth about Ocean. *She* should take the first step in reaching out to make up with him. He did acquiesce to his urges for self-pity. When Keith learned this, he loaned Carl his iPod with the "Breakup Mix" on it. While he decided against playing it, he did lay on his bed for a couple hours. He missed Susan, and it pissed him off that she had kept secrets from him. It felt like betrayal.

Soon he was back to normal activity levels and decided he better retrieve the remaining personal articles from the UR. He went on an evening when he thought Ocean wouldn't be there. He knew Susan had probably told Ocean all about the story and their ensuing fight, but it remained unknown how Ocean might've taken the news. When Denny let him onto the grounds Carl took it to mean that Ocean, at least so far, had stayed rational about the whole conflict.

It was a ritual he had done not six months earlier at Ogilvy & Standpipe. Carl gathered the things out of his desk, recorded a new outgoing voicemail message saying that he would be out for an indefinite time, typed out a resignation, and made one last pass through his Documents folder in case anything personal was in it. He did find a few reports he had never printed out for Ocean. While the work he did would never withstand a federal or state audit, any government attention would mean Ocean had larger problems. By 10:30 he had printed out an accurate balance sheet as well as a reasonable profit-and-loss statement and placed them along with his resignation on Ocean's desk. His hand lingered on the documents. There would always be costs associated with success, he thought. No one got off without paying some dues. When he turned to leave, Ocean blocked the doorway.

"I left you the reports for the rest of this year," Carl said.

"How do you know what's going to happen the rest of this year?" Ocean said. "Do you think we'll be shut down so soon there won't be any business for the rest of the year?"

"I mean up to the end of November."

"Of course," Ocean said. "That's big of you," he said, looking toward the statements. "Not that I will understand those reports." After a moment he said, "Susan sent me your story." He moved to sit behind his desk. He indicated Carl should sit.

No boss had ever fired Carl before. Could he be fired if he'd already technically printed out his resignation? He debated a moment as to whether it looked stronger to sit or to stand. Unable to decide, he sat.

"It was a good story. Worth writing," Ocean said. "Turning it over to the Bland Boys? That wouldn't have been my choice."

Carl crossed one leg over the other.

"Mom has always seen things a little differently," Ocean continued. "She's a conspiracy theorist down deep."

Ocean leaned forward, his elbows on the desk. "I'll take my hits if they come," he said. "It's not like you started an underground business."

"This has been a good job for me. I don't want it to go away. I need the money."

"Until that scholarship comes through, eh?"

"I have to tell you, it will be great for me, regardless of any collateral damage."

"Collateral damage to my business or your relationship with my mother? I guess it's both." He grabbed a pitcher of milk from the table behind his desk and placed it next to two goblets between them. "Sometimes I think Mom cares more about the rebellious nature of this company than I do. It had to be an anti-establishment operation or she would never have supported me getting into business. For me it's just a market advantage that allows me to charge more. Every day the challenges change, the market shifts slightly. It's dynamic," he said. He filled the goblets. "It's not the underground part that I like. Running a dairy isn't even a passion for me. I know I have a lot to learn, but I'm just intrigued by business. Don't tell my mom."

"Don't trust me with any secrets," Carl said. "I'm no good at keeping them."

"All of the management books I've read say if you can align the dreams of your employees with those of the organization, both will flourish. Guess there's no hope for reconciliation when the employee seeks his dream at the expense of the company."

Carl swallowed hard. He didn't want this to end too badly, but if Ocean wanted to burn the bridge, fine. He wouldn't sit there and endure insults. Best to keep it focused on the business. "The reason that management book maxim doesn't apply here is because the business is illegal. If you didn't have to spend all the money on security and secrecy you'd make a thirty-five percent profit."

"But what about the taxes?"

"I've accrued your tax liability. You're going to have to pay that someday.

124

"That's pretty good?"

"I've never worked for a business with a better margin."

Ocean nodded. "I should tell you, Mom actually felt relief after telling you that I am her son. I understood her motives for keeping it a secret, but it seemed vain to me. I can see how she might be embarrassed, having a kid at eighteen. But what could I do?"

"Yes. A good son plays along."

"I think she will really miss you. She liked your gravitas. You represented settling down to her. Jules Frye, my father, probably all the men in her life, were restless. She wouldn't let me be an English major for fear that Frye would ruin me somehow. Had to settle for French."

Carl didn't like the use of past tense, or being grouped in with her dead husband.

"You were the opposite of those guys. I can't now say you're reliable, but I have to acknowledge your pragmatism. Let's call it *raisonnable*."

Carl shrugged. "I guess we're done?"

"I have to let you go," he said. "The employees will need to know of the possible impending doom. I have to fire anyone who breaks the circle."

"I figured that would be company policy," Carl said.

"It's never happened before now, but I'm not so naïve. I know that it might help to have someone with your skills indebted to me. I might need your help finding something else if I don't have to go to prison."

Carl couldn't help seeing Don Corleone. *Someday, and that day may never come, I would like to call upon you to do me a service in return.*

Ocean clearly shared his mother's penchant for the dramatic. "I doubt you'll go to prison," he said. "If anyone finds out about the dairy and wants to take you down - a big if - the worst thing that happens after they shut you down is they hit you up for back taxes." Carl drank some of his milk. "All things remaining constant, you'll have the cash reserves to pay."

Ocean smiled and handed an envelope to Carl. "Official notice of your firing."

"Thank you," Carl said, though he wasn't exactly sure why. When he got home he unfolded the dismissal letter and 200 dollars of severance pay fell out. A handwritten postscript told Carl if he didn't feel right taking the money he could donate it to the Manhattan Chapter of Breast is Best. Carl didn't know how he felt about the money. What did Ocean have to gain by such a gesture?

His dismissal/resignation marked the beginning of a quiet interval. He found himself liberated from the largest claims on his time: his job and his girlfriend. He hoped to fill the gaps by hanging around with Frye, but Frye's writing had intensified, and only occasionally did he indulge Carl by letting him hang out in his office, pretending to wrap up his research on Sparky's accident. One afternoon he took the time to fully review the police files on the derailment investigation he'd received weeks earlier. He sat across the desk from Frye, who hammered away on his laptop in be-tween sips of slushy.

He came across the name of a group that the police had investigated but had led nowhere. It had the unusual name of Revolutionary Nipple. Apparently, a couple of people under that banner had picketed a warehouse owned by West Egg a few weeks before the derailment. A search for "Revolutionary Nipple" on Google turned up several sites with both words separately: one for a bicycle spoke company, another for a shield that prevents the irritating condition of "jogger's tit," and finally an erotic site devoted to Delacroix's *Liberty Leading the People*. He found nothing on Lexis-Nexis nor on any of the databases he accessed through the university library.

"Ever hear of the Revolutionary Nipple?" Carl asked.

Frye stopped typing. He interlaced his fingers and stretched them over his head. "You saw it."

"Saw it?"

"You're talking about Hirschman."

"Not everything I say has to do with Susan," Carl said. "I'm having trouble finding anything about it in my files, and I think it's related to the train crash. And do you know what Sparky's train carried, what the cargo was? A manifest said something about powdered milk."

He began typing again. "Carl, who here is the research assistant, and who is the writer?"

"I'd like to think we're both writers, one helping out the other. I just thought if you could fill in a few of the details that I could, you know, more effectively focus this research."

"I want you to see if you come up with the same findings I did. I think that process would be good for you."

"Thank you, Dad," Carl said. It seemed that Frye would always see Carl as a subordinate. "About what you said before. Is there something revolutionary about Susan Hirschman's nipples? Could that be why she never takes off her shirt?"

"So you don't know?" Frye asked.

Here was another place where Carl could be downgraded next to Frye. "We broke up before I ever got to see them."

"You broke up?"

"She kind of freaked out about the story."

"What did I tell you? I knew one of three things would break you up: drama, drama, or drama."

"I admit I understand it. Of course, she would choose her son over me," Carl said.

Frye made a sound like he just snorted slushy through his nose. "Her son?"

"Ocean's so pragmatic..." Carl realized he'd finally done it when he saw Frye's eyes. He'd told Frye something he didn't know. He must savor that moment. It felt energizing to be the tall kid holding the kickball away from the others.

Frye did not let him keep the ball for long. "Of course, Ocean is her son, not her nephew. That makes a lot more sense. That's why she keeps him so close."

"I assumed you knew," Carl said.

"She hadn't even told me she was married," Frye said. "I had to find that out on my own." He closed his laptop. "So why did she tell you that Ocean was her son?"

"I don't know. I'm not sure if she expected me to feel guilty about writing the story or what. You have a theory?"

"Projecting guilt onto you is in there. I think she did it to get you to fix things for Ocean somehow. More drama, manipulation, secrets. You ought to be thankful you're out of that circus. I know I am."

Did that mean he was glad that Carl was out of the relationship, or glad he himself was out of a relationship with Susan? Ultimately, of course, it didn't matter. They were both out.

Chapter 9
The Perennial Growing Putz

Nothing kept Carl in Manhattan for the weekend, so he figured he would attend his parents' annual pre-Christmas party in Kansas City. As he drove, Carl realized he had entered a new chapter in his relationship with Frye. Before, he felt the need to constantly show off the things he possessed that Frye didn't, like some information about Susan that proved the level of their intimacy. Now a kinship had developed that didn't require such posturing. Frye had looked out for him with Susan, had warned him about her. Now that he and Susan appeared to be through, it made him feel more like he and Frye were peers. Carl treated it like a rehearsal for when they were peers as writers.

He hoped his current lack of capital wouldn't get in the way of his plans to become Frye's true peer. He had saved a little money from his work at the UR, but it wouldn't last much past New Year's, especially if he had to keep coming up with half of the mortgage for the apartment in New York. He studied his budget. Unless he ate Ramen for three weeks straight or sold the apartment, he would probably have to dip into his 401k. But even as a writer, he still got nauseated thinking of the ten percent early distribution penalty. That money was not for short-term use. He might be able to get a loan from one of his father's banking relationships, but with no job and current market conditions, they would expect his father to co-sign, and his parents subscribed to the Krauthammer Teutonic Code: You cut off your kids financially at age twenty-five. Besides, they already had a home equity line on their house.

As he pulled into his parents' driveway his worries over broken relationships or money troubles vanished. All he could think of was the life-sized crèche (called a *putz*) that Carl's father, Klaus, had erected in their front yard. The decorations coincided with the "Annual Christmas Putz and Cheer," a cocktail party held two weeks before Christmas.

129

The party tradition had begun a month after his parents moved to the neighborhood in the early seventies. Eight disapproving members of the home owner's association came to serve Klaus with a formal order demanding that he remove the display for violating a codicil in the neighborhood's "Acceptable Holiday Decoration" code. According to legend, Klaus mistook them for carolers and invited them all inside for treats. Five hours later, the group had warmed up to the display and to the Krauthammers, thanks to the large amounts of pork *bratl* and *hefeweizen* they consumed. Every year since, Carl had watched the Putz grow with additional animals (Carl couldn't remember a polar bear being in any of the stories of Christ's birth), landscape elements (running water and enormous amounts of realistic-looking moss), and characters (like Galahad, grasping a garish plastic cup his mom Katrina had adorned with rhinestones to represent the Holy Grail). This year the putz featured a Barack Obama, replete with a blue suit and flag tie, smiling benevolently over the baby Jesus in the manger.

By 6:30 a solid crowd had gathered for the party. The invitation list had grown along with the crèche, because Klaus and Katrina never dropped anyone off the roster, including ancillary characters like Mr. Walkens, the Krauthammer's old plumber.

In one corner, Klaus spoke to Maurice Boris, the family's lifelong attorney who gestured wildly with his arms until beer sloshed out of his stein. The house looked the same as it did every year, with a gas fire in the fireplace, real greenery on the mantle, his boyhood stocking hanging next to those of his parents. From the edge of the steps that led down to the sunken living room, he had a broad view of the crowd. He noted a slight stir near the front door.

The Austen contingency had arrived.

First came the Governor and her husband, Ex-Elizabeth's dad. The Governor glowed, her pearl collection in full display: bracelets, earrings, brooch, and necklace. Next, where Carl and Elizabeth would have ranked, came Mary and her husband, television personality Bill Tawfee. Something must have happened for them to usurp Elizabeth, who entered next, wearing a revealing black cocktail dress. Carl's parents greeted everyone in the proper order. Elizabeth's dad and Carl's father walked toward the bar.

Bill Tawfee headed to the closet with the family's coats. Ex-Elizabeth spotted Carl, and then she, Mary, and the Governor exchanged words from behind purses, looking like football coaches, afraid the other team might lip-read their play calls. It was time to play nice to get her to sell the apartment. Carl walked down the stairs and crossed to the trio.

"Governor," Carl said. "Great to see you."

"Thank you, Carl," she said before another guest seized her attention.

He hugged Mary. "I don't think I have seen you since last year's Putz," he said. "How are you and the Tastemaker of Topeka?"

"He's just 'The Tastemaker' now. We signed with Harpo in Chicago. We're going into nationwide syndication in March. We have our offices one floor below Oprah's."

"Excellent news. How did this come about?"

"I managed to get him booked on Oprah to talk about what people in the Central Plains are reading. Now he has his own show and she calls him for his advice on what she should choose for her book club. They really hit it off." That explained the reordering of the Austen family's entrance.

"Elizabeth tells me you're between jobs doing a little writing in Manhattan?"

"Actually, an acclaimed author just took me on as his research assistant for his new book. Do you know Julian Frye?"

Mary blanched and held up a hand to quiet him.

Bill Tawfee, who had returned from dropping off coats, shook Carl's hand, and Carl instantly remembered one

131

of Tawfee's most annoying features. His thumb always swung free during a handshake.

"I remember Julian Frye," Tawfee said. "He used to be a writer."

"He's at it again," Carl said. "It promises to be an interesting story. Might be perfect for your new show."

Tawfee's nostrils clamped shut as he inhaled. "We don't do the Midwest anymore. Ours is a national show."

"The Midwest is still part of the nation," Carl said, but Tawfee was already leading Mary off to the bar.

Ex-Elizabeth shrugged and offered her square smile of perfectly white teeth. They hugged. She tucked her hair back with her index finger, but the Sequence of Gestures ended there.

"Elizabeth, you look beautiful." He noticed her dress looked similar to the one Susan had worn to the reception in Manhattan. Out of the corner of his eye he saw the Governor turn toward them.

Elizabeth took his hand. "I need you for a few minutes."

"And then you and I are through, I say," Carl said.

"Too funny," she said.

They headed to the guest bedroom and sat among the coats. It smelled of a thousand different perfumes. He wished they had gone into the kitchen instead. Scores of family photos obscured the walls, among them a portrait from Carl and Elizabeth's wedding.

"Nice picture," Ex-Elizabeth said. "Saw one just like it when I got home from New York. Our parents are hanging on hope until the divorce is final."

Carl considered it a crappy picture, too obscured by the soft filter the photographer had used. It featured them from the waist up, gazing at her wedding ring. Carl resented both the photographer for staging the pose and Ex-Elizabeth for insisting they buy prints for everyone. Copies of the picture hung on the walls of at least three guest bedrooms across Kansas City. If the photographer really wanted them gazing at an enduring material symbol of their marriage, Carl would have suggested a miniature model of their unsold apartment.

"I'm not sure if it's that they like the picture so much," he said, "or they seldom come in this room." He needed to stay on task, but he couldn't help himself.

"So tonight, it's Cynical Carl," she said.

"Would it be cynical to say I prefer the term realistic?"

She giggled curtly. "Yes."

Her smile began to transition to a look of – what emotion did he see there for a moment before she turned her attention to poking around in her purse? Its brevity precluded making any certain definition, but the condescending headshake gave him the impression of pity.

He said, "Aren't you going to ask me about my writing?"

"I already know about it. I understand you've won a full-ride scholarship. It's too bad you couldn't keep your girlfriend around to celebrate."

"Whoever your mole is in Manhattan doesn't quite have everything right."

She did not look up until she pulled a thick red envelope from it. "So you mean you got your girlfriend back?"

"I mean I don't have the scholarship yet."

"I have faith in you," Ex-Elizabeth said. It was the first time he could remember her expressing faith in him. Perhaps he had just lost the ability to tease the sarcasm out of her voice.

"I have this present for you," she said.

This was typical of The Natural. She probably knew he would come to Kansas City for the party after breaking up with his girlfriend.

She held out the envelope. "It's something we wanted to do. You can be as active or as inactive as you want. And now I'm going to go." She put the envelope down on the bed. "I wish I could stay but I'm taking West Egg's private jet to Wichita for their corporate Christmas party tonight."

Carl felt a little anger rising. Probably jealousy. But what did he have to be jealous about? He didn't want Elizabeth back. Who cared if she was still dating the Human Resources Director at West Egg? "Give my regards to Mr.

133

Fabulous. And make sure you read the employee handbook on alcohol consumption at company gatherings."

"Actually, he's out of town." She rooted through the coats for her own. "Bland invited me. We're finishing up work on a master plan for a takeover of a couple of regional dairies. He wants a monopoly, and, by God, at 255 bucks an hour, I'll get it for him."

The envelope had landed in a crater of a fur. It felt heavy when he picked it up. He peeked inside. It looked like some kind of legal document. "Is this a contract on the apartment?" he asked.

"No." She located a long black wool coat and put it on.

"Your will?"

"No, Carl."

He skimmed through a few pages and got the gist of it. It was a contract. Ex-Elizabeth was offering him a partnership in her firm, now called Krauthammer, Austen, Cotter, & Laird, KACL, Inc. Damn her, he thought. What was she up to? What would she expect in return?

He felt his ears redden. He had made strides in his life, and even though Ex-Elizabeth knew about them, her offer still suggested that he would never succeed. "You can keep doing this, Elizabeth. Refuse to sell the apartment. Offer me a partnership in your company. Keep pretending that we're not separated, that someday we might just move back into that apartment. What's different, what you'll have to eventually acknowledge, is that I have a life that doesn't include you."

She smiled. "Don't be offended. It's just business. I've included the basic information, but I imagine you'll want to do some due diligence. It's a real company now, Carl. Maybe it could replace some of the money you've lost from your accounting job."

She kissed Carl briefly on the cheek and left. He watched from the doorway to the bedroom as she stopped to say goodbye to both of his parents before leaving.

134

On the Sunday after the party, Carl stewed over the offer while watching the Steelers play the Packers with his parents. After the first quarter, Carl's father stopped trying to engage him in conversation about the game.

Right after she made that offer, Carl fantasized about taking the leftover guts from his father's homemade *bratl*, the parts of the pig too gross even to put in sausage, and wrapping them up in Ex-Elizabeth's contract. "There! That's what I think of your offer."

Why had she done it? Did she expect something in return? Did she just want to insult him? Was there some reason she needed him to be affiliated with her company? He seemed to attract women who operated with ulterior motives. Just like Susan trying to manipulate him into helping Ocean's business. If Ex-Elizabeth wanted to insult him, okay, mission accomplished. Yet the extent of her actions proved that insults couldn't be her only motive. In the past, she had demonstrated multiple ways of insulting him without engaging the services of a contract lawyer. She either had professional or personal reasons.

The Steelers went three and out. With the Packers on offense he wondered about her professional motivation. Did she really need him for the success of her company? Terry Cotter and Heather Laird offered no leadership from an execution standpoint. These people had plenty of competence, just no direction for it. But why make this bigger offer when he had refused any involvement a few months before? Did some recent development make her think he'd be more receptive?

When the Packers threw their second interception, he considered the personal angle. Did it have something to do with his relationship with Susan? Was this a way for Ex-Elizabeth to lobby for his affections again? She might have made the offer just so he would look at the partnership's financial statements. She might have wanted to draw the brightest line between herself and Susan. True, he hadn't been able to resist looking over the numbers. The company posted excellent cash flow, demonstrated strong receivable control, and a strong growth pattern, all without Carl's involvement. He didn't place her above gloating with a balance sheet.

Field goal, Steelers.

She could have sold a huge piece of work, something she couldn't execute without his help. Something to do with Bland's dairy acquisitions she mentioned? He let his head fall limp against the back of the couch. She hadn't used the word "acquisitions." She said "takeover" and "monopoly." And she mentioned his accounting job. At first, he assumed she meant his job at Ogilvy & Standpipe, but now he wondered if she meant the one at Ocean's business. Was this all about the UR?

At halftime, Carl gave up on watching the game and headed to the basement to go through the final box of his stuff he had shipped there from New York. He had hoped that his new life in Kansas would provide a respite from these sorts of conundrums. He craved delineation from Ex-Elizabeth and everything about New York. Why couldn't the partnership offer fit cleanly in a little circle labeled "Former Life?" That way he could dismiss it as part of the past. In a separate circle, he could place everything to do with his new life in Manhattan. His desired mental Venn diagram showed no gaps in either of the distinct circles.

But such a diagram depicted closure. The box, from a New York apartment that he still owned, demonstrated how such closure had eluded him. Each circle should look more like a letter C, half open so that the contents were left exposed and raw.

He had labored hard to create something new in Manhattan, but his successes felt obsolete outside of the town. He should have gloated more to Ex-Elizabeth about his work with Frye and the success of his story. She had chosen a vulnerable time to hit him with the offer. She hadn't allowed him to place his accomplishments in proper perspective. It nagged him that he hadn't acted with more self-confidence, hadn't immediately declined her offer. Was his hesitance just a leftover from his days as a contemplative accountant, a symptom of that lack of closure?

136

Did his behavior betray an emerging guilt that his small successes had already taken a toll, on Ocean and on Carl's relationship with Susan? Frye would call this thinking bullshit. He would discourage further consideration of Susan or Ocean, calling Carl weak for feeling guilty. Even Elizabeth would scoff at his "overactive conscience." But Carl considered guilt something that operated independently in the subconscious, regardless of a person's strength or weakness. Either you felt guilty or you didn't.

How strange to include Ocean, Susan, and Frye in his deliberations of Elizabeth's offer. Instead of focusing on things from his past, it was time to move on. As a symbol of this newfound resolution, Carl left the box in the garage with the trash from the Putz.

Classes drew to a close. Students and faculty began the holiday evacuation of Manhattan. Few pedestrians crossed Anderson Avenue between the campus and Aggieville. The parking lots held just a single car, usually with a Campus police ticket on the windshield. The Ole Smoothie Shop in the Union closed for the break.

Keith and Rosalie now lived mostly at her house, leaving Keith's place to Carl. He spent most of his time reading, alone in his room. Frye had recommended a stack of worn paperbacks from his own library. Pynchon, Cormac McCarthy. Oddly, he also had him read *You Can't Go Home Again* by Thomas Wolfe, the guy from way back, not the one who wrote *Bonfire of the Vanities.*

One afternoon he went to Frye's office. Like the campus, it had changed since before the holiday. It still had the stacks of material, but they had shrunk, as if someone had made off with the top third of each pile. Even the dumpster outside the window stood empty.

Carl snapped at the keys on his laptop, typing search phrases, but rarely clicking on any links. He leafed through police reports. He found nothing new about the derailment, but that was not his main purpose. He wanted Frye's take on Elizabeth's offer, and what it might mean for the UR. Frye would help him make sense of it. Things were clear-cut with Jules Frye. Carl knew he analyzed too much.

Soon Frye showed up wearing a white button-down shirt under the usual blazer. The flaps were stuffed inside the bulging pockets on both sides. One sleeve appeared to have brushed against something dusty. His hair looked like it had recently been cut. "Carl, what the hell are you doing here?"

"Just trying to finish up my research. I don't want to hold up your third act any longer."

"Fuck that, man." He waved his hand in a grand dismissive gesture that seemed to upset his balance. "You've done enough. I release thee."

Carl looked at his side of the desk, his stacked files, and his chair. "You mean my assistantship is finished?"

"That was more of a task for your own ed-i-fi-ca-tion." He shook his head. "You have no idea how hard that word is to enunciate after a few bourbons."

Carl watched him shuffle papers around on his desk. "His own edification." Had Frye seen something in Carl and concocted the assistantship just to have him around? Was it part of his mentoring, or had he recognized real talent in him? Either way it was flattering.

"Shit, I almost forgot," Frye said, doubling over the desk to extend a hand to Carl. "Let me be the first to congratulate you on winning the Bland Fiction Scholarship."

Carl shook his hand. "I got it? You're serious?" The information soaked in. It was official. He'd earned the scholarship. This represented the achievement of the short-term goals he set. It both shrunk his money problems and expanded the circle of those who appreciated his writing.

"We should celebrate," Carl said.

"You know I see other people," he said. "I have dinner plans with the Blands to celebrate right now. I've taken a page from the Carl Krautham-m-m-er book." He pointed down and to his left, emulating the voice of a stern parent in an anti-drug Public Service Announcement. "Where did you learn to properly celebrate the victories, Frye?" He turned around to face the other direction, and responded to himself. "From you! I learned it by watching you, okay?" Finally, in a voice that sounded like a cross between Don Pardo and Sylvester the Cat, he said, "Professors who celebrate victories have students who celebrate victories."

"You're celebrating my scholarship without me?"

"No, Carl," he said waving a finger, "I'm celebrating the completion of my book."

"Done?" Carl asked. "Like completely finished done?"

"Yessir. I have some minor editing to do, but the hard part is over." He took a single sheet of paper from his desk and held it before his face. "Here's the little bastard. The Blands and I are celebrating my deal with their publishing house, discussing this Promotion Plan." He sat down in his chair, but Carl couldn't tell if he meant to. His eyes settled on Carl. "But of course, you should be out celebrating your own victory, Krautham-m-mer." He reached in the pocket of his blazer and pulled out some crumpled bills, a shoehorn, and a receipt, all of which he cast across the desk. "Go out and buy a Fat Man on me." Carl hoped he meant the beer. Frye continued. "I shall give your regards to Messrs. Bland. I will also give them this important piece of paper." He stood, saluted, and left.

The next afternoon Carl wandered into the store called Excess Baggage, after randomly roaming the mall for an hour. He looked over the Executive Gifts Area, which offered things like a miniature desktop Japanese rock garden, magnetic sculptures, and those five silver balls suspended by fishing line that click back and forth as soon as you set one in motion. He also saw several items to practice putting on a carpeted floor. Frye didn't have room in his office to putt. None of this stuff looked appropriate.

139

He thought about all the things he had listed in his journal that Frye had done:

1. Motivated him to abandon his empty life for a more inspiring one as a writer,

2. Mentored him in his work,

3. Promoted him among those who could help him now (scholarship) and in the future (publishing?),

4. Looked out for him in personal matters (Susan),

5. Befriended him, and –

he had to open his journal to remember the last item -

6. Taught him how to make sense of the world.

The list below of potential gifts was disappointingly short:

1. Bottle of Woodford Reserve,

2. First edition,

3. Something from the mall.

The disparate lengths of the two lists embarrassed him. He had to do better than that. The Woodford Reserve was out, too impersonal. The first edition made the most sense, but he didn't have the money for that.

He came to the flasks. They had three kinds. The cheapest was plastic, clearly designed to appeal to the cost-conscious alcoholic. The second, a long tube hidden inside a faux driftwood walking stick looked like the perfect gift for a cross between Gandalf the Grey and W.C. Fields. The third one looked just about right, a chrome number wrapped in a thick band, which the tag called a "leatherette flask koozie." Sixty-five bucks. He took the top off, and for some reason sniffed inside.

"You're responsible for filling them up yourself, Krautman."

Carl turned to see The *Flanesser*.

"That's right," The *Flanesser* said. "I'm working here at the luggage store in the mall. Some of us need the money. You going to make fun of me?"

"I don't need to," Carl said.

He narrowed his eyes at Carl. "Are you going to buy something or not? You've been browsing for fifteen minutes."

"I don't know. I have to make sure it's right."

"Is this a gift for Frye?" He held his hands up on either side of his face, opening and closing his fists to emulate lights. "Newsflash, Krautman," he said. "You needn't continue brown-nosing Frye. You already got the scholarship!" His enormous beak wrinkled strangely. "Besides, not a flask. You can do better than a flask."

"No, it's for me." A man who looked like the manager of the store came up behind The *Flanesser* to listen to their exchange. "Perhaps you could recommend something that might bring you a better commission?"

The *Flanesser* snickered. "No, dillweed, I'm on a salary. I meant how about something more meaningful," he said. "For instance, I'm working on finding a sponsor for the EGSA Spring event. Soon enough he'll reinstate me as the true and rightful head of the EGSA." He continued blathering about rewarding academic duty and personal responsibility, but Carl stopped listening. The *Flanesser* unwittingly had raised an interesting point.

Perhaps he could do something for Frye, take some *action* that would demonstrate his understanding and appreciation of all that Frye had done for him. Maybe he could do something to help Frye raise the visibility of the department. He held up a hand to silence The *Flanesser*. "All right, sir. I acquiesce. Thank you for showing me the wisdom of leaving this establishment without making a purchase." He nodded at the manager as he left.

Sparky had the Lethargic Clown decorated for the holidays. He placed a wreath around each television. Errant sprigs of plastic evergreen obscured different parts of each screen. Some covered the clock in the lower right corner of basketball games. Others had the upper right covered where most NFL games had their scoreboard. Still others covered the entire bottom third, making it impossible to read the news ticker at the bottom of Fox News. One string of anemic

141

mini-lights hung from a wagon wheel on the wall, flanked by a menorah and a Happy Kwanzaa poster featuring a woman caressing a bottle of Courvoisier.

Sparky's shrine to Frye by the jukebox lacked décoration. Carl looked again at the display's focus, a picture of Frye with slightly less grey in his hair, sitting in a chair in the restaurant, surrounded by baskets of food. You could see the back of another man's head. He held a small steno notebook and a pencil.

"I'll never forget that interview," Sparky said, walking up to Carl. "When he first moved here the Chamber was booking him interviews with all kinds of magazines and newspapers. That's Bill Tawfee interviewing him."

Carl perked up. "The Tastemaker of Topeka."

"He wasn't called The Tastemaker then. He was on the news, had just come from a public access show somewhere, I think. The Chamber got him to do an hour special on entertainment and the arts around the region. Frye insisted that they do his interview here, a live broadcast. Frye sort of made a joke of the show. I mean he answered Tawfee's questions, he was just constantly eating the food we had made for the crew and raving about it. Practically a twenty-minute ad for us."

"How'd the Tastemaker handle it?"

"He was a nobody then, he was just in awe of Frye. Every year he does an anniversary show and plays a clip from that interview. And every year he says something snarky about how he's such a better interviewer now that he could cut Frye to ribbons in a rematch, if Frye ever started writing again."

Carl ordered food at the bar. While he hadn't seen the Tastemaker's new show, he wondered how a sparring match between the guy and Frye might play out today. It would make for great television, and the perfect gift for Frye. Who wouldn't want the national exposure?

And if the Tastemaker truly had Oprah's ear, such an appearance might lead to a book club selection. He ate his lunch, preparing to argue for booking Frye on the Tastemaker's new show. Why wait?

He searched for Mary Austen-Tawfee on his phone and called her. They talked for a moment and then he pitched his idea.

"You have to have Frye on The Tastemaker of Topeka's show."

"It might make your pitch more effective if you get the name of the show right, Carl."

"I'm sorry, I always think of him as a Kansas guy."

"We broadcast from Chicago, his hometown."

Carl knew the Tastemaker was born in Chicago and moved to Council Grove, Kansas when he was six months old, but he didn't contradict her. He needed to keep her happy. "This is worthy, Mary. Frye's a national personality. He had two best sellers."

"I don't see how I can make this sound appealing to Bill. Look at it from my standpoint," she said. "A fiction writer from Kansas who hasn't written anything in years?" She made fiction sound as if she were saying pornography. "Bill likes to have more conflict, more drama. If you don't have that, the show loses steam and peters out after the first ten minutes."

"There *is* drama here. Look at the reversal. Bill is on an upward trajectory. Frye's down. He's vulnerable. At the very least Bill can finally have the chance to cut him to ribbons as he's always dreamed." After Mary didn't speak for a moment, Carl looked at his phone to ensure they still had a connection. "At least part of the show?"

"You might have hit on something. At least I'll run it by him."

They hung up. This could be a monstrous publicity success for Frye.

"Monstrous," Carl said aloud.

From across the bar Sparky said, "On pasta?" He set down a bottle of yellow mustard next to Carl's plate of penne alfredo, laughing. "Customer's always right, my ass."

143

Susan had used the word monstrous to describe Carl's thinly veiled story about the UR. She hadn't yet been successful in making him feel guilty about writing the story. But he did think a lot about whether or not he should feel guilty. Had Bland connected the dots from his story to the UR? Would the UR be a natural part of the dairy takeovers Ex-Elizabeth had told him about? Carl recognized that such speculation served no purpose. He needed to know for sure whether or not Bland had designs on Ocean's dairy. He needed to put the whole damn thing to rest so it would stop nagging at him.

"Ackle ink, tee see here."

It took Carl a moment to parse out the phrase. He had reached ACL, Incorporated: Austen, Cotter, and Laird, Ex-Elizabeth's company. Terry Cotter had answered, T.C., his self-imposed nickname. It would never occur to Terry that people might not understand his cryptic phone greeting. Terry was a great IT manager. The guy possessed a preternatural ability to troubleshoot database problems and regularly billed forty-five hours a week. His phone greeting brought to mind the main reason Carl despised Terry. He lacked the ability to comport himself in a business setting. He intimidated by using obscure acronyms, berated clients he deemed stupid, and made ridiculous demands of his bosses.

"Terry, it's Carl Krauthammer. How was your Thanksgiving?"

"Oh," he said, "hello. Fine. I had turkey."

"Terrific. Listen, I'm doing a little due diligence on your company there, to determine whether or not I want to accept the generous offer you guys made to me." Carl could hear Terry's fingers typing away on the keyboard. "I got the financials, and the other stuff, but I want to know how sophisticated the firm's backend systems are. What's Elizabeth using for contact management and sales lead tracking? Did you put something together or did she go off the shelf?"

His typing stopped. "I created a solution, of course. She wanted to spend like a thousand dollars on something but I spent a week and banged out a superior product in Access with an ASP front end. Kicks the ass of any shrink-wrapped CRM system on the market."

"I have no doubt," Carl said. It was as Carl had expected. Terry spent a week of what should have been billable time, probably five or six thousand dollars worth, to save three thousand dollars. This was so easy. Play to Terry Cotter's ego and he'll tell everything.

Terry got rolling. "Before you say it, I know what you're thinking. 'Access blows,' and it does. I would have migrated it over to Oracle but we didn't have a seat license yet. It works. I had a friend who used to work at Microsoft tell me he'd never seen anyone get that kind of performance out of Access."

"I bet it's amazing. Are you using it for clients in addition to your own stuff? What if I wanted a dump of all the acquisition targets for a client, can you do that?"

"Simp," he said, resuming his typing. "By SIC code, geographic region, Experian rating–you name it."

"I wonder if you could run one of those for me, on, say, West Egg Holdings, so I could get an idea of the kind of systems you have in place." Carl had settled on the guise of performing due diligence on Ex-Elizabeth's offer as a way to get information on the Bland's intentions for the UR. If West Egg was after them, Ex-Elizabeth would have it documented.

"Elizabeth says I'm not to give you any sensitive information until you sign our offer and come aboard."

Carl hadn't seriously considered Elizabeth's offer yet. Divorcing the offer from the person who made it allowed him to become more rational. His decision came down to two considerations. First, being a partner in ACL would mean a salary. Combined with his scholarship, he would be able to build his reserves back up without taking on another job that might distract him from his writing.

145

Secondly, access to Ex-Elizabeth's work would help Carl learn for sure whether or not the Blands planned to target the UR. Certainty here would allow Carl to stop worrying about the possibility that he had screwed Ocean. It had begun to affect his ability to write by sabotaging his concentration. Two pros and no cons.

Why wait? He didn't have to be active in the company. He could resign just as easily as he could accept it. There was no downside.

He would take the job.

Ten minutes after verbally accepting the offer from Ex-Elizabeth, Terry's report appeared as a spreadsheet in Carl's inbox. In a cell next to the names of each company she had entered a two- or three-letter code. She used the same abbreviations they had used at Ogilvy.

TO meant takeover. She'd put this next to most of the companies on the list.

TKO meant they would Technically Knock Out any competitor with this designation. It meant they had identified a vulnerability that would take the company out of contention. Carl had only seen two TKOs in his career at Ogilvy. They had taken out one manufacturer by seeding a class action lawsuit against the company. For another they sent an anonymous letter to the New York State Attorney General regarding some questionable stock option deals with the firm's executives. In both cases the acquiring company purchased the assets and client list at a quarter of the cost had the scandals not occurred. The only company with that designation on Terry's report was "UR." In the Notes field, next to UR it said 'KSDA. Q1.' Bland and Ex-Elizabeth meant to derail the Udderground Railroad by calling in the Kansas Department of Agriculture sometime after the New Year.

146

Sitting alone at the Lethargic Clown, Carl decided he needed an outlet to deal with the guilt he felt for his role in the future demise of Ocean's dairy. He thought back to his conversation with Frye the first time he went out to the Konza prairie. Frye said that writing had always helped him make sense of the world, and his place in it. Carl decided he could use a little of that therapy himself. He would outline a story about Frye's book. Even though he had yet to read a page of it, he knew it was about Sparky, a real person. Throughout the process he would draw a comparison to his own situation with Ocean. Susan played the part of the offended person in both situations.

With Keith out of town to spend Christmas with his mother in Colorado, and Frye wrapped up with revisions to his book, Carl had few things to distract him. He removed everything from the magnetic whiteboard by his desk: a Gumby's Pizza coupon, the Progress Report, and a copy of his dairy story. The markers in the tray had lost their rainbow organization, but Carl ignored this, anxious to gain insight from the experience.

To form the skeletal shape of the story, Carl identified the three basic points of view it would include: that of Sparky (the subject of the betrayal), that of Frye (the writer who betrays while trying to create good fiction), and Susan (an unrealistically pious observer).

He began by writing out two paragraphs summarizing the three positions. This he would take from real life. For Frye's position, he pulled together some things Frye had said, and some things he had said himself. Mainly, the point was that Frye had nothing to do with Sparky's situation. The writer is not responsible for the real-life situations he writes about.

Capturing Sparky's character proved difficult. Sparky was more of an innocent victim than Ocean, simply because Ocean had made the conscious decision to embark on an illegal business. Carl wondered what exactly had compelled Frye to write about Sparky. He really took no action in the events that surrounded the train accident. Certainly, Frye would have addressed this early on.

While outlining the arguments Susan had used when they had their fight, Carl came across an interesting idea for a scene. Susan claimed that Carl did Ocean a disservice by not telling him in advance that the story might harm him, so he could prepare somehow. Would Frye come tell Sparky about the book he was writing? Again, Sparky as the protagonist in the story posed problems. This conflict made the author character appear monstrous because Sparky had taken no part in causing his own problems.

Carl leaned back in his seat. The case was not the same with Ocean, who had contributed to his own demise. Ultimately, he bore the responsibility for starting an illegal business. That should have taken some pressure off Carl, yet the guilt he felt didn't abate.

Carl knew West Egg and ACL were going to tell the KSDA about the UR. Did Ocean deserve to know that the investigators were coming? Perhaps he could prepare for it, though Carl was not sure what he might be able to do. Either way, it was the only way to get Ocean's problems off his mind.

Chapter 10
Christmas with the Holsteins

The next day, Carl passed the empty security booth at the UR gate. It was Christmas Eve, so Denny was off. He rolled down his window and punched in his old passcode on the keypad at the gate. Snowflakes melted on his eyelashes. The keypad buzzed and the gate slowly swung open. the system. The wipers swept we Apparently, Ocean had never removed Carl's credentials from t slop across the windshield onto the ground beside the car.

He parked and followed two sets of tracks in the snow from Ocean's truck toward the main barn. Almost four inches of snow had fallen, smoothing out the bumps and clumps of the grass.

The milking facility was a long building with a vaulted ceiling, brightly lit by caged bulbs, which swung languidly over two rows of stalls on either side of a wide central passageway. The clean layer of sawdust that obscured the floor made it smell like a lumberyard. Carl stood at one end of the room, opposite an enormous wooden door that hung on a sliding track.

He pushed up his sleeve to see it was almost 4:30 in the afternoon.

The door shrieked as the iron wheels picked up momentum on the track. The stark silhouette of a man pushed the door the rest of the way open. It looked like Ocean. The cows lumbered in. Stirred sawdust shimmered in the light as they made their way to their stalls. The lead cow aimed her surly snow-covered muzzle toward Carl and snorted. She swung her head toward the stall closest to Carl as if to double check the name handwritten on the wall over the bin inside it. Apparently satisfied that it said, "Mrs. O'Leary," she walked on in.

Each cow, save one, ambled into her own stall, like a lackey to his cube. Ocean shoved the troublemaker into the proper slot. He performed the correction like a good business owner, gentle but firm. A soft grunting rose as each cow

149

began to eat the grass in her bin. Ocean headed toward Carl, leaving the door open. He stopped briefly when he spotted him, showing no surprise.

Ocean tenderly swatted the cow asses up one side of the passageway, then down the other, finishing with Mrs. O'Leary, who responded with an extended rear hoof as a warning.

"*Joyeux Noel* to you too, Madame O'Leary," Ocean said.

Carl moved up and rested his arms on the half wall that comprised Mrs. O'Leary's stall, peeking over to watch as Ocean slathered on disinfectant. She didn't notice, or care, as long as she had grain to eat. He connected the hose suction cups. So that's a teat cup, Carl thought.

Ocean moved five cows down and hooked up another set of hoses, repeating the process for two cows on the other side of the center passageway. After re-checking the four cows being milked, he took off his hat. He wiped his forehead off on his sleeve. It steamed in the cold air.

"What brings you here?" he said.

"Bad news," Carl replied.

A small green four-wheeler came around the corner and through the large door. When the driver removed her helmet, Carl saw it was Susan. She frowned when she saw him. She began unloading the hay bales on the trailer attached to the four-wheeler.

"Carl says he's come with bad news," Ocean said, helping unload the bales.

She stopped and pulled a strand of hay from her hair. "I'm not surprised he has bad news, just that he's here to deliver it personally. Normally, he lets me discover this kind of thing for myself."

Carl coughed. "I'm not here to have this argument again."

"We have a lot of work to do here, Carl," Ocean said.

"Let me help," Carl said. He walked over and grabbed the last bale. A sharp end of the bailing wire poked his glove and immediately drew blood. He dropped the bale instantly back on the trailer.

"I'll get that," Ocean said. "Just tell us the news."

"I've learned the Kansas Department of Agriculture is going to launch an investigation into your dairy. They're going to shut you down after the first of the year."

Ocean looked to Susan, who snorted and shook her head. "How? What happened?"

Susan said, "You know what it was. It was his story."

"Bland's company is behind it," Carl continued. They're eliminating competition with their own dairies, legal or not. It probably was my story."

"I knew it," Susan said. "I knew no good could come…"

"All right, Mom," Ocean said. He sat down on one of the bales and removed his gloves.

"I wanted to let you know. In case, maybe there was some way to prepare," Carl said.

"What kind of preparations can I make in a week? Shut down?" He looked to Carl, as if expecting an answer. "You didn't come just to tell me this, right? You've come back to tell me how we're going to fight it. You've come to repair your collateral damage."

"I don't think there is a fix," Carl said. "You could write a letter to Bland or the KSDA, or possibly a blog?"

"A writer is not going to be able to fix this," Ocean said. "I need a business solution. If you can't help, then I guess we're on our own."

Carl started to say that he was sorry all of this happened. When he opened his mouth, Susan shook her head and put her arm around Ocean. "Don't worry about the mess you've made, Carl. We'll figure out how to clean it up."

On his way back to his car, he walked in footprints that had mostly filled in with fresh snow.

The Christmas holiday involved his parents and two cousins from Pennsylvania who'd flown into Kansas City on their way to spend a week in Cole Camp, Missouri. After a series of large meals, a present exchange with his folks (they

151

gave him a sweater), not much was left except for a few bowl games, which he watched with an open book on his lap.

For short intervals, his thoughts would flit from one bit of unfinished business to another: the apartment, Susan, the dairy, his inability to write. Most of the time he settled on Ocean and Susan. His attempt to help had done nothing but alienate them further and actually intensify his guilt. If he were to retrace his steps back to when he first considered writing the story, in the very beginning, were there things he should have done differently?

If Bland and Ex-Elizabeth made a strong enough stink, the state might decide to make an example of Ocean and put him in prison. After all, his was a big business, not just a family farmer drinking the milk from his own cow...

Of course, Carl thought. There *was* a business solution to Ocean's problem. He had one week. He just hoped that was enough time.

On the morning of New Year's Eve, Carl stood in the UR milking barn. It had filled with people affiliated with the UR: Customers, employees, and suppliers. Almost all the 350 locals they had invited milled around the stalls and shook the sawdust from their shoes, a remarkable turnout considering the short notice. Ocean had intrigued them with a cryptic invitation, a flyer rubber-banded around his milk bottles for three straight deliveries:

Keep the government off the family farmer's back. Don't miss your chance to claim your share of the UR.

Ocean did not look nervous on the makeshift stage of stacked hay bales. His lips moved slightly as he rehearsed his speech one last time.

Carl and Ocean had spent the days since Christmas with attorneys and bankers, formalizing Carl's idea for reinventing ownership of the UR.

152

As Ocean moved to the microphone the crowd pushed slightly forward. They quieted down as he inhaled to speak. "Today is a momentous day," Ocean said. "No longer do you have to drink your milk in the darkness. No longer do you have to consume your raw cheese in delicious seclusion. And you may cast off the yoke of fear you wear as you eat your morning yogurt."

Carl winced at this last line, one he suggested that Ocean leave out or at least work on a little more. But the attention and energy had emboldened him, and Carl had to admit, the audience seemed to like it, no matter how ludicrous it sounded.

"That's right, *mes amis*," Ocean said. "Today this railroad goes aboveground." There was a slight audible gasp from the crowd. Ocean had inherited a talent for cranking up the drama.

"I want to introduce my good friend and ally. Come up here, Carl." He motioned for Carl to join him onstage. Carl stepped up, careful not to let his foot slip in the gaps between the pieces of plywood. Once he got his balance he looked out over the audience. He recognized many faces. He saw Sparky, Lady McKinley, and finally, Susan. When they locked eyes, she gave him an encouraging nod.

"Carl Krauthammer has come up with a plan that will thwart the jackbooted thugs of the KSDA. He will describe how we can beat their swords with Cow Shares." It was another line Carl had suggested leaving out, but the crowd loved it.

Carl stuck to the script he had written. He described how the reinvented company would work, how each customer would own shares in the dairy's cows. He showed them that their ownership in Cow Shares, L.L.C. made it legal for them and their families to drink the milk produced by their own cows. All they needed to do was sign a short legal agreement, fill out some paperwork, and get their shares. Ocean had started the process of getting licenses and permits. They hoped to close the offering before midnight so that they could start up under the new ownership before the KSDA had a chance to take any action.

He hadn't counted on the effect his words would have on the crowd, or how their applause might affect him. For half an hour people surrounded him and congratulated him on his plan. Almost everyone had signed the documents before leaving. They expected a fifty percent participation rate, they already had ninety percent of the locals on board.

He saw Susan, lingering off to the side after many had left. She wore a puffy white parka with the hood up, framing her face in synthetic fur. She put her arm around his waist and hugged him close. "What are you doing New Year's?" she whispered in his ear.

The limp wreaths hanging from the light posts showed the holidays were about done for. As Carl drove home from the dairy, he couldn't help feeling a little cocky. The UR Cow Shares plan had come together beautifully. He had saved Ocean's dairy and possibly won back Susan in the process. She had asked him to meet her at the White House Supper Club that evening. Carl didn't know what to expect. Did she have more in store than her stated objective of thanking him? He could still feel her whisper in his ear.

His cell phone rang.

"Carl, it's me," Keith said.

"Uh oh," Carl said. "Are you already back from Colorado? Did Rosalie say something to piss off your parents?"

"No, quite the contrary. My mother loves her. Says she reminds her of Rita Moreno," Keith said. "Rosalie took that better than you might think."

"Great news. Is that why you called?"

"No, I just wanted to know whether or not you and Hirschman might have miraculously gotten back together."

An odd question, Carl thought. "Jury's out on that. We're going to dinner tonight though."

"I just got some disturbing information about her."

"Disturbing? How?"

"Calm down. She's not a transsexual."

"Is this a joke? I better hang up. It's hard for me to talk on the phone and read my email while I'm driving."

"I'm trying to prepare you for the real information, loosen you up with a little humor. Rosalie says I have a way of dropping bombs on people without properly preparing them," which was the first time Carl remembered Keith ever taking advice from a girlfriend. "Susan lifted some parts of her book from someone else's work," he said.

"What?"

"I got an email from my buddy in Emporia, who was to help us edit the book. He's kind of a stickler regarding academic ethics. Hell, he calls it plagiarism if you don't footnote your text messages. He's got proof. I forwarded the email to you. Says it was a former student of his that he had worked closely with, like twenty years ago."

"I have a hard time believing it," Carl said. "Who is this guy, Rain Man?"

"I know. Maybe it's just a misunderstanding. We can talk about it when I get home in a couple of days. Better go. Rita Moreno has convinced my parents to try sushi for lunch today."

Once he arrived home he read the email. It sounded accurate, but Carl couldn't fit the information in his head. Susan a plagiarist? Why would she risk her livelihood? What did it mean? He turned his car toward campus. Frye was probably in his office. He was going to flip his shit over this.

Carl told Frye everything he knew, how Keith's friend happened to remember her (he had saved a few of her papers from helping her apply to larger universities) and how one section of Susan's introduction contained three sentences pulled verbatim from one of those papers. Frye acted uninterested until Carl described the student as a "sort of radical breastfeeding advocate at Emporia State at the time."

155

Frye immediately knew who it was. "Suzanne Sherman." Then he laughed, a staccato "Huh!" before a look of concern crossed his face. "Has anyone mentioned this to Susan?"

"I don't believe so. Why?"

"I don't want it getting to her yet. Tell Keith and his friend to keep it quiet for now."

"Why?"

Frye sat on the edge of the big desk. He took a breath before launching into the story. "In the early 1980s, Suzanne Sherman is Emporia University's premiere advocate for breast feeding at age eighteen. She's a great speaker: inspirational, motivational, a bit of a radical. She leads a few rallies against hospitals that give formula samples to new mothers. Stuff like that. When the news comes out that West Egg Holdings is doing some subcontracting for Nestle out of Wichita, it sends Sherman over the edge. Now Nestle is making babies sick by sending free baby formula to poorer countries. Turns out not everyone has access to clean water in the third world. It's one of the reasons they're not considered the first world. Babies start getting dysentery. Sherman and a few fellow wingnuts form a protest group, a sort of unsanctioned militant wing of La Leche League called *Pezon Revolucionario,* or as you've heard of them, the Revolutionary Nipple."

"The ones who threatened West Egg before Sparky's train derailed?"

"Yep. Sparky's train was carrying baby formula to San Diego, eventually bound for South America."

"So that's how you know about her. She figures into your book."

"This Suzanne character–she's called Emily in my book–tampers with the track and causes Sparky's train to derail."

"Really?"

"The police can't find any leads on *Pezon Revolucionario,* but Bland's insurance company is very interested. They get a court order for her to appear for questioning. She vanishes. No one's seen her since right after Sparky's accident. Of course, Bland's insurance company is the only one looking, since the investigators listed 'operator impairment' as the official cause of the derailing. But what if she did it? What if she's making those anonymous guilt payments to Sparky every year? The pathos, my God, the pathos."

"Sounds like a wonderful book you have there. I look forward to picking up a copy at Costco when it comes out, but why don't you want Susan to know she's been caught plagiarizing?"

Frye tapped his pencil on a coffee cup for a minute. "Let's just assume that this Suzanne person did derail the train," he said. "She's in hiding. Has a new life now, worried that charges may someday be filed. Susan is in contact with her and they decide to surreptitiously work together on this book."

"There sure is a lot of assuming going on in this conversation."

"But it's all possible, right? Did you ever see Susan with a strange woman?"

"No."

"Their contact must be in secret," he said.

"By that logic we should assume she's in league with Al Qaeda based on the evidence that I never saw her talking to Osama Bin Laden."

"To defend herself against the charge of plagiarism, Susan would have to blow Suzanne's cover, and then people might wonder where Suzanne's been. Then maybe the police do want to question her after all."

"So?"

"So? Then the story that I made up turns out to be true and gets told in the news. Suddenly I've been scooped by Nancy Grace and Katie Couric. I don't want the thunder of my story pilfered by Katie Couric, Carl. That would just be too much for me to bear. No, you have to keep this quiet."

Carl did not like the idea of withholding this information from Susan. For one thing, all of Frye's surmising could be completely fallacious, and Susan could have used the research without attribution, mistakenly or not, possibly assuming no one would remember this Suzanne person. If the book came out and people connected the dots to Susan, exposing her as a plagiarist, she and Keith could lose their jobs. At the very least their reputation could be tainted by that kind of charge, even if Susan did find a way to explain it. But certainly, Frye wouldn't let things go that far. Carl would eventually tell her, so it wasn't to be a secret for long.

Frye looked out the window. "It's like a pattern with Susan and Ocean. 'Fuck up. Cover up. Repeat with increased drama."

"I'm sorry," Lady McKinley said. "We have no booths available, just two-tops..." She stopped when she spotted Carl. "You two are together?"

"Yes," Susan said, putting her arm through his. "We're together." Her proximity to him felt warm.

"Based on this morning's presentation, Mr. Krauthammer, you can have a booth here anytime. That dairy means a lot to us. Thanks for being its savior."

"My labors hardly rise to the biblical terminology, but if it gets me a booth, I'll take it."

Once they were seated, Susan said, "Everyone is excited about what you did. I can't contain all the things I feel: happy, proud, relieved." Her face backed up the statement. Her skin looked softer across the forehead. Her eyes looked back at him with warmth. "The whole thing shows me your strength to resist the evil that is Julian Frye."

"Hallelujah and all that shit, but I don't think I like the implication," Carl said. "The guy has some rough edges, but evil?"

She closed her menu. "Let me rephrase. I'm glad your path has diverged from Frye's. You've seen the light." Apparently sensing no understanding in Carl's expression, she continued. "You have not become Frye redux."

Her demeanor showed that she meant the words as a compliment, yet to Carl they sounded like a rebuke. "Don't be too hasty," he said. "I'm not completely formed yet." He

158

thought of the plagiarism charge. "Just because I helped Ocean doesn't mean that the caring businessman has won out over the cold and calculating writer."

"No, things aren't so binary. I don't buy that every action proves a person has made a definitive character choice." She rolled the stem of her empty wine glass between her thumb and forefinger. "Wedging people into one box or another usually proves a futile exercise. Ultimately, we're an amalgam, a Big Fat Ball of everything we've ever done."

"Yet you'll refer to Frye as evil."

"I can be hyperbolic. I teach Romantic literature, for Christ's sake. He's a Big Fat Ball of everything he's ever done, also. It just happens to all be evil."

Carl thought of the buried documents. "Didn't he say he would change for you?"

"I don't believe in that sort of thing, in people rein-venting themselves. From what I've seen it's like Indiana Jones, right? Running from that Big Ball of the past, hoping to arrive someplace else, as someone else, before one gets flattened."

Carl gripped his menu. "But I have reinvented myself."

"I didn't realize we were talking about you," she said. "I should have said 'one.' When I met you, I didn't exactly see you as a complex person, I just saw stability. You just seemed like the opposite of the other men I had known. Accurate or not, I imbued you with the characteristics that those men all lacked. Then I started to see Julian working on you. I saw his influence when you wrote the story about Ocean. Just as I had seen you as perfect, then I deemed you as hopelessly imperfect. I wrote you off as unsalvageable, just as I had done with Julian." She reached across the table and grabbed his shirtsleeve. "I wanted to apologize. It was unfair to hold you to a code more stringent that the one I hope people use to judge me."

"I would hope the people around me aren't judging me at all," Carl said.

"I don't know. In some respects, I think there's not *enough* judging going on. I mean overall in a holistic way,

159

as a total package, all actions taken together: Are you a good person, doing the best you can, muddling through to find your way without harming anyone else? That's the criteria, not whether you did something wrong, made one mistake and that defines you as bad forever."

Again, he became confused as to whom "you" referred. She wouldn't look right at him, and he wondered if she weren't talking about Suzanne Sherman. It certainly fit Sherman's situation and whatever actions she took that might have derailed the train. Was Susan making the case that Suzanne should not be judged by her one mistake, the actions she took that derailed the train? "So where does motive fit in here?" he asked. "What about one's intentions?"

"I didn't really look at your motive too closely, Carl." Apparently, she was back to talking about him. "It's too easy to get distracted from what your Big Ball tells me." At that moment, their server approached, and upon hearing Susan's last line, turned to help another table nearby.

They both laughed. Carl asked, "So what does my Big Ball tell you about me?"

"Your Big Ball tells me you helped Ocean because you felt guilty."

"Does that lessen the impact of the action, doing the right thing because it makes me, I mean *one*, feel better?"

"I look back to the reasons you felt guilty. Your Big Ball says you're a cold, caring, calculating, pragmatic, writer businessman."

"My Big Ball sounds like the work of a bad beat poet."

Around midnight Carl stood in Susan's bedroom, looking out the front window. He could hear the coughs and shouts of people beginning to gather across the street. Susan had invited him up to watch the small fireworks display put on every New Year's Eve by a small group of guys in Pioneer Park. He continued to ruminate on her theory as more people arrived, bundled against the cold in parkas, mufflers, and ski masks. Overall it made sense to Carl. He saw how it dovetailed with her policy of "full disclosure," letting someone know, for instance, that you were married and had a kid, so that you could know enough to judge that person's character and evaluate your own attraction to that person. A few firecrackers acted as a preamble to the display.

Susan went in the bathroom, and based on the way the evening had gone, he figured she would come out wearing nothing but her shirt. He felt a little disingenuous being there, having not come clean about the plagiarism. If they were to have sex, would he have to fully embrace the policy of full disclosure before they did it?

The bathroom door opened and closed behind him. He heard her sit down on the bed. Outside the full force of the display began. Each burst seemed to burn a little brighter than the previous. He turned around and a red burst illuminated Susan. She sat there naked except for a T-shirt.

"I have to tell you something," he said. "I know all about Suzanne."

He couldn't tell if the noise he heard was a "shit" from her, or the *shht* of a bottle rocket. He crossed the room and sat next to her.

"It was Frye, wasn't it?" she said.

"He filled in some details..."

"I was going to tell you, Carl. Tonight I was going to do this." She crossed her arms and grabbed the T-shirt at the bottom and took it off over her head. "I hope you can forgive me."

He did not understand what she said to him. In the dim light he saw the dark splotch on her left breast. It was the tattoo.

When a series of glittering white bursts erupted outside, Susan closed her eyes, as if afraid to see what effect her complete exposure might have on him. "I was going to tell you everything. I'm not a bad person."

Carl looked closer. The tattoo looked very much like the La Leche League logo he'd seen on the back of her car. It had the same silhouetted woman holding a baby-shaped bundle to her breast. But the woman on this tattoo curled her left hand into a fist extending up in the air. Before the room went dark again, he read the caption below: *Pezon Revolucionario.*

Chapter 11
The Revolutionary Nipple

Carl had trouble focusing on one thing. It jumped between many possibilities. Was she part of Sherman's gang? Did she add the tattoo recently out of solidarity? He turned on his phone and examined the tattoo closely in the light. Its colors had all faded to old-tattoo green. His mind settled down and he knew.

She leaned over and turned on the bedside table lamp.

"I always thought an alias should vary from the real name," he said.

"I told you my husband wasn't creative. He named our son Billy Ocean for God's sake. He was better at making close copies than coming up with anything original." So her ex-husband had used his forging skills to get her the new identity. She re-started her life, this time as an academic, complete with a forged B.A. With that she went on to earn a real M.A. and Ph.D. The plagiarism made sense now–you can't get in trouble for borrowing from your own work.

He watched her put her shirt back on. She scooted back against the headboard and pulled the covers up to her waist. "Were you really going to tell me tonight, if I hadn't brought it up?" he asked.

"I wanted to. I meant to a bunch of times."

"But?"

"But I probably never would have. Out of respect for our relationship."

"*Respect*? What kind of relationship would that be?" he asked. "Although when you've skewed your whole life into a lie, maybe that changes your concept of what's moral or respectable."

"I told you most of the truth."

"Except for a few little details like how you were responsible for Sparky's train."

"Why did I need to tell you that? Sounds like Jules handled that."

163

Carl laughed. "That's original. Why be honest when someone else will spill it for you?" Why had he felt any guilt over this woman? How had her good points ever stood up against all the drama and secrets? It was like marrying someone with a split personality because you feared commitment.

"I didn't even intend to derail that train, just delay it."

"I don't even care at this point." Carl stood and headed for the door.

Susan kept talking, the covers falling away from her. "The railroad had plans to rebuild that section of track so they had spaced out a load of ties every two miles or so. My idea was to move each pile onto the tracks. My theory went like this: Either as the train got back up to speed after clearing one pile, they'd have to stop again, or crews would have to go clear all of the piles at once. Either way they'd be slowed down and annoyed.

"We had the schedules that showed only trains from Bland's factory used that three miles of track before you got to the main line. No train was slated to go until the next morning, March 16th. The four of us had two piles up, working on the third. We placed them on straight stretches of track, well past any curves, so that the engineer would have plenty of time to see them and to slow down."

She was practically crying.

"They weren't sticking to the schedule," she said. "Why would they? We'd made threatening calls. The factory sent out shipments at odd hours to circumvent any delaying protests like the one we were setting up. It was almost midnight, six hours before the scheduled train departure, when Sparky came down the stretch. At night in the dark, he couldn't possibly see our piles far enough in advance to stop. I never told Frye that."

"I figured that much," Carl said. "He's completely clueless about all of this." Carl sat back down on the bed. He wouldn't rush to Frye with any of this information. When he extricated himself from Susan, he wouldn't obsess like Frye, constantly keeping tabs on her. "I won't tell him about your 'secret identity.'"

Susan looked confused. The wrinkle in the bridge of her nose looked deeper in the light from the lamp. She sat up slightly taller. "But of course, he knows I'm Suzanne. You said he told you all about it."

Carl laughed again at the absurdity of the whole situation. Frye's book was about to go to press and he completely got the story wrong. "He told me all about Suzanne. He hasn't yet figured out that it's you."

"He knows that because I told him," she said. "That's why I asked him to destroy notes. He started to write a book with a character based on me. It was creepy stuff. He was always observing me and writing down everything I did." She moved a few strands of hair from her face and tucked it behind her ear.

"But the notebooks he buried that broke you two up, they were about Sparky."

"No, he was writing about me, about how I derailed the train, my life in hiding. And he didn't bury them. He burned them," she said. "That son of a bitch better have burned them."

"But..." he said.

"Carl? Do you feel all right?"

He did not feel all right. "I think I've done a bad thing. I think I've helped Frye write his book about you."

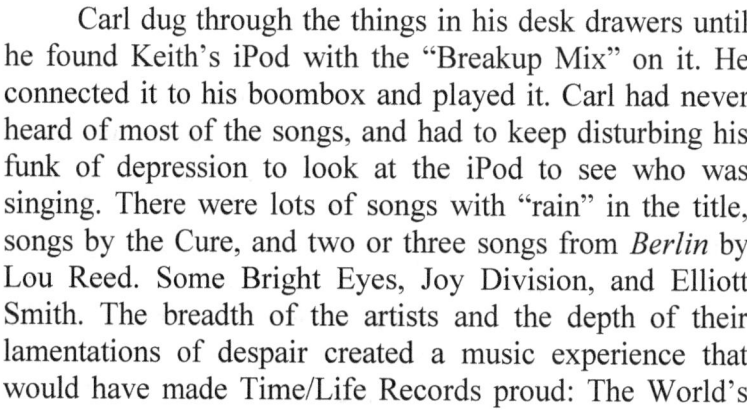

Carl dug through the things in his desk drawers until he found Keith's iPod with the "Breakup Mix" on it. He connected it to his boombox and played it. Carl had never heard of most of the songs, and had to keep disturbing his funk of depression to look at the iPod to see who was singing. There were lots of songs with "rain" in the title, songs by the Cure, and two or three songs from *Berlin* by Lou Reed. Some Bright Eyes, Joy Division, and Elliott Smith. The breadth of the artists and the depth of their lamentations of despair created a music experience that would have made Time/Life Records proud: The World's

165

Most Depressing Music. The playlist provided the perfect capper to his self-imposed three hours of guilt-indulgence.

As he listened to the maudlin musings of the Smiths on "Please Please Please Let Me Get What I Want," he reflected on his sham of a new life, how Frye had duped him, and as a result, how he had betrayed Susan.

He checked his watch: twenty more minutes of self-flagellation. He concluded that ego was the core cause of it all. He had assumed Frye wanted him around because he liked him, but it was so he could provide access to Susan. He acknowledged his own prurient interest in telling Frye private things about Susan. It amounted to gossip. Even in his state of *mea culpa* he preferred to think of it as "idle talk."

Carl had enabled Frye to keep writing Susan's story after they broke up, provided the intimate details of how Susan reacted to her estranged husband's death, how she handled her relationship with her adult son, what her continued desires were for her life in Manhattan - all details Frye could no longer ascertain after their breakup. Frye had used him, just as Bland had used him in the Sellars deal. Carl Krauthammer hadn't progressed at all in his new life. He'd only repeated the same mistakes in a new venue.

He dozed off to the sound of Lou Reed's nasally singing/talking: *How do you think it feels/When all you can say is, "If only?"*

"You bought this set of CDs because you want or need something special out of life. But in today's hectic world, no one's going to hand you a silver platter. Arnie Becker here, attorney with McKenzie, Brackman, Chaney and Kuzak. Whatever you're after, a favorable divorce settlement, maybe that raise you feel you deserve, heck, even that dual-deck VCR you've had your eye on at K-Mart, all can be yours. The first step? Make sure you negotiate with the right person."

Carl stirred, vaguely aware the playlist had ended and prompted the CD changer to start playing whatever disc was

166

in the tray. It took him a moment to figure out what he heard. It must be disc one in the series *Negotiate Your Way to Financial Freedom the McKenzie Brackman Way* (featuring the cast of *L.A. Law*). Corbin Bernsen's voice hovered over him.

"How do you know if the person across the table from you is the right one? First, ensure they have control over what you want. Make sure that the real decision-maker doesn't lurk in the shadows, uninvolved in your direct discussions."

The disc had lain dormant in his boom box for years, ever since Ex-Elizabeth had given it to him. He took it as a sign pointing him to his next move. He needed to negotiate with Jules Frye to get things fixed. When it finished, he put in Disc 2: *Give the People What They Want*.

"One of the biggest mistakes people make when attempting to achieve their goals in life is failing to consider what the other party wants." Carl listened to the words, delivered in character by Jimmy Smits. "If you go around just asking people to give you what you want, chances are, they'll resist. For instance, if you went up to a friend and asked them for the latest Bangles compact disc, your friend probably wouldn't just give it to you. Now if you did your homework and found out that she wanted the *Dirty Dancing* soundtrack, now you have something to negotiate with. Better yet, digging a little deeper, you might find out she prefers listening to the music from *Dirty Dancing* in her Walkman. So you tape your copy of *Dirty Dancing* and trade it for the CD you want. Suddenly you're 'walking like an Egyptian,' and it only cost you the price of a blank cassette."

The advice he received didn't contain much information he didn't already know, but he decided he should hear all the distilled wisdom of McKenzie Brackman. He listened to Disc Three: *Leland McKenzie on Achieving Balance* in the car while on the road to Frye's house. A couple inches of snow had fallen, making it look like a smooth plane from road to prairie on either side.

The voice of Leland McKenzie was both comforting and firm. "By the time responsibility for a negotiation comes to the desk of a Senior Managing Partner, it means all the other methods have failed," he said. "Not that the other attorneys in our practice hadn't tried. Arnie had done a good job of identifying his client's needs. Victor had compiled a list of the opposition's requirements. Stuart Markowitz had run through the financial implications, and even Benny knew it wasn't yet time to resort to professional arbitration.

"Yet even still, neither side had made any movement toward an acceptable agreement. In short, things stood still. The approach I recommend instead is balance," Leland said. "You can only do these things if you seek an equilibrium between all parties. You needn't head for a collision–instead you can all head the same direction, toward everyone getting what they want the most."

He turned off the stereo when Leland finished. Then he turned off the ignition. These words made sense to Carl. At Ogilvy & Standpipe, even here in Manhattan, he had approached every situation in terms of winners and losers. He always made sure he was on the winning side, when he should have considered that they all could win. The Sellars didn't have to be losers in the Heartland deal. Ocean didn't have to lie down and die for Bland to come out on top. Ex-Elizabeth didn't have to win at Carl's expense. He didn't have to forsake his old life for one in Manhattan.

He should have worn boots. The snow caked on the bottom of his Nikes.

When Frye opened the door, he called to his dogs. "C'mon you two. You always want to sic 'em." Merkin wagged her tail uncertainly. Taint didn't even bother to get off the couch, resettling his muzzle in his paws with a disappointed sigh. "They terrorize Bland now. Guess they can only hate one person at a time."

Once they sat down, Carl said, "What's happening with your book?"

"Off to the publisher yesterday. The final edits are complete. My book comes out on March first!"

168

Under the coffee table, clumps of snow-turned-slush slipped off Carl's shoe onto the rug. "Why did you do it, Jules? Why'd you write it in the first place?"

Frye cocked his head. "We're back on that, are we? My inspiration? My motivation? I shouldn't have to tell you, Grasshopper."

Carl spoke by rote. "Because it works as a story. It's compelling. A story like that deserves to be told." He continued, "But that theory only works in a vacuum, where your actions don't have real implications."

Frye put a cigarette in his mouth, never breaking his sad-eyed stare from Carl's face. "Our little boy's growing up. He's figured it all out for himself," he said. "The effect on Susan isn't my concern, as a novelist."

"Or as a person," Carl added. "You had the story. You observed it all yourself and wrote it down in your buried notebooks. Why bring me into all of it?"

"The notebooks held the premise of my story. A premise in equilibrium does not make a compelling story." He started looking for a lighter but gave up when his pockets didn't produce one. "It isn't interesting until the turd hits the water." He sat forward with his elbows on his knees. "It fascinated me to think how she would deal with those kinds of disturbances. Take your arrival, for instance. How would she deal with this new person, someone she could settle down with? How would she balance him and her son?" He tried to take a drag on the cigarette, looking surprised to find it unlit.

"So that was my role? I'll overlook being called a turd, but I was only a McGuffin for your novel?"

"You were much more than that. You provided a continuing source for details and unexpected twists for my main character. You get the largest entry in my acknowledgements. My God, I couldn't have done it without you!"

Carl shook his head. "Don't put it on me. Had I known the real situation, I'd never have participated."

"Bullshit. You thrived on doing it. You loved running to me every Monday morning with news of Susan," he said.

"And stop acting like you'd never do something beneficial for yourself if it might hurt someone else. You would. You have." He stood up, bending over to point across the coffee table. "That's why I picked you. You have all the requisite qualities. You'll turn on your best friend to make a deal happen. For evidence, I only have to mention those poor bastards who owned that dairy. You may have had reservations about hanging them out, but you still did it." He took the cigarette out of his mouth and waved it dismissively at Carl. "Don't give me that pathetic look. I thought with the right influence, you could become a great writer. And look what happened. You wrote your dairy story." Frye crossed to the bar and poured two shots of Woodford Reserve.

"See," he said, "this is nothing to be ashamed of." He closed one eye and toasted Carl. "You should view this, all of it, as a victory. Something to celebrate."

"This isn't about writing. Not every successful writer is a prick."

"I'm talking about successful businessmen. Isn't that what we are?"

"If you felt so confident in my capability for selfish action in the name of becoming great, then why not tell me the truth about Susan if you know with such certainty what kind of a person I am?"

"People don't work that way. It's too direct."

"The people I know act that way."

"Did Susan voluntarily trust you with the truth before you figured everything out? Did your Elizabeth tell you she had other desires before she went out on you?"

For a moment Carl's breath failed him. Only a squeak came out, like a stepped-on dog toy. "That's a bullshit low blow, even for you."

"It is nonetheless accurate." Frye drained Carl's shot without asking. "You talk too much. When you found out that my book was about this Suzanne person, I bet you ran right to Susan and told her. All part of your 'information as power' shtick."

"This is not about writing, and it's certainly not about me."

"Who then? You think it's about me?" he asked. "I get it. You thought, 'This one time maybe I can get him not to be Jules Frye. Maybe he'll listen to reason, see the error of his ways?' Pardon the clichés, but I'm trying to accurately capture your predictable thought processes here. Maybe you thought I'd voluntarily pull the book? Maybe re-bury it out there? Possible in theory, but that ground's frozen now."

"As much as you want this all to be about me, how quaintly naïve I am, trying to change the incorrigible Jules Frye, it is about you. I see it."

Frye spread his arms wide. "Then enlighten me, Carl Krauthammer, C.P.A. Tell me what I lack. Tell me all of my deficiencies."

"I don't have to. You have just one big fat deficiency, and you know all about it."

Frye's arms, suspended in mockery, fell to his sides.

Carl continued. "You didn't even know at first that you'd lost it. Like an empty paper bag that retains the shape of what it used to hold, you could practically touch the void. Pardon the poetic language, but I'm trying to capture your thought process."

"Don't apologize. I'm enjoying the performance."

Carl sat forward on the couch. "Here you had a great setup for a story, a premise, a tragic main character, but no idea how to disturb that setup to shape a real situation into a dramatic story. Those skills had abandoned you. Your imagination left you hanging."

Frye stood up and moved toward the front door. "Terrific. Penetrating. Insightful. Top-quality personality audit there, Krauthammer, complete with all the subtlety of solid black and bright white. This has been rewarding, but I have to get started on my next..."

"Keep shitting on the people around you," Carl said on his way out the door. "I'm sure eventually we'll all change to suit you."

As he made his way back to his car, he heard Frye shouting, "You'll never suit me, you fucking ingrate. Hack!"

The situation remained in stasis over the remainder of winter break. Carl decided against taking Frye's section of "Avoiding the Creation of Soporific Long Form Fiction."

Rosalie helped him drop the class and petition to get into Dr. Grey's "Anatomy of Prose Forms."

He took a total of nine hours, wanting to take advantage of the full scholarship, filling out his schedule with Dr. Fabresi's "Gallops 'N' Trollops: Horses and Fallen Women in England, 1850-1877," and a modern lit class with an adjunct professor.

The semester looked busy, with lots of reading. He could handle that. He quit the EGSA. No longer having a mentor also freed up his time. Carl had deleted Frye from his mobile phone and removed his email address from his laptop. He now thought Jules Frye was an asshole, which constituted a major market change, allowing him to reprioritize the goals on his Progress Report. He no longer defined his ultimate success as becoming Jules Frye's peer. This goal became "Make a living as a writer," and moved to number two. He moved the second goal up to number one: "Do the right thing for close relationships."

He returned the Progress Report to the magnetic board, and his gaze settled on the box in the middle of the room. It contained Carl's things from his drawer in the double desk. Frye had packed them up and had an undergrad deliver it a few days earlier. The box sat in the middle of his bedroom for weeks. He would walk around it, sometimes Dick-Van-Dyking it like it were an ottoman.

Susan continued to plan for the upcoming semester, even though she knew she wouldn't carry out that plan after Frye's book came out. Dread and an acknowledgement of its futility had killed Carl's desire to try and convert Frye.

They simply wouldn't ever agree when it came to Susan. Carl had accepted his own culpability–his indiscretion in revealing her personal details had caused her harm. Though Frye had described Carl's actions as ruthless in pursuit of his own success, did that label fit? Did he use information as power? Did he manipulate people that way?

Maybe, he thought.

All right, yes.

He had to acknowledge it. How had turning on Susan and Ocean been any different than what he'd done to the Sellars in the Heartland Dairy deal? He could blame Frye for the impetus, but not the results. Hadn't Frye ever learned that trampling over the people in one's life had consequences? He had, Carl thought. At least he said so on the Konza that afternoon. He said Manhattan would be different–that he wanted to live here. Had he changed his mind? That formed the fulcrum of their disagreement, each of them on opposite ends of a board, balanced in stillness as long as no one moved. If nothing had changed, if Carl didn't reorder his priorities, he knew that eventually Frye's side would rise as Carl headed down.

Chapter 12
The Ides of March

A snap of warmth hit Manhattan in the middle of February, turning the campus into a vat of mud. Those veering from the concrete paths and sidewalks risked having their boots sucked off. Carl stayed on the sidewalks, slicked with water running from high ground to low. He held two smoothies from the Ol' Smoothie Shop in his hands, extending his arms for balance. He was heading to Susan's. Frye's book was coming out the next day, and when he'd talked with her on the phone he determined she needed a pep talk.

From the outside, Susan's house looked like a greenhouse, the windows opaque with moisture. Inside, Carl smelled something musty. At first, he thought it might be the mud from his boots he'd removed on the entryway rug. Once he found Susan in the kitchen he figured out the smell's source: potatoes. Various containers overflowed with them throughout the kitchen. A white plastic scrub brush sat atop a wet pile of fifteen or so, unpeeled and glistening in a massive wooden bowl by the sink. Another pile, fresh out of boiling water, sent curls of steam up into the diffused light of the fogged windows. He couldn't help thinking she looked like she had acquired some kind of specialized Obsessive Compulsive Disorder involving root vegetables.

Using the end of a peeler, she poked out a potato eye and adroitly flicked it into a paper bag at her feet. As she peeled, most of the brown strips tumbled into the bag, a few falling onto the tops of her shoes. She had her hair back in a ponytail but a lone strand kept falling across her face.

"Does a Berry-licious Smoothie go with boiled potatoes?" he asked.

She smiled, but kept her attention on the potato. "*Everything* goes with potatoes. These are to be mashed." She wiped away the hair strand with the back of one hand. "My mother always wanted them for her birthday–it was her family gathering recipe. Serves thirty. I was never able to effectively reproduce the taste by dividing it into a smaller

174

portion. I know it's strange, but even though she's gone – has it been nineteen years - I still make them every February twenty-eighth."

Carl handed her a smoothie and took off his gloves.

"I wore a disguise to her funeral–a light blond wig, dark glasses, big black floppy hat. I know it probably wasn't necessary. I thought some investigator might show up looking for Suzanne Sherman."

She looked at Carl for the first time. Her eyes looked a little red on the rims. He imagined her wearing a wig and enormous black sunglasses, standing by a freshly dug grave like Karen Black in *Family Plot*. Behind her on the stove, the lid of an enormous pot rattled. Steam condensed and hissed down its side.

She grabbed an oversized split fork and waved it up in the air, saying, "Irrational and a little paranoid, I know," before stabbing a potato which she transferred from a bowl into the pot.

"I also feared my husband might have shown up. I sort of dreamed he was still tracking me down in those early years of my new life."

"Your paranoia wasn't too far off early on," he said. "The file I read said Bland's insurance company wrote a letter every year to check up on the case, to ensure it was kept open. That lasted about five years."

She replaced the lid on the pot. "Then I ended up here in Manhattan. I was certain no one sought me but I couldn't exactly drop my new identity. It was now completely tied to my job. Some new life." She let the fork clatter into the sink.

"I don't know," Carl said. "You aimed yourself in a more positive direction. You teach, you help support Sparky, and you volunteer with the Best Breasts."

"Breast is Best," she corrected, taking a few scraps of peel from the floor and dropping them in the sack. "It was a moment, my mom's funeral. A watershed. I'd seen what came of rebellion. It hurt people who I didn't want to hurt. And it had absolutely no impact on the formula trade to the third world. I decided never to run again, just to make damn sure it never got out and never came back to affect my son. I guess I was the only one fooled."

She glanced at the windows clouded over with condensation. "Ultimately, it might be the best thing for me if–I mean *when*–people make the connection between me and the character in Frye's book. That's true full disclosure. No more annual tithing for Sparky, lying, being paranoid. I've had a portion of my brain reserved for being afraid and ashamed for so long. It might be nice to put it to a different use. Sure, I'll be in prison, but I'll feel better."

"Will people care? I mean, there's a statute of limitations on the actual crime."

"No, you're right. The police won't care about the original accident. But what about Sparky, the university, Bland? They all have reason to hate me in varying degrees. Some might have grounds to sue."

"You already know they'll care at the university. You have no illusions they'll keep you on under these circumstances."

"Of course not," she said.

"But you've made Sparky whole by giving him the money for a new hand. Frye's a wild card. He might like the publicity, but he wouldn't want people knowing he's lost his gift for fiction."

"He's like a cockroach," she said. "The world blows up and he'll crawl out of the rubble and write nonfiction. What about Bland? You told me that his memory stretches back forever."

Carl wondered about Bland. He should be so focused on getting his publishing business rolling that he wouldn't care about any old fraud allegations. But Bland's blind spot was his vindictiveness. He would press the people at the KBI to do something–collect back taxes, find new fraud charges, or convert it to something with no statute of limitations. Something like attempted murder.

"Bland will come after me," she said.

"No jury would convict you. You look great on paper. If it were me on trial for all I've done? A corporate-type who

176

manipulates people and uses information as power? They'd already be warming up the electric chair."

She straightened up from bending over the sack, her hands on her waist. Her eyes looked less red, and the blue stood out her pupils. "Bah," she said, "manipulation and information brokering? Those things aren't inherently evil. You just have to do them for the right reasons, for the right people. Then you get a job in congress."

"I wonder if I even have the morals to know what's right."

"You wouldn't feel like shit if you didn't."

"I don't recall telling you I feel like shit."

"It's obvious, darling. You wear guilt on your face. But feeling that way wastes time and resources if you don't act to change things."

"What can I change at this point? Everything's been set in motion."

"I was talking about myself," she said, "the changes I made."

But Carl wondered how much that applied to him. He had resources upon which he could draw. He still had information that would be valuable to certain parties. And still others might be interested in ensuring that information didn't get out. He thought again about Frye and himself on the teeter-totter. He visualized the cheap playground trick where one person leaps off and the other hits the ground. The key was hopping off before the other guy got the same idea.

The night before Frye's book came out nationwide in Costco and several independent booksellers, they threw a signing party at Auntie Mae's. Carl had seen flyers for it at the Dusty Bookshelf in Aggieville. Carl and Susan chose to skip the party, spending the evening at home watching basketball.

During halftime, as Carl went to the kitchen for a beer, his phone rang. It was Mary Austen-Tawfee, his ex-sister-in-law.

"Where are you, Carl?" she asked, before he even finished saying hello. "I was sure I'd see you here at Julian's party."

"Huh?"

"We're all here. Don invited everyone on the mailing list and all of his Twitter followers."

Don? It took Carl a moment to figure out who she meant. "Hold on a sec." He went to the dining room and checked his email. All messages from The *Flanesser* had become casualties of Carl's falling out with Frye. Carl had created a rule that took any message with The *Flanesser's* name in any field and moved it directly into an email folder he hadn't opened in weeks. "I'm a little behind."

He opened the folder where he found forty unopened messages from Mary, The *Flanesser*, Chancellor Schroeder, and others. The rule had silently moved them all.

"When will you be here?" Mary asked.

"I'm not coming," Carl said.

"You're missing a great party. It started small, but it seems to be picking up momentum. We'll see you at tomorrow's public announcement, right?"

"Public announcement?"

"For the show with your friend Julian Frye?"

Carl felt panic as he clicked one of the messages from the Chancellor, promising use of the Weber Hall livestock arena for the taping of *The Bill Tawfee Show*. Everyone agreed interest among alumni would be huge.

"Don is really terrific. He wants this thing to happen as much as you do!"

Mary stopped talking, leaving a gap where Carl would have echoed her enthusiasm, had he still wanted the broadcast to take place, had his priorities not changed.

"Don't you have anything to say? Aren't you excited? Aren't you," she cleared her throat and continued, "grateful?"

"I don't know, Mary. Are you sure you want to do this?" he said. "Is Frye a big enough name? Maybe your gut had it right about people not reading fiction anymore."

"What?" Mary said.

"And will this show be dramatic enough for Bill? I just don't know."

"Do you have any idea what I had to go through to get Bill to even read Frye's damn book? I worked my ass off talking to the producers, getting Oprah herself to sign off on the expense of putting a remote show together in the middle of Kansas." Her tone turned dismissive. "This is happening. It has momentum now. You clearly haven't seen the advance reviews. People are gushing. Bill Tawfee will tape his show in Manhattan on March fifteenth with his guest Julian Frye."

The mention of Oprah Winfrey's association with Bill Tawfee's show sparked a rumor that spread from Manhattan to Junction City to Topeka, and all the way to both coasts. Carl heard from a former co-worker in New York that Oprah Winfrey had selected Frye's book for her book club, and that she would do her show in Kansas. Before Oprah's spokeswoman and Bill Tawfee quelled the rumor, people bought thousands of copies of Frye's book from their neighborhood Costco. Bland had extra copies sent to Kansas City where supplies had sold out quickly.

Carl knew he had to read Frye's book, but he delayed. He hated for Frye and Bland to have any of his money. He kept checking the used bookstore downtown in hopes that someone had turned it in. The university library had two copies, but the waiting list was so long, it would be late 2017 before he would have a chance at it. He finally caved and ordered one from Costco. He decided he would loan it to as many people as possible until the per-reading value of money he paid had diminished to near worthlessness. Or, he would just burn it.

The book engulfed him. Over two days he neglected everything else in his life. He missed a class, skipped four meals, let his phone die, and forgot to take his multivitamin. Frye had put everything in the book. He reproduced some conversations verbatim. The climax of the story comes as Emily, the character based on Susan, decides to leave town when someone threatens to expose her true identity. In one particularly emotional scene, she says goodbye to her son, who owns a bakery. She decides that her double-life has done enough damage to her, and she would no longer let it affect her son. The dialog was perfect, the blocking of the character's movements superbly staged, and the emotional impact wonderfully crafted. It was one of the best scenes he'd ever read. This was Frye's masterpiece.

Carl loved it, and hated himself for it.

When he finally plugged his phone into the charger it immediately rang with a call from Ocean. Someone had begun mounting a hostile takeover of UR.

When he arrived at the dairy, Susan met him in the parking lot. "Is it Bland? It has to be Bland, right? He's the one trying to take over the dairy!" She led him into the boardroom where Ocean sat at the conference table across from Lady McKinley.

"Why don't you run through it one more time for Carl," Ocean said.

"This is the third time, for God's sake," Lady McKinley said, thumping the sheet of paper. "We got this tender offer for our shares and we want to know if you can match it. Otherwise we take it."

Ocean handed the letter to Carl.

It was indeed a tender offer, signed by Elizabeth Austen as an agent for West Egg Holdings.

"Bland is offering real money. Total, for my one percent, is five thousand dollars," Lady McKinley said.

"If you take this offer, you won't be able to buy milk or cheese from the dairy," Carl said.

"I'm not convinced I'm going to sign, but I wanted to hear your response. The best thing would be for you to pay us, and then we could continue being customers," Lady McKinley said. "But we bought our shares for a dollar. That's a hell of a return. I love UR Camembert as much as anyone, but with five grand I can buy my own cows."

"Think about West Egg's motive here," Carl said. They're just trying to buy off our customers. Let's say half of the people take the cash..."

"Everyone I've talked to plans on taking the money," Lady McKinley said. She thumbed through a copy of the shareholder agreement. "However, if the money's comparable, I think everyone would rather sell to you guys under the, what's it called here, 'right of first refusal?'"

She referred to the option for the dairy to buy back their shares first, at a comparable price that was being offered by a third party. It was a standard clause.

Carl had never dreamed anyone would offer real money for the shares. He blew into his fist. "All right. We'll consider this. We have seven days from this notification to decide."

Lady McKinley nodded. "That takes us to the fifteenth of March."

Carl felt like he was trying to insert the large colored toothpicks into the Ker-Plunk cylinder while someone else pulled them out faster. Whatever he did brought on a cascade of marbles.

After Lady McKinley left, Carl did the math for Ocean. The offer valued the dairy at half a million dollars. That was high. Though essentially if Bland wanted merely to have a controlling interest, say fifty-one percent, he could get that for 255,000 dollars, and not have to spend any more. But that didn't make sense for two reasons. If he bought up all the outstanding shares from customers, in other words, from people other than Carl, Ocean, or Susan, he'd only have 46%. They had broken the shares down this way so that no one could mount a takeover bid without their consent:

Ocean: 40%
Susan: 9%
Carl: 5%

It was the perfect strategy to come out of a partnership between Ex-Elizabeth and Bland, at once ingenious and vindictive. They'd found the perfect loophole: Pay your competition's customers to go away.

Back at his apartment, Carl stumbled on the box of his things Frye had packed up from his office. He needed a mindless activity so he could think. Unpacking the box sounded perfect. He turned on his boom box for some music. Instead he heard the last disc in the *L.A. Law* series. He left it on, thinking perhaps it would help him come up with a way to fix his problems.

"By the time responsibility for a negotiation comes to the desk of a Senior Managing Partner, it means all other methods have failed," Leland McKenzie said.

The box had the disorganized appearance of having been hastily packed. Carl thought perhaps Frye had just dumped the drawer's contents into the box and then taped it up. Carl organized the materials into piles and got loose sheets of paper back into their proper folders. As he listened, Carl took the books he'd found in the box, ordered them alphabetically, and put them on his homemade shelves.

Leland described the signs of stagnating negotiations while Carl worked down to the clipping file he had on Jules Frye. Leland McKenzie quieted down. Carl had learned nothing new from this second listening. He flipped through the pages of articles, noting all the places Frye had been before fouling his nest by writing a book critical of the people who lived there. Bloomfield Hills, Bloomington, Strong City, and now Manhattan. He had certainly written a book to alienate the people around him here, even though he had said he wanted to stay. Was he lying about wanting to stay? No, Carl decided. Frye had probably come up with a way to make the people he alienated leave. He probably guessed that Susan would cower in the face of full disclosure and leave, perhaps taking Carl with her. If she stayed, she might face punishment for her crimes. Either way, Susan would leave. How do you negotiate with a guy like that?

As if in answer, Leland McKenzie started talking again. "You're still here?" he asked. "Perhaps you still need a little more advice. I know, you've tried everything and still your opponent seems determined to see you suffer in the negotiations."

What was this, a hidden track? On a business CD? Leland's voice had changed. Whereas before, Carl had visualized Leland relaxing in a wingback leather chair, now it sounded as if he leaned on the boardroom table, gorilla-like, with his knuckles boring down into the wood.

"Achieving balance has failed. The other side refuses to let you create a win-win. They play the bad cop, they play hardball, and they play to win at any cost. That's when you go for the nuts. That's when you undermine everything they hold dear. Work to destroy it or render it unwinnable. My advice to you is to grab them by the balls and squeeze until they give in." The CD ended for real this time. Carl looked at the CD case to see if Tipper Gore had deemed it explicit, but found no such label.

Leland was onto something. His words dovetailed with something Susan had said, that he needed to use his skills for the benefit of the right people. And that meant using those skills to the detriment of the other people. He needed a plan. He went to the closet and found his personal shredder. He plugged it in and began feeding it each of the Frye clippings, reducing the Twitter stream, the blog posts, and the articles to tiny diamond-shaped bits.

Chapter 13
The Burn

Carl had performed some perfunctory research about Weber Hall and the attached arena where *The Bill Tawfee Show* broadcast would originate. The website had few specifics about the arena, but it did explain the variety of smells exuded by the structure. Apparently, it housed a complete USDA meat processing facility, including a 400-pound meat-smoking chamber, something called a Baader desinuator, and several different sizes of meat mixers.

Acknowledging that this information was not going to help, he needed to see the facility in hopes that he could figure out how to disrupt Frye's show, now just two days away. He observed a thin column of blue smoke rising from the center of the main building, clearly emanating from the smoking chamber. Outside, the place smelled a lot like a barbeque restaurant.

At the loading dock, he spotted a few of the Philosophy students who kept the English department out of Dickens Hall. They resembled the Mario Brothers. One, mustachioed and squat, wore a dark puffy coat and black pants. The other, tall and wan, lacked a chin and also wore black. They pushed a cart of boxes, covered with a black cloth. He followed them from a distance. They pushed their cart up a ramp and toward a lobby area where people would enter the arena. The Mario Brothers looked in all directions, trying to tell if anyone had discovered them. Carl ducked around a corner, just into a large hallway that led to seating and the main arena where he could still watch them.

The thin man unlocked a small closet with some effort (he possibly picked the lock) while the chubby one removed the black cover over the cart to reveal about twenty cardboard boxes. They stacked the first two boxes in the closet with some effort. This would take them a while. Each had a single word written on it. Carl couldn't make the whole thing out, but he did read the last half of the word: "maniac." Carl wondered what these guys had in mind. Were the Mario

184

Brothers planning some kind of disruption too? If so, he might be able to use their help.

Down the hallway toward the arena he heard the unmistakable voice of The *Flanesser*. Carl followed the voice to a small knot of people walking past the opening of the hallway into the arena. He recognized the EGSA.

"The mayor of Manhattan will sit here, flanked by members of the Kansas Bureau of Investigation and various other people Frye has used as sources."

After they passed, Carl came down to get a look at the arena. It smelled like cows and new carpet. They had laid plywood over the dirt arena floor, and three men worked on their knees covering it with blue carpet. On the half that had been carpeted, two women placed grey folding chairs in neat rows, facing a nearly completed wooden stage. Three wooden platforms of similar construction rose from among the folding chairs. Carl guessed those would eventually hold cameras and their operators. As the EGSA approached the stage, Mr. Clean asked where he would sit during the broadcast.

The *Flanesser* waved vaguely up at the 2,000 or so bleacher style seats in the arena. "We have standing room only for dignified alumni and faculty as it is. You'll have to watch it at home later that afternoon, like the rest of the unwashed masses."

The Shush-Sneezer raised her hand. "But I thought the show was broadcast live."

"Of course you did, you rube. Since it airs at different times throughout the country it couldn't go out live. They shoot it live-to-tape, which means they do it in real time, with gaps for commercial breaks and everything. Security will be watertight. No one without one of these will get in." He held up a laminated pass that hung around his neck in a leatherette passport pouch he probably procured from the travel store.

"Now let's go up to the lobby."

They began to head toward one of the other hallways that led to the lobby, where he knew the philosophy students were still unloading their boxes. Carl stepped out in the open of the arena, hoping his movement would gain the attention of the EGSA.

"Let me reiterate. No unauthorized visitors will be allowed. That means people like you, Krautman."

The EGSA turned to look.

"I have as much a right to come as anyone," Carl said.

"I have explicit instructions. You are forbidden to attend the proceedings. They want no disruptions."

"Who doesn't want me to come?"

"Bland and Frye. And you might as well add me to the list. In fact, I'm not too happy that you're here now. Where's that twit from security?" He fumbled for a small radio attached to his belt.

The Mario Bothers walked right in front of The *Flanesser* as he barked into his radio, "There are all sorts of ruffians about. Get it nailed down!"

A few warning signs along the side of the road alerted drivers that smoke from the prairie fires could hinder visibility. The burning of the Konza had begun. The flames rose no more than two feet high, delineating charred black on one side, tall golden grass on the other.

Carl didn't yet have a solid plan of attack in mind, but he had called Mary to see if there might be some opportunities. He knew he would have to be at the taping to do any good for Susan. As he drove out of the burned area, about where he turned off Highway 177, a mass of smoke completely obscured Carl's view of the road. He impotently turned on the wipers, but after a moment the cloud blew off to the east on its own.

Even the day before the show, Frye kept to his Thursday schedule of sitting out at the Konza. His BMW sat in the gravel parking lot, right next to the path. The grass that edged the path appeared to have been burned sometime earlier. It didn't smell overtly smoky, just a little, like someone had burned leaves somewhere in the neighborhood. The limestone outcroppings looked more exposed without the tall grass to soften their edges. Frye stood on the same rock they had sat last summer.

"You caught me," Frye said, his eyes on the blackened horizon. "I think my next novel will be named *The Hills Like Burned Marshmallows.*"

"I'd read a novel called that," Carl said.

"I'm supposed to be picking out my new office today. I shall demand a view."

"New office?"

"In the soon-to-be-minted Bland Center for Literary Pursuits."

"Sounds dreadful."

"Don told me you were poking around Weber Hall earlier today."

"Yes, and he told me you're not going to let me in the taping. I'm coming to the show. I want to see what will happen."

"I'll tell you what will happen. I'm going to talk about my book, about how hard I worked on coming up with the people in it. I'm going to describe how it marks the return of the Jules Frye post-modern work of intense imagination. I have gone over everything. Nothing's going to get in the way of my performance."

"What if I show up with Susan?" Carl asked.

"If you're thinking about sabotage, forget it. Why would you bring Susan?"

"So she could make her own case. To preemptively deflect any fallout that might come her way."

"Preemptively?" Frye said. "It's a big leap to think people will make the connection between her and my character."

"You have put too much faith in your own ability to obscure reality," Carl said.

"Tell me," Frye said, looking at Carl for the first time, "for whose benefit would it be to have her story come out? Yours, so you could get some kind of revenge on me?"

187

"Susan's. To let her tell her story *her* way, as a counterpoint to your book."

"At what cost?" Frye asked. "How will she benefit if Bland has her arrested?"

"Bland doesn't have any case against her about the derailing."

"No, of course he doesn't. It was technically an accident. At any rate, she'll have to answer a lot of questions about forging her teaching credentials. She'll have a tough time convincing the KBI it isn't fraud. At any rate, she won't be present for much of the show."

In his frustration, Carl thought of the Philosophy students. "There are others who would want to disrupt any event that makes the English department look good."

"This is a warning? So I'll be prepared?" Frye asked, with no change in expression.

"Take it however you want."

"I take it for what it is. The sound of desperation," he said. "If you take part in any of this, even showing up at all, Bland will make things uncomfortable for you."

"I don't live in his world anymore."

"You're wrong. He can make you look bad," Frye said. "Things that you've done. Maybe even conflict of interest in the dairy deal."

"Anything he says about the Heartland Dairy deal will make him look worse than me."

"I'm talking about Ocean's dairy."

"What conflict of interest?"

"You were a shareholder in both the dairy and your wife's company. You convinced Ocean to divide up the company, which made it easy for Bland to put them out of business. Then you get a scholarship from Bland? It looks like a reward."

"That is ridiculous. It's just a small dairy. No one's going to care about it," Carl said. "Besides, it will implicate him as well."

"He's got that figured out already. That little affair between his H.R. manager and your wife will provide enough of a distraction to where all of the focus is on you and the people you care about."

"Let him go for it. Let him sue me. I don't have any money, and I no longer care for people who'd be bothered by that kind of stuff."

"You don't think the extra-marital affair your wife is having with the manager wouldn't make her family look bad? Her mother the Governor wouldn't care for that kind of publicity. And what about Susan? You don't think it might get to her that you and the almost ex have conspired against her son's dairy? And now you tell me–this is perfect, Carl, even better than anything I could ever have come up with– you want her to come to the broadcast tomorrow, where Bland is certain to have her arrested before she gets to say anything to anyone. You think then she'll grasp the subtleties of your actions and how they've impacted her life?"

Frye was right. Bland's version would be hard to refute. Bland had cornered him, again. Maybe it would be best if Susan and Ocean just left town and started over somewhere else. No one would find out about Susan's past, and Ocean could recreate his dairy almost anywhere. Carl could leave at any time–nothing kept him in Manhattan if Susan left. Maybe keeping things status quo would be the best for everyone.

But he knew he could never advocate that. He had a choice to make. He no longer enjoyed being cornered by people like Bland and he wouldn't allow Julian Frye to bully him. A plan began to take shape in his head.

"Since you appear to be Bland's message boy," Carl said, "tell him to go ahead and spread the word about what I've done." Carl climbed down from the rock. "Tell him I'll see him at the broadcast. Tell him Susan and I will both be there."

"Will do," Frye said.

"And you can forget about getting tenure after all this shit is over. I'll have quite a story to tell Dr. Grey."

Frye laughed. "I already have tenure. Have had it since I started here. But you never checked into that, did you?"

He headed toward his car, adding over his shoulder," Fuck off then. That's for you, but it goes for Bland, too."

When Carl got home he called the Governor to tell her he had the perfect way for her to honor her deceased father.

The next day at noon, Kansas State played Kansas in the first round of the Big 12 basketball tournament. A crowd formed at the Lethargic Clown to watch the game. The place was rowdy, perfect for the appointment he had made.

Terry waved Carl over to the table where he and the rest of the Li'l Apple Elite sat watching the game, drinking PBR, and eating peanuts.

"Where the hell is your pal Jules?" Terry said. "He's never missed round one of the tournament. His absence gives some of us in the group complex feelings of rejection."

Ray crushed a beer can in his three-fingered hand. "He too good for us now? You tell that guy to fuck off."

"Interestingly enough, I did that yesterday," Carl said.

"Is it because of his recent success that you two no longer have anything in common?" Dawn asked. She had done her hair in pigtails, spraying out dyed blond hair on either side of her head. It gave the impression that her head was leaking. Carl noticed her shirt. It said "Lactivist" on the front.

"That shirt." Carl said. "Where'd you get it?"

"Do you like it?" She turned around to point at the back. It had the title of Frye's book and his website address. "I just loved it, didn't you? So imaginative. All my girl-friends love it. I heard Oprah loves it too!"

"I didn't make it past page seven. I hated the way he described Manhattan," Ray said before someone coming through the door distracted him. He said, "There's some heat coming in, gentlemen." They all turned.

Dawn shook her head.

Carl saw Ex-Elizabeth at the door. She looked around the room.

190

Terry laughed. "She looks like she smelled a fart. What the hell is she doing here?"

"She's my new girlfriend," Ray said. The Li'l Apple Elite laughed.

Carl crushed his beer can and left it leaking on the table-top. He stood up. "She's mine for now, folks."

They laughed again.

Ray said, "You going up to talk to her? Two beers say you can't keep her attention for twenty minutes. Not with that mood you're in."

"I'll take that bet," Terry said.

"Good luck," Ray said. "I'll give one to you if I win, Carl!"

At the mention of his name Ex-Elizabeth turned and her lips parted in a half smile. They met halfway and she leaned in to kiss his cheek. "Is this the sort of place writers frequent?"

"Why not?" he said.

As they walked over to the bar, she kept looking at the bottom of her shoes to ensure that what made the floor so sticky hadn't rubbed off on her. She searched the bar top for an acceptable place for her purse. She hung it back on her shoulder.

"Thanks for agreeing to come all the way down here, Elizabeth."

"You said you had some transactions to discuss. What better place to talk than in a bar where people drink beer with lunch?"

Sparky finished with another couple and walked over. He waved at Carl but kept his eyes on Ex-Elizabeth.

"This is my wife, Elizabeth," Carl said, barely remembering to skip the "Ex" before her name.

Sparky shook her hand and she started at the touch of his artificial grip. "Let me buy your first drink of the day. It's a new special I made up for the ladies."

He held a can of PBR and turned it in his artificial hand. After he poured the beer into a pint glass he continued

191

rotating the hand 360 degrees until the can was back upright again.

Carl thought it was a great trick, but it made too much foam in the glass.

Sparky produced a shot glass and filled it with Smirnoff vodka. "When you're ready, drop this in the beer and chug the whole damned thing. You want to know what I call it?"

"Not really."

"A Pabst Smir."

Ex-Elizabeth's face returned to the smelled-a-fart look. "I know what's happening here. Though you've mistaken me for a writer, I'm in fact a business consultant." She leaned forward, as if in confidence, and whispered, "We usually wait until after one before we chug."

"All it takes is a little practice. Look at the wonders we've worked with Carl here." He laughed and ducked into the kitchen.

"So you mentioned we had a transaction to discuss?" she asked.

"The broker in New York called me. There's an offer on the apartment. I think we should take it," He said.

"Is it over the minimum amount you wanted to get?"

"It's over my minimum," he said, "by exactly a dollar. Makes me think the broker told the buyer what my minimum was."

"To agree with this sale, I would have to receive something in return."

Carl nodded. "Of course you would."

"I want a divorce. Expedited."

"This is a new development. What's changed? Your H.R. Manager ready to share his benefits with you?"

"Yes," she said, looking at him sideways. "How did you know that?"

"Because it's how you operate. I don't have to mention that we'd already be divorced if you'd have let us take the first offer on the apartment."

"You don't have to bring that up, Carl. You have more tact than that," she said.

"I'll let you have your expedited divorce, if you're really in that much of a hurry," He said. "But I'll need an extra $10,000 of the proceeds from the house."

"Deal, as long as you agree to relinquish your shares in Krauthammer, Austen, Cotter, and Laird."

He wondered at her motivation. It didn't matter to him, but it might make things look better against Bland's conflict of interest allegations. "I'll do that, if you will scuttle Bland's offer for the UR dairy."

"Whoops. Non-starter there," she said. "If Bland's offer for the shares gets picked up by over 40% of the shareholders in the UR, Bland has offered to acquire ACL."

"That's why you wanted me out? You're selling? Were you planning on telling me this before I signed the document to sell my shares?"

She performed the Sequence of Gestures. "Don't get your panties in a bunch." She leaned forward and scooted the shot of vodka toward Carl and took a drink of the PBR. "I was going to tell you before we signed everything, when you were feeling good about the deal."

"That's so Disc One," he said. "Arnie Becker would be proud."

"How do I know that name?" she asked. "The discs. You listened to them?" She stopped for a moment. "This place. You picked a location for negotiations that would throw me off, but where you'd be comfortable?"

"Yep," he said, and took the shot of vodka.

"And you've been asking for the order as well. Disc Two, Jimmy Smits. I'm impressed."

"Hold on, we're not finished yet. I have some information for you, *gratis*."

"Nothing's *gratis*, Carl. I'm guessing you have something uncomfortable to tell me, while I'm feeling good about the negotiations?"

"Uncomfortable for both of us, actually. Bland's going to Lee Majors you." When Susan showed no signs of understanding he continued. "Lee Majors was in *The Fall Guy* in the late 1980s. Mean anything to you?"

193

"You need updated reference material," Elizabeth said.

"He's going to use you and your H.R. pal as the fall guys in his plan to expose me as a conspirator against the dairy. My guess is that his faux outrage over your relationship means you've broken his ethics clause. That would make it convenient for him to get out of making a deal with you, knowing you wouldn't want it to go to court. Think of all that nasty publicity, and you and I still married."

"That's all bullshit. He can't back out on my deal. I have a written contract that says he'll buy."

"I guarantee he buried an ethics clause in there. Remember your special friend telling us that's always his escape hatch for a deal?"

Ex-Elizabeth let her face fall slack. "For the first time in my life I feel overmatched." She drank almost half the beer in one swig. "Not by you, Carl, by Bland."

"So much for not chugging before one," Carl said. "I agree, it looks pretty bad, but I have a plan that just might work out with regards to your agreement with Bland. We're going to give him more than he's asked for. We're going to give him the dairy, the whole damned thing."

The next morning, he received a FedEx containing some legal documents. They covered the house and the agreement to relinquish his shares in ACL. He glanced over the numbers to make sure they lined up with what the broker had told him verbally. They did. Once he took out real estate commissions, the balance on the mortgage, and added in the bump for releasing his shares to Ex-Elizabeth, Carl would get a check for 36,000 dollars.

He thought about the success he had enjoyed in his negotiations with Ex-Elizabeth. He hadn't expected it to go so well, that he would get everything he wanted. He owed it to McKenzie Brackman. He assumed the timing had worked in his favor–their needs to move on from each other had lined up naturally. But now, looking at the numbers on the contract, numbers that came out better than he expected, he could see that focusing on his needs made him a tougher opponent, as Ex-Elizabeth had suggested. Had he really changed?

He sat at his desk and uncapped a pen to sign the contracts. He glanced up at the whiteboard in his bedroom where he'd outlined his plans for the taping of *The Bill Tawfee Show*. His success with Ex-Elizabeth had spurred him to be more aggressive.

But something about the contract gave him pause. It wasn't really a contract so much as an agreement to abide by a quitclaim deed. She was basically paying him $36,000 to relinquish the apartment to her, just as the housing market in New York was starting to rebound. Carl's irritation did not last long. He signed the papers and moved on to the next part of his plan.

He had two hours to convince Susan to go to the broadcast.

Carl found Susan at her desk, in her railroad-car office surrounded by open-flapped boxes of books and rolled up posters. She dropped her pen when she saw him and stood to greet him.

He pointed at the boxes. "You moving offices?"

"Just preparing." She closed the flaps on a box and moved it to the floor for Carl to sit. "I was just updating my notes on my class. I'd hate for whoever takes it over to spend too much time getting it going again. That wouldn't be fair to my students."

"So you're drawing upon your resources to do what you can?"

Her face smiled, but her eyes appeared unmoved.

"Someone once suggested I do that, too," he said.

"And how's that working out for you, Carl?"

"Good and bad thus far. I got some money out of my house, got divorced."

195

"Congratulations." She rolled up a "Breast is Best" rally poster and snapped a rubber band around it.

"That's the good. I figured we'd defer celebration because of the bad part. My efforts have also gotten me stonewalled, blackmailed, and banned from Bill Tawfee's broadcast."

"You weren't planning on being there anyway, were you?"

"I was, actually. I am."

She wedged the poster in a box in front of the couch and moved the whole thing out of the way to make room for her desk chair. "What good would come out of that?"

"Everyone wants a show: Frye, Bland, Bill Tawfee, The *Flanesser*. They just don't understand that I'm the one who's going to give it to them."

"That doesn't sound noble."

"My purpose is noble. My techniques are opportunistic."

She sat in the desk chair and maneuvered in front of the couch. "Sounds intriguing."

"I had hoped you'd say that. I need you to be there, too."

She scooted back slightly. "Why?"

"Bland and Frye have threatened that the KBI agents will be there and they'll arrest you if you show up. At the same time, Frye wants to keep up the illusion that his quirky story came only from his imagination. But if I get your story out as part of the show…"

"I'd be *on the show*?"

"I know that everything I've done has been an unqualified disaster for your family. I exposed your son's business to certain ruin. I aided a man in exposing your secret past, which should have stayed secret. Now I'm complicit in making all of these events national stories. But it's not just you. I've even exposed the Governor's family to potential scandal. You look at my Big Ball from the outside and I look like a terrible person. But all of those things happened when I worked to achieve something for Julian Frye and myself. I want to see what happens when I aim my intentions in the right direction. What can I actually achieve with this one event? How can I twist what's happened so far into what I want to occur, into what's best for the people close to me? Look at my great Big Ball from the perspective of someone who knows my intentions now, and I don't look too bad. But it's not just my intentions. I'm actually going to achieve some results here."

Susan shook her head. "Carl, you have taken my life and smashed it into pieces. You've ruined just about every aspect of it: my job, my son's business, my son's privacy, my privacy, my life, for God's sake. Ultimately, I wonder if that was a life that needed breaking, like a flawed mold that just kept cranking out bad statues. An odd analogy, I know. In your defense, you're the only one who has come back. My husband bolted after the train incident. Frye only wanted to write about me after we split up. But you keep coming back. I guess I have to trust you. Besides, I don't want to go to prison without a boyfriend."

They kissed. She said, "I guess I need to practice my speech for the show?"

"Yes. Think of it as Suzanne's last act of rebellion."

"No, this is Susan's last act of resistance."

They hugged. "There's one more thing," he whispered in her ear. "I need you to sell all of your shares in Ocean's dairy to Bland's company."

He tried to release her so he could look in her eyes but she wouldn't budge.

"Don't fuck this up, Krauthammer."

197

Chapter 14
Kansas Knows How to Make a
Chicago Guy Feel Welcome

An unpleasant odor surrounded the livestock arena attached to Weber Hall. Carl stood near the entrance, in the rain, trying to determine whether it smelled more like the leftover brisket he discovered in the backseat of his car, or the small container of cottage cheese that had gone unnoticed in his refrigerator. The rain and direction of the wind kept it subtle, but occasionally a stiff breeze strengthened it.

A purple Town Car pulled up in front of Weber Arena, sporting a magnetic seal on the passenger-side door that marked it as part of the University Motor Pool.

The driver emerged first, opening a large golf umbrella. Carl recognized him as the guy with the permed mullet from his writing class. He wore an old windowpane-patterned suit, dating from the mid-Nineties, like the one Carl wore when he interviewed at Ogilvy. Mullet guy rushed around to the passenger side and opened the door. Chancellor Schroeder emerged, wearing an open trench coat that revealed a blue blazer with gold buttons, a blue oxford, and khaki pants: Midwestern Nice. The choreography of the arrival broke down early, as mullet guy stood too close to Schroeder in order keep the rain off his fluff of white hair while Schroeder tried to open the back door. The guy finally moved around and shielded the guests of honor as they emerged from the vehicle. Mary Austen-Tawfee wore a grey sweater and skirt, her husband black slacks and a grey collared shirt, buttoned to the top. Tawfee seized the umbrella and held it over himself and his wife.

Carl put down the hood of his rain jacket so Mary could recognize him. She waved him over to join them as they walked toward the entrance to the arena. The space she made for him under partial cover of the umbrella relegated Chancellor Schroeder to complete exposure to the elements.

"Bill, you remember Carl, Elizabeth's...," Mary said.

"Hello Bill. I'm married to Elizabeth for," Carl said, checking his watch, "four more hours."

"Of course, Carl," said Bill, offering the same old Tastemaker of Topeka handshake, with the errant thumb. "That odor, Carl. Do you know what it is?"

Chancellor Schroeder quickened his pace to get closer to the group. "That is our USDA meat processing facility here in Weber Hall," Schroeder said. "State-of-the-industry, it is."

"Let it be known, that I have not lost my nose for irony. My first remote as a nationally syndicated talk show host will take place next to a slaughterhouse. And I thought I had gone so far from that meatpacking plant on Topeka Boulevard next to the studios of KKOW-TV."

"I think they're cutting and deboning today," Chancellor Schroeder offered. Tawfee just closed his eyes and clenched his jaws.

"You're here to convince us the show shouldn't go on?" Mary asked. "We roll tape in 45 minutes.

Carl turned to make sure Schroeder was out of earshot. "Actually, I've come around. I think I have a few ideas to increase the drama of the subject matter."

Bill cocked his head in a manner that reminded Carl of a dog hearing one of the few words that got him excited. "The show is all laid out now, Carl. We would need a strong reason to tinker."

A momentary wave of apprehension washed over him. He had concentrated all his efforts on the broadcast. He had no plan B if they said no, or if Frye and Bland had gotten to them. He knew his only play was to The Tastemaker's hunger for conflict.

"What if I could give you the real-life people from Frye's book?"

The Tastemaker snorted. "What, is there a woman here who derailed a train?"

Mary joined in. "Or perhaps we could meet the one-handed bartender who used to drive trains."

"They're both on their way here."

199

The Tastemaker stopped walking. A quantity of water splattered off the front of the umbrella onto the sidewalk.

"Come on, Carl," Mary said, "these are just people he loosely based the characters on, right?"

Carl shook his head.

"He's serious," The Tastemaker said. "These are real people!"

"If you can promise them a slot, maybe the final segment? Then I'll have them here."

Tawfee started walking and the group followed. "We already have a final segment, about the raw milk cheese craze. Someone is bringing a wheel in."

"No, you don't want to get sick...or sued," Carl said. "Instead, let's get these people on your show. They have a great story to tell."

Mary said, "We'll have to run it by Frye."

"You don't have time for that," Carl said.

"He thinks we should blindside Julian Frye?" Tawfee walked forward, looking as if he liked the idea more with every step. "We should blindside Julian Frye."

Mary said, "It does add another dimension to the show."

The Tastemaker agreed. "At the very least it will give our audience insight into the fiction writing process. How much is real? How much is made up? Get them here, Carl. We'll find a place for them."

They arrived at the entrance to the arena, their way momentarily blocked by the back of a security guard. He turned around and Carl recognized him from the UR.

Denny held up a hand to halt them. "Sorry folks, I have to check your names against this list."

"This is Bill Tawfee and I'm Mary Austen-Tawfee."

Denny screwed up his face into an expression of doughy mistrust. "You need to have a pass." He consulted the clipboard.

Inside the arena, Carl saw The *Flanesser* running down the hall, waving his arms.

"We'll talk tomorrow, Mary. I'll have them here," Carl said.

200

"Can't we talk now?"

He headed back down the sidewalk just as The *Flanesser* greeted the group.

Carl could hear him saying, "Denny? Is that your name? For God's sake, don't you recognize Bill Tawfee? Let them in, let them in, you idiot. Not everything has to be done by the book." His voice changed to a more solicitous tone. "Welcome! Welcome! Mr. Tawfee, Mrs. Austen-Tawfee. Hello again, Chancellor Schroeder! Isn't this *fun*?"

Carl sat in the passenger seat next to Susan in the parking lot. The driver-side windshield wiper splayed out like a bloomless black bouquet.

Susan said, "I had a wig and a fake passport in my purse. I took them out before we left."

Carl ran a fingertip down her arm. "You're not going to jail, O.J. I've taken care of everything."

"Carl, while I love you, your assurances do not give me confidence."

Two trucks with strange antennae atop masts dominated the parking lot. Men in coveralls smoked near the open back doors of vans from local television stations. He did not see any limousine or the Kansas Trooper entourage that usually accompanies the Governor.

Carl felt he had done as much as possible to ensure that his plans came off without any glitches, but he also understood that he was not in control. There were simply too many variables. There was no categorizing these things, no numbers to place in the neat columns of ledgers, no way to ascertain a probability of success. Would Frye refuse to participate if he sensed something had changed? Would Bland have Carl tossed out and Susan taken into custody before the show even began? Would the Governor's schedule actually allow her to show on time? Having no answers to these questions did not make him nervous.

Rather, he felt a peace. He had used his resources and called in favors.

"It's out of our hands now."

At the entrance to the Arena, Denny pored over his clipboard. "The only name I have on my Do Not Admit list is a Carl Krautman, which is not you, Mr. Krauthammer." He held out his arm in a gesture of welcome. "It says here for Dr. Hirschman to go straight to makeup."

As they walked to the seats Mary had reserved for them, Carl saw several of the Philosophy guys in black T-shirts scheming quietly. He had forgotten about them. He worried they might try to stop a show that Carl now needed to go off without disruption.

A voice chirped out from behind Carl. "What the hell are you doing here?"

Carl recognized it as The *Flanesser*. He was coming up behind them. Susan grasped Carl's forearm. They froze, unable to do anything except keep walking forward. But suddenly, The *Flanesser* was past them and waving his hands at the group of Philosophy guys.

"I never said you could sell T-shirts."

"You said concessions," offered the chubby fellow Carl had seen the other day.

"Concessions means popcorn, sodas, Jujubes. I gave you the concession contract to keep you from ruining this show. No high-markup profits for you," he said. As the *Flanesser* directed them down a different hallway to the arena, Carl saw their T-shirts read, "Hegelomaniac."

A man in faded Levis, a short-sleeve dress shirt, and a double-eared headset crossed to the center of the stage. He

202

held a microphone close to his mouth. Carl could hear him tongue a lozenge off to one side of his mouth.

"Two minutes," he rasped. "Two minutes, people."

Carl could hear Susan's breath deepen. She straightened up. Her gait became more confident. He thought she just might keep it together.

The set for the on-location version of *The Bill Tawfee Show* looked similar to the set for the one in the studio, excepting the show's logo, which hung by two strands of barely visible fishing line in front of the draped-fabric background. It featured a wedge of road–including the dotted center line–stretching off to the vanishing point. A stylized version of the red, white, and blue interstate badge hovered over the horizon, emblazoned with the words, *The Bill Tawfee Show: On the Road!* The furniture was basically a living room set, a long sofa and a matching overstuffed chair angled around a glass coffee table. Two coffee mugs on the table also sported the *On the Road!* logo.

He wished Mary hadn't placed them in the VIP seating. He would have preferred some less conspicuous seats offstage, or even in the livestock pen they had converted into a backstage area.

Forrest Bland stood offstage to one side, scanning the crowd with a faint smirk. His gaze stopped and he winked. Carl followed his line of sight to see Ex-Elizabeth sitting on the front row of the regular seats on the floor. She smiled, performing the Sequence of Gestures toward Bland. After Bland's gaze left her, she leaned forward in her seat and looked toward Carl with crossed eyes. They shared a smile, the first genuine one he'd seen on her face in months. He'd just received a text message that their divorce had become final.

She sat back and Ocean, sitting next to her, gave Carl the "OK" sign with index fingertip to thumb.

"Thirty seconds to studio."

Carl regarded the crowd and picked out a few others in the assortment of faces: Sparky, Mrs. Sparky, Mr. Clean, Rosalie, and Keith.

Monitors flanking the stage faded up from black to show *The Bill Tawfee Show* open as his theme song blared over the speakers. The thrum of the crowd turned quickly to applause that grew as the open transitioned to a live shot of the crowd in the arena, taken by a camera on the end of a large arm, swooping just over the heads of the audience. The cheering kept getting louder. The crowd slowly adopted a standing ovation as Bill Tawfee jogged out onstage, with his right hand raised in triumph.

"Thank you!" Tawfee said, followed by a truncated whistle of feedback. "Wow! You people here in Kansas really know how to make a Chicago boy feel welcome!" This sent the crowd off on another clapping jag lasting thirty seconds while he turned around and made his way to the overstuffed chair. A man with a handheld camera darted in front of the stage to get shots of the audience. He focused on two men in suits who sat next to Carl.

Bland spotted Carl and Susan. He kept his expression completely neutral as he whispered something to an assistant next to him and pointed at them.

The red tally light on one of the cameras lit, and Tawfee spoke, reading the teleprompter. "Today we're doing our show from Manhattan, Kansas, the home of an author I first encountered years ago. He's the author of four books: *The Voortman Trifecta, Faulty Cradles, Again with the Voortmans,* and *The Atomic T-Bones.* His work has received two National Book Awards and one National Book Critics Circle Award. He creates quirky characters in quirky settings, and their stories surprise and entertain with wit and imagination."

Susan sat rigid in her seat and squeezed Carl's hand.

Tawfee held up a copy of the book. "But his latest novel, *The Philistine Prophecy,* supersedes all of the others in its Julian Frye-ness. Can I make up a word like that?" At this the crowd applauded, cameras catching a few people waving their personal copies of the book, others pointing to their "Lactivist" T-shirts.

"It's the story of a woman who did everything for her son. You'll be touched. You'll be scared. You'll sympathize with the mother, even when she attempts murder in the name of her political beliefs."

"Jesus," Susan said under her breath.

"Did you love the book?" Tawfee asked the crowd. The applause gave Carl the idea that half of the people were there for the spectacle rather than for Frye's book.

"Shall we bring out the author?" They clapped some more.

Frye came onstage wearing a black turtleneck and faded jeans, looking like Steve Jobs with a ponytail. They shook hands, each with an expression of mutual admiration.

He settled forward on the edge of the couch, legs crossed at the ankles. "It's clear you're beloved!"

"This is my turf," Frye said. "These are my people. I'm impressed at how they've taken to you, as an outsider."

Carl thought he saw an "Are you fucking with me?" expression on Tawfee's face. "You've had some great successes in your career."

Frye scooted back on the couch. It looked to Carl like Frye was trying to appear at ease. "Have I? You think so?"

"Come on, Julian. I've followed your career for almost twenty years. I know you aren't modest." Tawfee gazed out over the crowd looking for some backup, which arrived in the form of minor tittering.

"I've had some success. My characters have resonance. The things I write just–oh how should I put it–they just work, you know?"

"I love that. 'They just work,'" Tawfee said.

Carl rolled his eyes and pretended to put a finger down his throat in front of Susan. She just kept watching the stage with a clenched expression. She looked pale, in spite of the amount of make-up she wore.

"I want to know how you describe the story of this book. For those who haven't read it yet, what happens?"

"Basically, it's the story of an idealistic woman who falls in love with a man who is equally as idealistic. He tends toward the more extreme kinds of protest. Together they form a cell here in Kansas, and they sabotage a train as it comes through Manhattan."

"A freight train, not a passenger train," Tawfee reassured the audience. "But a man is injured."

"Yes, the engineer of the train loses his hand."

They spoke more about the plot of the book, and as the segment came to a close, Tawfee said, "When we come back, Julian Frye will read some for us. And later in the show, we'll give you a few surprises about the events depicted in the book. We'll be right back."

When they stopped clapping, the audience buzzed with conversation.

"I don't think I can do this," Susan said. "I'm getting nervous. I'm going to throw up."

"Just remember why you're doing it. This is the best way for you to get everything out in the open."

"Back in sixty," the guy in the headset and jeans called out.

"I know why I'm doing it. I can and will do it," she said. "I still might throw up, though."

"Everything's going to be all right," he said.

"At least it will be resolved one way or the other," she said.

When the show started up again, Frye read an excerpt from the part of the book about Susan's life in hiding. He described her panic, her worry of being caught as "a dull throbbing pain just under the surface, like that from an invisible pimple, waiting for the right moment to erupt and become public."

The audience responded enthusiastically to the reading. Even the people who just came for the show appeared to like it.

Tawfee clapped. Carl marveled at the host's ability to make Frye comfortable. He had no idea what was coming. "That was my favorite passage. I am amazed at how fully realized your characters are in the second half of the book. It's as if we know this woman. There's a realism to her that's almost frightening. And the pimple, what an image!"

206

"Thank you."

"It's so real. She's so real. By the end of the book, she became the hero of the story."

"Hero sounds a little extreme," Frye said.

Carl could feel Susan stiffen beside him.

"Clearly what she did was wrong," Tawfee said. "But the character that you create in the present, the involved woman who teaches Philosophy here at Kansas State, the lactivist, it's almost like derailing that train was what was out of character, rather than an act that defined her character." Tawfee looked out to the audience. "Didn't you think she was a hero?" The crowd enthusiastically agreed. "She did everything for all the right reasons. As I read the second half, about her life of hiding, I wondered how you were able to capture a female character in this situation so convincingly."

"To borrow a phrase from GE, it's imagination at work, Bill."

"I envy your students," Tawfee said. His fawning was quite convincing.

Frye read again, an excerpt from the part of the book where Susan chooses to keep her son's identity a secret from even the new romantic interest in her life. Frye held them rapt.

Despite his feelings of disgust for Frye, Carl enjoyed hearing the audience grow completely silent after the first paragraph and let out a collective exhalation at the end, as if no one had breathed through the entire passage.

Afterwards, Tawfee proclaimed that this new passage was actually his favorite. He stood to address the camera as he walked across the stage until the crowd filled the screen behind him.

"When we come back we'll further explore the real-life inspiration behind Frye's story."

Bill Tawfee left the stage as soon as the video monitors showed black. "Away for two minutes," the guy in the headset said. Frye's smile dissipated with the applause. He looked to Bland, who pointed him toward Carl and Susan.

The author and publisher met at the edge of the stage and crouched in front of Carl and Susan.

"What do you think you're doing? There are representatives of the KBI here, and I have instructed them to arrest anyone who gets in the way of this broadcast." Bland straightened up and hailed The *Flanesser*, who spoke into a walkie-talkie after recognizing Susan and Carl.

"Have you fucked this up for me?" Frye asked. "I don't have to take this. I don't have to stay."

"No, you don't," Carl said. "But I know you don't want to be the one who leaves this time. You want to see what happens next. And besides, you haven't asked for the order yet."

"He's right, Julian," Bland said. "Let the authorities handle this inconvenience. You need to ask Tawfee to suggest your book for Oprah's Book Club." He buttoned his jacket. "Besides, here comes help."

Through the door to the arena came four state troopers, followed by the Attorney General of Kansas, whom Carl recognized from the newspaper. Susan's eyes widened.

"Forty-five seconds back to studio."

"Not feeling so cocky now, Krauthammer? Got nothing to say?" Bland said. Then to Susan: "You're going to jail."

After the entourage of lawmen came Mary, escorting Victoria Austen, the Governor of Kansas, followed by two more troopers. They crossed to an open set of seats off to one side of the VIP section.

"Holy shit," Frye said. "Looks like Bland called out the big guns."

"Thirty seconds."

The theme music came up and the monitors showed a taped ad encouraging people to send in for tickets to the studio show. Frye sat down on the couch. Bland resumed his frown at his offstage post. Susan bore her fingernails into Carl's hand.

Carl had averted the first crisis. If Frye had left after this segment, the show might not have continued. If Frye could get through this next part, Carl thought, he would have served his purpose.

Tawfee snuck back into his overstuffed chair and looked straight at the camera when its tally light illuminated. "Welcome back. We're talking about a new book here, live in Manhattan," he yelled, "Kansas, that is." The crowd responded with waves of cheers. As their noise dwindled, he continued. "We're talking with Julian Frye, author of *The Philistine Prophesy*, a brand new book from West Egg Press. Julian, before the break, you mentioned the role of imagination in your work. Elaborate, won't you?"

"Every author uses his imagination..."

"Every *fiction* author."

Frye waited to see if Tawfee had something else to say before he continued. "Every author takes inspiration from real life." Frye's glance darted toward Susan, or possibly toward Carl. It happened too quickly to tell.

Tawfee continued, "Let's take the Emily character, the woman who derailed the train. Does she exist in real life?"

"She is inspired by a true story, yes. But I added details to render her unidentifiable."

"Like what?" Tawfee said, a froth of spittle gathering at the corners of his mouth.

"Her hobbies."

"So the real Emily does not quilt?"

"No."

"Did she derail a train carrying powdered formula?"

Forrest Bland shifted on his feet and re-crossed his arms.

"Yes," Frye said. "She did."

"And she has a son, she split up with her activist husband, and started a new identity in Manhattan as a professor, staying involved in breast feeding advocacy?"

"Yes, but..."

"And the character named Lightning. Did you make him up? Did your imagination spawn his artificial hand?" Tawfee yelled now, and the crowd made no sound.

"No..."

"Julian Frye, I feel duped. It is difficult for me to sit here and treat you civilly any longer. Your book, as brilliantly

209

rendered as it is, does not qualify as a created story of imagination. You have hoodwinked thousands of readers because your story is a contrivance of *truth*. Your story isn't inspired by a true story, it *is* a true story." He turned to one of the cameras and spoke loud to be heard amid the gasps of the audience. "When we return, we'll meet the real-life characters who appear in Julian Frye's book. We'll be right back."

Carl caught Ex-Elizabeth's eye across the way and mouthed the word "Now" to her.

The guy in the headset yelled, "Away for four-and-a-half minutes. I need Sparky and Susan Hirschman in the wings please."

The audience broke into a buzz of confused disorder. Event security appeared at the front of each section to reassert control. Carl, Susan, Sparky, Ocean, and Ex-Elizabeth all showed their passes and made their way up on the stage.

Forrest Bland crossed the stage, headed directly for Carl. If he had gotten all the way to him, Carl was sure Bland would have hit him. Instead, Ocean stepped in front of him and said, "Maybe this isn't the best time, but I have some great ideas on how we can incorporate probiotics in your products."

"Who the hell are you?" Bland said.

"I'm Ocean and I'm coming aboard with the UR dairy acquisition."

"Yes, Mr. Bland!" Ex-Elizabeth said. "Every shareholder accepted your offer, and your H.R. Director offered him a job."

"We paid for *all* of the shares?" Bland said to Elizabeth. "Why would we have done that? I don't want him working for me. You're fired, Ocean."

"That's fine, too," Ocean said. "I negotiated quite a severance package. Let me tell you about it." They steered Bland off the stage.

"Two minutes back to studio."

Frye stood up in front of the couch. His initial expression of disorientation from his treatment by Tawfee had now given way to a discomfiting grimace.

Tawfee leaned forward and Carl heard him ask, "You had enough, Julian?"

Frye tweaked the grimace on his face, softened it in some subtle way. "Hell, no. I never leave spectacles in the middle. It's wonderful – orchestrated and melodramatic. I have a feeling it's going to be very good for sales when Susan is taken out in handcuffs."

"Fuck off, Julian," Susan said.

Carl grabbed Susan's arm and they walked just off-stage where Bland had stood just moments before.

Once Susan got on the set, Frye moved down the couch and let her tell her story. She described how she hadn't intended for the accident to happen, how she now hoped coming on the show she could finally take responsibility for it. Overall, she got a favorable response from the crowd. She no longer sounded like a scoundrel on the lam. Everyone got to see her great Big Ball. She vindicated herself and Tawfee loved it. He had achieved the joining of literature with Jerry Springer-style tearful confessions.

Frye said nothing during this portion of the show. Occasionally, the camera caught him nodding, or expressing intense interest in the answers Susan gave. It surprised Carl that Frye hadn't lashed out at Tawfee. Perhaps he would have, had Susan not appeared ready to go on the show. Frye's own cynicism had served him here. He clearly realized that he didn't need to have an outburst. Susan would provide the emotional drama that sold books to the people who watched this show.

"When we return, Susan faces off with Sparky, the man she caused to lose a hand."

"Five minutes back to studio. We need Sparky up here."

Sparky delighted the crowd with tricks from his hand while he detailed the history of his arrival in Manhattan. He described meeting his wife, and how the town had taken him in as one of their most respected members of the community, electing him to head up the Aggieville Business Association. He mentioned the annual delivery of cash he received from

211

the mystery benefactor, and the amount he received last year, which allowed him to buy his new hand.

Tawfee said, "There's a remarkable passage in the book where, Emily, what the hell, *Susan*, talks about the money. Would you read it for us, Julian?" He handed the open book to Frye, who took it without objection or comment.

He read in a higher voice. "'Did I hope to bribe Lightning, to buy off my own guilt? I thought I had taken responsibility by providing for a new hand, but the opposite was true. It was vain and selfish for me to determine what would make him whole again.'"

As Frye read, Carl watched Susan, but a sudden movement from Sparky caught his attention. Sparky looked out to his wife sitting in the crowd. She nodded, and Sparky looked down. Something unscripted was happening.

"'Ultimately,'" Frye read from the book, "'I would ask him to look at me as a whole.'"

"I guess I should say something," Sparky said.

Mary shook her head at Carl, indicating she had no idea what was coming.

"I have something to confess. I was drunk that night. I had polished off a pint before I started the train moving. I'm not sure I would've had the reaction time to stop the train, but I am guessing I would have at least minimized the damage. Susan, you did help me out. I gotta tell you I have gotten more mileage out of my new hand than you could ever imagine. It has changed my life and brings people into my business. I forgive you. Do you forgive me?"

They hugged.

Frye cleared his throat. "And now I assume this carefully orchestrated performance will tie up the only remaining loose end, the investigation into the derailment."

"Of course," Tawfee said. "Governor?"

One of the cameras swung around to capture the Governor as she stood up, straightened her jacket, and approached the stage flanked by two state troopers. One of the troopers handed her a sheet of paper and she read from it. "Susan Hirschman, alias Suzanne Sherman, I am issuing

212

you a full pardon on any civil or criminal damages related to the derailing of the train in 1989. I have also authorized the Douglas Austen Foundation to commit four million dollars to Breast is Best."

Susan shook the Governor's hand and gave her a hug. When they parted, Carl could see Frye, seated on the couch. He looked at Carl with an expression of head-shaking admiration.

Bill Tawfee addressed the camera, amid the jubilation and bewilderment of those onstage. "This issue of passing truth as fiction is not about accurate labeling or the misrepresentation of one author. It is a case about how much value contemporary culture places on the very idea of fiction. And I believe that fiction matters."

The stage manager in the jeans said, "We are gone."

The *Flanesser* barked over a microphone, "Show's over people. Let's strike this stuff because there's a cattle insemination demo here in four hours."

Chapter 15
Augustine of Hippo

Six months later, Carl and Frye sat in folding chairs before the newly remodeled English Counseling Services Building. Frye refilled Carl's paper cup with a shot from a bagged pint of Woodford Reserve.

"If we keep this up I'll be too drunk to make it to Keith and Rosalie's wedding," Carl said.

"I'm already too drunk," Frye said, slouching in his chair and closing his eyes. "No regrets, though. That wedding is about them. This event is about you, Carl." They clicked plastic.

On a small platform in front of the building, Governor Austen's voice echoed over the portable PA system, "My father-in-law, to whom we dedicate the building behind me, moved to Tonganoxie, Kansas, with a dream to work for a horse-drawn dray service. But by 1920 he was selling automobiles for a man named Henry Ford."

"Perhaps you can humor me, Jules," Carl said, smiling. "What did you really think of my *Breast of Show* story? Did you really like it, or was it just part of your plan with Bland to use me?"

Frye cleared his throat. "It sucked. Good premise, but it just didn't work."

Carl's smile did not waver. "I thought you might say that, so I had Mary run it by Bill Tawfee, anonymously, for his opinion."

"No shit? What did he say?"

"He hated it," Carl said.

"He did?" Frye poured himself another bourbon that snapped over the ice cubes. "Knowing that, you have no regrets on your new pursuit?"

"None. Why do you ask? Did Bland change his mind about me?"

"He still dislikes you for all the money you made him spend on Ocean's dairy, but no one can argue with what you did for my book. He definitely wants you working for West Egg Press."

Carl noticed the small group of people clustered around the platform, listening to the Governor. Several of them wore T-shirts with *The Philistine Prophecy* on the back. Carl had suggested they rechristen the book as narrative nonfiction on the second printing, and add a disclaimer that Frye had based most of it on real people. As a result, Tawfee agreed to suggest it for Oprah's Book Club, as long as Frye worked out the rights with Susan and Sparky. Carl worked out a profit-sharing plan to everyone's satisfaction. Frye had sold two million copies and a hundred thousand T-shirts that read simply, "Inspired by a true story" on the front.

The Governor continued. "Soon Douglas managed the Ford dealership in Tonganoxie, becoming the most powerful businessman in town, and a natural candidate for mayor. They say the surname Austen relates to St. Augustine of Hippo, a philosopher and a thinker. I can't think of anything more appropriate for a center for the literary arts."

The Governor struggled with a pair of oversized scissors Chancellor Schroeder handed her. Finally, she cleaved the stretch of yellow tape before her. A few camera shutters clicked.

From then on, the building was called, "The Austen Center for Literary Arts."

"I guess I won't ever know what it feels like to be a great writer," Carl said.

"But you'll know what it's like to work with a great writer as a publicist and acquisition manager."

"I hope West Egg can find such an author here in flyover country," Carl said.

"Piss off, Krauthammer."

Carl's voice blared over the DJ's P.A. system. "So in closing, my toast for the newlyweds." He aimed the plastic champagne glass toward Rosalie and Keith, sitting at the

215

Lethargic Clown. "To the bride. Rosalie. You finally tamed the man who proclaimed he would never marry." Some in the group laughed, notably Keith's parents. "And to the groom, for finding favor with a woman who is too damned selective as to who she's nice to." More laughter. "I love you both and wish you the greatest success in your life together."

As the group raised their glasses to drink, Sparky and Ocean shuffled onto the improvised dance floor in front of the jukebox, carrying a huge piece of cardboard between them.

Sparky motioned with his head that he had something to say into the microphone. "Before we start the music up again, I want to remind you to take care of your waiters and bartenders tonight."

Carl pulled the microphone away from him.

Ocean clamored for a chance. "*Mesdames et Messieurs,* as you may or may not know, Sparky has invested in my new side business, and we'd like to present the newlyweds with our gift, something for their new house." They unfolded the piece of cardboard, which looked like a giant coupon, complete with dotted edges. "It is forty percent off a brand new kitchen from our shop, Uncle Tom's Cabinetry."

"Some hero you turned out to be," Susan said to Carl as they danced.

"I got you a multimillion-dollar foundation to run. You don't think I did right by you?"

"You didn't tell me it would be such a pain in the ass. Never in my life did I think I'd deal with human resource issues. I wish I'd never heard of human resources." She pulled him tighter to her.

Carl kissed her. "You don't get to hire an H.R. director."

"You turned out okay, Krauthammer," she said.

"You like what my Big Ball is saying about me?"

"I do."

"It's time for the bouquet toss," the DJ boomed.

"Let's grab another glass of Sparky's cheap champagne, walk home, and take our shirts off." They headed out the door as the bouquet smacked Carl in the back of the head.

He didn't even turn around.

Acknowledgements

Thanks to: Whitney Terrell–without your influence, I never would have finished this book. Also, Michael E. Benson, Michelle Boisseau, Scott Ditzler, Matthew Eck, Daniella Mallinick, Phil Nel, Michael Pritchett, Jennifer Phegley, Robert Stewart, Lisa Tatonetti, Dayane Taylor, Anne Wertheimer, my workshop classmates at UMKC (the margaritas are on me), and Rusty Coats for getting me writing fiction again. Special thanks to the Stanley H. Durwood Foundation

Cover photo and author photo by Julia Shapiro Photography + Art www.juliashapirophotoart.com

Thank you for reading this book. If you enjoyed it, please tell your friends and review it on Amazon.

Contact the author:
Email: steve@revare.com
Twitter: @slrevare
Facebook: facebook.com/slrevare.author
Web: RawTheBook.com

Thank you for reading Raw, A Novel. Did you know most writers don't write to make money? Most writers write for the love of words and the love of making people laugh, cry, and think. The best way to encourage a writer to keep writing is to leave a review for the book at the place where you purchased the book, Goodreads, Facebook or your own blog. Our authors welcome honest but fair reviews.

Of course, money does help pay for the coffee…

For more fine books, please visit

Inknbeans.com